ALMOST PERSUADED...

"I'll buy the cabin from you," Michael insisted. "You can take the money and buy a house closer to town."

"I'll stay in my cabin," Jenny said.

"You could stay with the McLeods," he continued. "Duncan and I are gone for weeks at a time on patrol. You'd be company for each other."

She shook her head. "That would be too much like charity." She turned to walk away from Finnegan to put distance between them. Just his standing next to her addled her thoughts.

His hand clamped around her elbow, and he yanked her to face him. "You're smarter than that, Jenny, and it makes me furious to hear you belittle yourself."

"Then don't listen."

His grip on her arm softened. His arm slid around her waist and drew her close. She thought for a moment he would kiss her, but his other hand cupped the back of her head and pressed her cheek against his shoulder.

The thump of his heart was comforting beneath her ear. She shoved aside intruding thoughts of tomorrow and next week and concentrated instead on all the places his body touched hers, tucking the memory away to remember on long, lonely nights.

He released her suddenly and walked to the fireplace, where their supper lay oozing blood onto the hearthstones. He squatted down, speared the fish with a stick, and propped it above the embers to cook. "I fight a battle every day with my past sins," he said softly. "Some days I win, some days the past does. But I never stop trying. I can't go back and undo the things I've done. Neither can you."

Dear Romance Readers,

In July of 1999, we launched the Ballad line with four new series, and each month we present both new and continuing stories set everywhere from medieval England to the American West—the kind of passionate, romantic stories you love best, written by the most gifted authors. At the back of each book, we tell you when you can find subsequent books in the series that have captured your heart.

First up this month is **After the Storm,** the final book in Jo Ann Ferguson's heartfelt *Haven* series. When a mother in search of her children finds them with a man who has become like a father to them, will he become a husband to her, as well? Next, talented Kathryn Hockett introduces us to the third proud hero in her exciting series, *The Vikings*. Raised to be a scholar, he never expected to be an **Explorer**—until the fate of a young woman falls into his hands, and her love burns in his heart.

Men of Honor continues with Kathryn Fox's emotional tale, **The Healing.** Can a desperate woman on the run from her past fall for the mounted police officer who intends to bring her to justice? Finally, Julie Moffett concludes *The MacInness Legacy* with *To Touch the Sky,* the gripping story of a woman born to heal others who discovers the strange legacy that threatens to harm the one man she has come to love.

These are stories we know you'll love! Why not try them all this month?

Kate Duffy
Editorial Director

Men of Honor

THE HEALING

Kathryn Fox

ZEBRA BOOKS
KENSINGTON PUBLISHING CORP.

http://www.kensingtonbooks.com

ZEBRA BOOKS are published by

Kensington Publishing Corp.
850 Third Avenue
New York, NY 10022

Copyright © 2002 by Kathryn Fox

All rights reserved. No part of this book may be reproduced in any form or by any means without the prior written consent of the Publisher, excepting brief quotes used in reviews.

If you purchased this book without a cover you should be aware that this book is stolen property. It was reported as "unsold and destroyed" to the Publisher and neither the Author nor the Publisher has received any payment for this "stripped book."

All Kensington titles, imprints and distributed lines are available at special quantity discounts for bulk purchases for sales promotion, premiums, fund-raising, educational or institutional use.

Special book excerpts or customized printings can also be created to fit specific needs. For details, write or phone the office of the Kensington Special Sales Manager: Kensington Publishing Corp., 850 Third Avenue, New York, NY 10022. Attn. Special Sales Department. Phone: 1-800-221-2647.

Zebra and the Z logo Reg. U.S. Pat. & TM Off.

First Printing: September 2002
10 9 8 7 6 5 4 3 2 1

Printed in the United States of America

Chapter One

Yukon Territory, 1898

"Jenny, darlin'. Put the gun down."

He grinned at her from the open door. Bits of snow swept past his feet, skittering on the plank floor.

"No, Frank. You're not coming in this time." She raised the revolver and her hands trembled from the unaccustomed weight. He saw the momentary hesitation and his grin changed to a confident leer.

"You wouldn't shoot me, girl. Not after all I've done for you. You belong to me, Jenny, and so does that brat in your belly."

"We don't belong to anybody. Least of all you." Fear hammered through her. He'd forced her into a path she could neither change nor desert. The next few minutes would play out exactly as she'd imagined them for the last six months.

"I'm going to kill you, Frank. In cold blood. Right here." The words came hard, with effort. And saying them made the task at hand even more surreal.

A flicker of doubt passed through his eyes and he blinked. "You ain't got it in you to kill nobody, Jenny girl. Let me have that pistol and we'll sit down and talk about this." He extended a hand and took a step forward. Jenny clicked back the hammer.

"Don't come any closer."

He hesitated. "You think you're just going to kill me and run off with my son? You think the Mounties won't hunt you down? There's law in the Yukon now, law brought here just for the likes of you."

"I didn't say I was guiltless, Frank, but I'm not going to let you come back in here again. Or bring in any more of that."

She nodded in his direction and he glanced down at the sack in his hand. He looked up at her, a slow smile spreading across his face. "This is what we came here for. This is it." He held up the sack and thrust it in her direction. "Thousands of dollars in gold. All for us, for you and me. We can go anywhere, do anything." He took another step forward. "And there's more where this came from."

She was in it as deep as he, there was no denying. And she was indeed guilty of thievery and lying and cheating and a thousand other small crimes.

THE HEALING

But another life depended on her now and soon would need her even more. She had to draw a line someplace. Gold fever had long ago robbed Frank of his good sense and morals. The only shred of decency she could attest to was an overwhelming wave of protectiveness when the baby moved within her. It deserved a home free from suspicion and deceit and guilt. This tiny flicker of life had had no part in the crime wave she and Frank had begun, then ridden to riches. Now, it was either the baby or Frank.

She raised the gun again, struggling to force her mind not to leap ahead and bombard her with images of Frank's faceless corpse stretched out on the cabin floor.

"You won't shoot me."

Was that a note of hesitation she heard in his voice?

"How can you shoot the man who loves you so?"

The tone of his voice slid from threatening to cajoling—soft and sultry, deepening to the whisper she remembered from so many firelight-softened evenings.

She mentally slammed that door and locked it. Frank Bentz was a cruel man, a man who would use words or anything else at his disposal to get what he wanted. And he had no fear of trampling all who stood in his way. Once he had the prize, he'd move on to something bigger, more expensive, more sought-after. And, if she allowed him, dragging her along behind.

"You don't love me, Frank. You love yourself. And money."

He smiled. "Of course I love money. So do you or else I wouldn't have found you flat on your back selling your best asset—or renting it, I should say."

"The difference between us is that I know when enough is enough."

He smiled again, deepening the dimples in his cheeks, dimples she'd allowed to lure her from her comfortable, if not legal, home in Seattle's red light district to this lonely cabin amid the gold fields.

"That's not what you tell me in bed. There, you can't get enough. Or so you say."

The day Frank Bentz walked through her door had been a dream come true—or so she thought. Clean, dressed in the latest fashion, pockets bulging with gold dust, he was a cut above her usual customers. And he'd easily convinced her to leave her whoring days behind and become his woman, to trail after him from one scheme to the next. At first, life was perfect. *He* was perfect—charming, gentle, a passionate lover, and a clever con man who kept their every whim satisfied. But as the months went by, his greed began to exceed his abilities and suddenly there was never *enough* money, *enough* gold, or *enough* liquor.

"I want out, Frank."

He spread his hands. "All you had to do was ask. There's no need to be pointing a gun at me. You can leave right after the baby's born."

Jenny shook her head. "I can't wait that long. This baby deserves a home, a good home."

"What makes you think I can't give him . . . and you . . . a good home? We'll move down to Seattle. I got an uncle there someplace. We can get us a little house. I'll even get a job."

She shook her head. His words probably sounded sincere to an unpracticed ear, but she knew the moment she lowered this gun, she'd feel the back of his hand across her cheek and the bite of the rough-board floor scrape across her face. Frank Bentz had become a cruel man, or perhaps he always had been and she'd been too cow-eyed over him to see the truth.

She shook off the foggy memories just in time to see him step toward her, murderous fury in his eyes. She squeezed the trigger and the recoil jerked her arms upwards. For an instant she saw his surprised expression, then he crumpled to the floor, oozing a pool of blood. She'd aimed for his forehead and missed, hitting him in the chest. Trembling, she reached down, hesitated, then finally touched his neck. No pulsed jumped beneath her fingers. She put her fingers underneath his nose. No warm breath raced across her skin.

She'd killed a man.

She'd killed Frank.

Cold terror seeped through her. Doubts and memories fled, chased into dark corners by hard, cruel reality. She was a murderer. She shook her head to clear the hysteria coming to claim her.

Laying the gun on the table, she sank into a chair before her legs gave way beneath her. Half a glass of liquor sat where Frank had left it this morning before he went to Dawson. Her fingers closed around the glass and she brought it to her lips, trembling. The amber liquid burned over her tongue and down her throat.

At her feet, the pool of blood widened, spreading like red silk across the floor. She wished she'd made some plans as to how to dispose of the body. She glanced at the window, where snow fell at an increasing rate. She'd have to bury him somehow.

An hour later, she piled the last stone on his grave. She'd done little better than scratch a shallow depression from the nearly frozen soil near the porch, drag him into the grave, then cover him with heavy stones. With each grunt as she hefted a rock, she wondered if she harmed the baby sleeping within her womb.

She trudged back to the cabin, grateful for the warm, yellow light shining from its windows. But one step inside the door sent a family of shivers up her back. The thirsty, rough floor boards had greedily soaked up the blood and now bore the evidence. A wide, smeared path led to the front door. No amount of scrubbing would ever rid this house of its shame.

Panicked, Jenny threw her few clothes into a carpetbag. Then she paused and forced herself to think calmly. She'd need money and a place to hide, at least until the baby was born. Underneath the table, Frank's bag of gold waited, abandoned in the scuffle. Jenny reached down and picked it up. It was blood money, stolen or won in rigged card games. But it was money just the same and she had to think of the baby. She stuffed the sack into her carpetbag.

Then she remembered more of Frank's drunken bragging. He'd once said something about winning a mining claim from some poor, drunken slob in a game of five-card stud. She dropped the bag, went to the bedroom, and lifted the mattress. There, tucked neatly beneath, were several papers folded together. She paused with them in her hand. No matter what they were, Frank had gotten them at a cost to someone else and no one but Frank knew what that cost might have been. The baby moved again, as if reminding her they needed to flee. She hurried to the other room, stuffed the papers into the bag, then gathered Frank's clothes from a trunk and committed them to the dancing fire. She watched his fine clothes burn, haunted and grateful at the same time as a carefully starched collar charred and then blackened. She was free. But free to go where? *Where* didn't matter, she decided, as long as it was away from here.

Outside, the sky darkened with night but she couldn't spend one more minute in here with Frank's blood and Frank's memory. There were neighbors up the canyon, miners who'd be glad to see a new face. Perhaps she could hide out in one of the tiny communities that had grown up around a stream generous with its gold. Frank and his money would soon be missed in Dawson City and if the Mounties lived up to their reputation, they'd quickly be on the trail, wanting to know what happened to Frank Bentz.

With a last look at the cozy cabin, she vowed to take with her only the memories of warmth and plenty, of feeling her child move within her. She would leave behind all traces of Frank's cruelty, all memories of his fist connecting with her jaw and his booted foot on her backside. She would never again bring to mind his rutting in bed and the way his emotionless thrusting robbed her of the last remnants of any affection she'd once felt for him. She closed the door and stepped into the snow-filled night.

"And I suppose that's my driver." Constable Mike Finnegan toed a heap that snored at his feet.

Superintendent Sam Steele slowly shook his head and stared down at the fur-covered body curled peacefully on the floor of the Gold Nugget Saloon. "Meet Alfred Nantuck, dogsled driver."

Finnegan reached down and tugged at Alfred's arms. "Get up, Alfred. We've got mail to deliver."

Alfred mumbled into his fur coat and rolled over on the damp, dirty floor to recurl himself into a warm ball.

"Sure, and I don't think Alfred and I will be enjoying each other's company today." Finnegan straightened and pushed back his Stetson. Twenty sacks of mail waited outside in Alfred's dogsled, mail destined for lonely miners in the gold fields up north. The postal service had been overwhelmed in May when the first wave of miners clogged the routes to the Yukon, desperate to reach the gold-rich fields; hundreds of sacks of mail waited in Skagway and Dawson City. The Mounties had stepped in and now faced the daunting task of delivering the piles of months-old letters.

"I'll see if I can find another driver. Might take a few days," Steele said with a sad shake of his head. Sam Steele was a man who expedited matters whenever possible. Another delay was sure to chafe his good humor.

Finnegan turned and walked out into the morning sun. A team of wolf-dogs waited, yellow eyes peeping above bushy tails as they lay curled in the snow.

"What do you say, boys? Are you willing to take an Irishman to Eldorado?"

A few tails thumped in greeting, but the team remained huddled against the cold. Finnegan had seen the native drivers come and go through Dawson with their teams. He'd even begged a few lessons on off-duty hours. The sound of the runners sliding across the snow; the cold air whipping by his face; the joy of overwhelming solitude. His heart began to pound with anticipation.

"Constable, are you sure about this?" Steele asked, stepping to his side and eyeing the waiting team.

"Aye, Superintendent. The mail's piling up."

"I won't risk a man's life to deliver the mail."

Finnegan gripped the handles of the sled. He could almost feel the strength of the dogs through the wood. He put one foot on a runner and the team sprang to their feet and surged forward a foot or two.

"Hike!" The dogs sprinted forward, their tails curled over their backs.

"Haw!" They swung in a wide circle, throwing bits of snow from their paws.

"Take care, Constable," Steele called, then followed those words with more instructions, but the rest of his comments were lost in the wind as Finnegan headed north.

Finnegan swung his dogsled wide to miss a churned puddle in the center of the path that served as the main street of Eldorado. Snow covered the rickety, dark buildings, lending them a beauty they didn't deserve. Figures hunched against the cold raised their heads as he passed and he knew that soon there'd be a crowd surging against the doors of Cranston's General Store as he unloaded the long-awaited mail.

Deep cold had done little to slow activity in the mining town. Mud-encrusted boots had been traded in for snowshoes, but the saloon still did a raucous business despite storms that came and went. Vice and desire seemed to have no seasons, he mused as he ordered the team to a stop.

"They been asking when you'd get here," Robert

THE HEALING

Cranston said, stepping out onto the porch of the makeshift post office. "With Christmas coming, they're all looking for word from home."

Finnegan stepped off the sled's runners and gripped the handles for a moment longer as his knees unlocked and trembled from fatigue. "Got a late start in Dawson," he said, stomping his feet to restore circulation. "Lost my driver."

Cranston grasped the bulky canvas bag. "Go on down to the Dead Horse. I'll start sorting this. Word'll travel fast you're here."

Finnegan shoved open the glass-paneled doors of the saloon and the odor of unwashed bodies and smoke immediately assaulted his cold-sensitized nose. He breathed deeply of the offending odors and stepped into the warm interior.

"Constable Finnegan," George the bartender called, swiping at a spot on the counter. "You're the most asked-about man in the Yukon."

Finnegan leaned against the bar and unbuttoned his fur coat. He inhaled again, taking deep the biting odor of liquor, stirring his demon to life. "I got away late from Dawson and had some trouble crossing the river."

George sat a glass in front of him, the amber liquid within winking and flirting with him. "This is on the house . . . to warm your insides."

Finnegan stared at the glass and the old thirst rose, stronger this time. He swallowed back the temptation. Again. "I think I'll just have a cup of that coffee I smell brewing in the back."

George removed the glass and poured the liquor

back into the bottle, the golden pleasure trickling down the sides, staining the paper label. "Suit yourself, Constable. Watch the counter for a minute, will you?"

Finnegan nodded, forcing his eyes away from the bottle sitting so tantalizingly close. In a few minutes, George returned, a steaming cup in his hands. Finnegan wrapped his hands around the warmth and sipped the evil concoction. Thick and strong, the taste jolted him, putting temptation a little further away.

George leaned his elbows on the counter. "I ain't never seen you take a drink, Constable. I reckon it's allowed, being as it's so cold and all, ain't it?"

Finnegan looked up into eyes silently assessing him, eyes accustomed to judging weaknesses and strengths. "Some of the lads take of the spirits. I don't."

A spark of interest passed through George's eyes and awoke the bloodhound within him that sniffed through life stories and sought tasty bits of drama to fill empty days. "Any particular reason why?"

Finnegan smiled, clasped the cup tighter, and stared down into the dark liquid. "Never developed a taste for the stuff."

"An Irishman that don't drink? God never made such."

"Well, he made this one."

With a final assessing glance, George leaned closer. "I might have some business for you."

Finnegan looked up.

"Frank Bentz ain't been seen for a week or two."

"Frank Bentz?"

"A gambler turned miner. Lived up there on Quartz Creek with a whore. He usually comes in here once or twice a week. Buys some drinks, buys a woman. Ain't nobody seen him lately and there's talk."

"What kind of talk?"

George leaned closer. "There's talk he's been stealing gold from sluice boxes. Ain't nothing been proven, but most folks feel he ain't willing enough to get his hands dirty to dig out all the gold he spreads around."

"What about the woman?"

"The whore? Ain't nobody seen her either."

"What makes you think something happened to them? Maybe they just moved on."

George shook his head. "Folks think he's got it too good here to leave. Plenty of women, liquor, new pigeons coming through town all the time he can cheat at cards, her waiting for him at home. She ain't a bad looker."

"Maybe she left and he followed her."

"Strange woman, that one. She's got a bellyful and she says it ain't Bentz's. Told everybody who'd listen that she was going to make a home for the baby, once it's here. Said she was going to give up the trade and settle down." George chuckled. "She ain't been in the business long enough, I reckon, to know that a whore's always a whore."

An uneasiness settled over Finnegan. A pregnant whore. A gold thief. A twisted love affair. There was enough chaos right there for a crime. Enough to warrant him looking into George's tale. His return trip to Dawson City would have to wait. "Can you give me directions to their cabin?"

Huddled beneath a huge hemlock, the tiny cabin appeared deserted. Vacant, curtainless windows stared out at the unmarred blanket of snow. No sound rivaled the quiet of the forest.

Finnegan ordered his team to a stop and the dogs lay down. He stepped up on the porch and peered in a window. A cold fireplace stared back at him. Rags and bits of household goods lay strewn across the floor. The door protested his shove with a deep groan and swung open. A table sat to the left, dishes placed haphazardly on its dusty top. A red silk dress hung across the back of a chair, its bold color in stark contrast to the grayness of everything else. Someone had left in a hurry.

Acknowledging the bristling hair on the back of his neck, Finnegan drew his revolver and walked to the tiny area curtained off from the rest of the room. He shoved aside the dull bit of rough fabric to reveal a bed, tousled and unmade, sheets and a rough blanket still in place. A woman's high-button, black shoe sat under the bed. Two depressions, side by side, sank into the ticking of the mattress.

He picked up the shoe. It was almost new—barely scuffed and carefully polished. Turning it in his hand, he marveled at the smallness of the fit and the pointed heel—completely out of place in the rough Yukon. A tool of her trade? A subtle lure? A symbol of helplessness and fragility, meant to appeal to the protective nature of a man? Or meant to give rise to the very erotic images now spinning in his head?

Carefully, he replaced the shoe and moved to the fireplace. Long-dead ashes lay scattered across the hearth, tiny rodent tracks crisscrossing the fine, gray powder. A dark stain on the floor caught his attention and he squatted to examine it better. Thirsty, dry boards had quickly absorbed the stain, taking it deep within the fibers, but there was no mistaking that it was blood. And a lot of it.

Finnegan rocked back on his heels and pushed back his Stetson. Who had done in whom? He returned to the bedroom. A man's clothes hung on a nail on the wall. A fancy brocade vest hung atop carefully tailored pants and a smooth, black coat. Not something a gambler would leave behind, Finnegan reasoned. But except for the shoe and the red silk dress, no women's clothes remained.

He looked outside, into the graying of twilight. New snow coated everything, covering tracks and any other evidence. With a last glance around the cabin, he stepped out onto the porch. A dark smear, matching the one on the cabin floor, skimmed across the threshold onto the porch and to the steps. Bending, he brushed aside the snow to reveal the same dark swatch dribbling down the steps until it was lost in the dark soil below.

A small clearing surrounded the cabin, obviously

built as a temporary home. No frills had been wasted on its construction and foot-high stumps dotted the yard beyond. Out near the edge of the yard lay a churned area, barely discernible in the darkening day. Finnegan slogged through the snow until he stood amidst uprooted rocks and sprayed dirt.

Wolves.

He knelt and poked at the dislodged stones. Faint lumps beneath the snow, they formed a roughly oval pattern, as if someone had intentionally placed them there.

Perhaps as a grave.

He turned over a few, brushed away more snow, but no body lay beneath them and the area was so disheveled he couldn't tell if anything had ever been buried there. If so, wolves had probably dragged the body away. He stood and peered out into the woods. A faraway wolf's call raised the hair on his neck. His dog team stood, their noses quivering. Whatever had happened here, there was nothing to go on now. The couple was gone, leaving only faint clues behind. Snow had covered their sins, if indeed there were sins to obscure.

The sky was quickly darkening and the short day would soon fade into the long, winter night. The trail back to Dawson City would be long and cold and lonely. He took his place on the sled, spoke to his dogs, and swung back toward Eldorado. His lead dog stopped the team and looked back over his shoulder at Finnegan just before they left the clearing, as if questioning the decision to leave this mystery unsolved.

"There's nothing we can do here, boy," he said, and the dog turned his attention back to the trail. As they sped off, Finnegan pushed the cabin and its small drama to the back of his mind, concentrating instead on next week's long run to Skagway.

Chapter Two

The contents of the slop jar sloshed against its sides, threatening to splash over onto Jenny's hands before she reached the back door. Holding her breath against the stench, she fumbled for the doorknob with one hand. Miraculously, it opened before she touched it.

"I hate to see you doing this kind of work," Thelma muttered, wrenching her face away from the odor as Jenny hurried past and down the path to the outhouse. Thelma beat her to that door, too, and held it open while she dumped the putrid contents into the dark hole. Vile odors rose and Jenny hurried out while Thelma slammed the door closed.

"I don't know why the customers can't go to the outhouse here same as they'd do anyplace else," Thelma muttered as Jenny yanked on the pump handle until a thin stream of water poured out. Quickly she rinsed the enameled pot and lumbered back to the outhouse to dump the contents again.

"Miss Lucille wants to make them feel as comfortable as possible, I guess. Pampered and such." Jenny put a hand to her aching back and trudged the well-churned, snowy path back to the brothel.

"Still, you shouldn't be a-doing this kind of work, what with your condition and all."

"Nobody wants a pregnant whore, Thelma. I'm just thankful to have a job." Jenny stepped into the moist warmth of the kitchen and inhaled the aroma of roasting meat.

"Git out of my kitchen with that nasty thing." Loni turned from her stove, wiping her pudgy, black face with the end of a dirty apron.

"I'm sorry." Jenny tucked the chamber pot behind her back. "It's always so warm in here. I couldn't resist."

Loni's expression softened. "Go put it back and wash your hands. Then come and see me." A wide grin split her generous face. "I got a surprise for you."

Her stomach rumbling at the mention of food, Jenny slipped through the parlor unseen and crept up the stairs to the Egyptian room. Vacant, the room still stank from the chamber pot. Replacing the pot behind the screen, Jenny yanked up a window and pushed the curtains aside to let the pure, clean air pour inside. She breathed deeply, none of the Skagway street smells reaching the second-floor window. The air here came straight off the snowy peaks gleaming pink in the western sky.

Turning from the window, she yanked the soiled sheets off the bed and replaced them with clean ones, leaning around her protruding stomach. When she was done, she ruffled the tasseled bedspread over the bed and tucked it neatly under the pillows. Then, she stood back. In the four years she'd worked in various whorehouses, she'd never gotten accustomed to the odors. The musky scent of lovemaking didn't bother her, somehow seeming natural. But men visited whorehouses for more than just sex, and alcohol always played a role. Too much alcohol left a mess for her to clean up—at least since she'd started working as Miss Lucille's house girl. But she wasn't complaining. Most madams wouldn't give a pregnant girl a second look when they came begging for work. Miss Lucille was different, offering her the only job available with profuse apologies. And Jenny had leaped at the chance. After all, in a few months, she'd have another person to think about.

She glanced around the elaborately decorated room, marveling that Miss Lucille had managed to get such wondrous and odd things here to Skagway. The mounted head of some beast hung over the fireplace, great tusks sprouting from its mouth. Cavorting, golden figures danced half-naked across the dark-green wallpaper. Above, candles burned brightly in a chandelier made entirely of moose antlers. The *coup de maître*, as Miss Lucille liked to say, was the golden sarcophagus propped up in the corner. It had once been an Egyptian king's coffin, she'd explained, but the only girl who'd use the room after that was Thelma, who professed no fear of anything. Miss Lucille was a smart woman, well versed in what appealed to men in rut. Men lined up to use the room on Saturday nights and Thelma had to go out and buy herself a set of scales to weigh gold dust. Some, Thelma had said, even wanted to make love *inside* the coffin.

Shaking off the spell the room always cast over her, Jenny hurried downstairs, remembering Loni's promise of food. She ate when it was offered and tried to save her money, existing on one meal a day.

Loni's kitchen was always warm and fragrant, perhaps the homiest place in the otherwise austere house. Miss Lucille's decorating tastes ran to the odd and the dark. In addition to the Egyptian room, there was the Texas room for those who fancied themselves cowboys; the girls wore nothing but chaps. And the London room, where gentlemen had the privilege of peeling away layers of high-necked, constricting clothes from girls that acted as virginal, proper English ladies.

"Sit down right there, Miss Jenny." Loni motioned with a spoon at an empty chair, then ladled steaming food into a bowl with the same spoon. "Did you wash your hands?"

Jenny dashed to the pitcher and bowl that always sat by the door.

"Use plenty of that soap."

Jenny lathered her hands and arms and rinsed,

embarrassed to have forgotten so important a task. Loni insisted on cleanliness for all who entered her domain. No sex-tousled girls were allowed in for midnight snacks, not unless they'd bathed since their last customer. Jenny wondered how Loni had ended up so devoted to Miss Lucille as she hurried back to the table, now a slave to her grumbling stomach.

"Now try this chicken soup and tell me if it needs more salt." Loni set a generous portion in front of her, far more than was necessary for a "taste."

Jenny had swallowed three gulps before she thought to look up and mumble, "It's fine."

Loni grinned as if the comment was a compliment from the queen herself. A gold tooth gleamed in the front of her white teeth and Jenny took another spoonful, closing her eyes as the delicious broth slid down her throat.

"You don't eat enough to feed that babe," Loni scolded, her expression quickly darkening.

"We're all right," Jenny reassured. "I don't get that hungry."

"Hungry or not, that baby gotta eat." Loni's voice held the hint of an exotic accent. She'd come from the Caribbean on a ship with big, white sails, a tropical place where flowers bloomed all year and sudden storms brought spectacular rainbows. Jenny could sit for hours and listen to Loni's stories of a land completely surrounded by water.

"You hear me, girl?"

"What?" Jenny blinked and found herself staring straight into Loni's face. Seated across the table,

Loni leaned beefy elbows on the table, her eyebrows knitted together in concern.

"I say, do you hear me?"

"I promise I'll eat more."

"Miss Lucille ain't gonna charge you for your meals."

Jenny shook her head as she devoured another spoonful. "I'm not one of the girls. I just work here and I have to pay for my food."

Loni tapped a finger on the table. "You let me talk to Miss Lucille. We see about that."

"Talk to Miss Lucille about what?" Lucille Turner stood in the doorway, her conservative dark-green dress tastefully draped around her still-trim figure.

"About feeding this child."

Lucille looked from one to the other, obviously perplexed.

"She don't eat but one time a day. She's saving her money, she say."

"Heavens, Jenny, you don't have to pay for your meals here. Not with the work you so cheerfully do. You'll eat with the girls whenever they eat and more often if you're hungry." Lucille stepped into the room, letting the swinging door close behind her. "Have you been under the assumption you were supposed to *pay* for your meals these weeks you've been here?"

A wave of perfume enveloped Jenny, a soft, soapy scent, as Miss Lucille approached and leaned over her. "Where on earth did you get such an idea?"

"I . . . heard you tell one of the men that came

to do the garden . . . that he had to pay. . . ." She let her words drift off as amazement filled Miss Lucille's face.

"Good heavens, Jenny, he was somebody I hired off the street to do odd jobs. I mostly wanted to discourage him from coming inside the house. Have you thought all this time . . . and done without. . . ." She blinked rapidly before raising her eyes to Loni.

"Don't worry, I took care of her."

Lucille smiled. "You have the most apt talent for appropriate sneakiness, Loni." She returned her attention to Jenny and placed a hand on her shoulder. "I came to find you, Jenny. May I see you in my office a moment? After you finish your meal, of course."

Miss Lucille's office was as odd and exciting as any other of the rooms she decorated. Lavish tapestries covered the rough board walls and thick, colorful Persian carpets lay on the floors. A soft glow filled the room, light given off by candles held in opaque glass globes that sat about on tables like stars fallen to earth.

Jenny fidgeted on the stiff, upholstered chair, wishing she'd had the time for a bath, sure she still reeked of chamber pots.

"I'm sorry, my dear, just a little business to clear up before we open tonight." Lucille bustled into the room and closed the door behind her. She rounded the baroquely carved desk and settled into the velvet chair like a queen ready to rule her kingdom.

THE HEALING

"I'll come right to the point. I have a proposition for you. You are under no obligation either to accept or refuse. When this request came to me, I immediately thought of you."

Jenny nodded and waited.

Lucille picked up her eloquent quill and ran the soft ridges of the feather through her fingers. "One of our best customers lost his wife and son in childbirth a little less than a year ago. I am given to understand that the circumstances were tragic and he has never quite gotten over the pain of losing them. He has seen you about and come to me with a request."

Fear slipped into Jenny's blood like a cold, slithering snake.

"He would like an evening with . . . a lady . . . a pregnant lady."

Jenny sucked in her breath.

"He only wants a supper in one of our rooms, some pleasant conversation. He said specifically that he did not want . . . relations."

Suspicions began to grow.

Lucille held up a hand. "I know it sounds strange and if it were not . . . who it is, I would have refused. I believe that he simply wants the company of someone who reminds him of his former life. He is a prominent man in Skagway with interests in Dawson City as well and he has always conducted himself as a gentleman while under my roof." Miss Lucille smiled. "Over the years, I've become a very good judge of people and Mr.—, the gentleman, is quite normal in his tastes, I'm confident. He's offered to pay very well and you would keep fifty percent, just as the other girls do. I wouldn't have come to you with this if you weren't ... experienced."

Jenny's thoughts spun. Something niggled at the corners of her mind about a request so odd, so poignant. Out-and-out strangeness she could handle, but this situation seemed rife with emotion and uncertainty. And yet, there was the money. She mentally tallied her secret cache, safely hidden beneath a loose board under her bed. Just a little more and she'd have enough to buy her way to Dawson and maybe some left over for a room for a week or two.

"I'll do it," she said, snapping open her eyes.

"Don't you want a little more time to think it over?" Lucille studied her closely.

"No. When?"

"Tomorrow night. I'll have Thelma alter a dress to fit you."

"Thank you," Jenny said as she rose and started for the door.

"Jenny, wait."

She turned to face Miss Lucille's worried face. "If anything ... untoward should happen ... I'll be close by."

The room glowed softly, Lucille's glass globes lent for the occasion. The girls called this the Virgin Room, used mostly when fathers brought their sons in for their first taste of illicit love. The decor was

THE HEALING 31

homespun, with soft quilts on the bed, white curtains at the windows, and a fire softly burning on the hearth. Nothing erotic or adventurous here, the emphasis only on comfort and the deed at hand.

Thelma had altered a soft, pink gown, one of her personal dresses, a garment meant for life outside the brothel. The bulge of Jenny's stomach was almost concealed, just enough to be tasteful and yet revealing enough to satisfy the mysterious visitor's careful instructions. Loni had set a lovely table in the center of the room, complete with white tablecloth and a softly flickering candle. As soon as their guest arrived, supper would be served.

As the minutes ticked past on the mantel clock, Jenny grew more uneasy. Every intuition she possessed was rebelling at the thought of what she was about to do. And yet, logic told her this was a simple meeting with a simple purpose. She'd conjure, and then soothe, his memories, allowing him his fantasies. Why was that any different from any other meeting? Somehow, though, it was.

Maybe it was this room. Jenny rose from the rocker and paced to the hearth. Red rugs, red curtains, and nauseatingly baroque furniture belonged in a brothel. Quilts and rockers did not. They belonged in a home with loving parents and children.

The practice of a father acquainting a son with his own particular variety of sin had never sat well with her. When they became men, they might frequent brothels for whatever reason drove them to do so. But it would be their decision, made in adulthood, not encouraged in adolescence. Fathers should encourage their sons to seek wives, start families, contribute to their communities. But, none of the men she'd known were ever such upstanding specimens.

A soft knock interrupted her thoughts. She arranged her face and her dress and turned toward the door. "Come in."

The door eased open and a young man stepped inside, his hat in his hand. "Are you Jenny?" he asked softly.

"Yes, I'm Jenny." She walked toward him.

"My name's Percy. Percy Sage."

The owner of the new Sage Bank and Trust, whose brand new plate glass windows were probably already lettered with his name.

Jenny swallowed and pasted on a smile, liking this arrangement less and less with each second that dragged past.

Percy laid his bowler hat on the top of a dresser and slowly closed the door, latching it with a soft click. He turned, firelight reflecting in his dark eyes. He was a handsome man, a single dark curl dangling over his forehead. His clothes were the latest cut and a pleasant whiff of men's cologne drifted around him. A chill ran up Jenny's back.

"When are you due?" he asked, moving toward her. He stopped, inches from her, and laid a hand intimately on her belly.

"In December, I think."

He spread his palm across her stomach and his

THE HEALING

eyes drifted closed. "My wife was seven months along when she died. We could feel the baby move." His eyes opened to stare straight into hers. "Can you?"

"Yes, I can. Sort of like tiny butterflies fluttering around inside me." She covered his hand with hers and felt him flinch. Despite his appearance or what Miss Lucille said, there was a dull madness in his eyes, a pain so deep it had ripped open his soul and let demons inside.

His other arm slid around her shoulders and urged her closer until her protruding belly pressed against him. He sighed, ruffling her hair with his breath as he pressed his temple to hers. "We used to make love," he whispered, "Cecilia and I, after she was as far along as you. She was so big, she'd have to be on top. And when I'd slide inside her, the baby would kick and I could feel him there, pushing against me."

"You shouldn't be telling me these things, Percy," she whispered, the oddity of his words prickling down her spine. "They're private between Cecilia and you."

"They can't be private anymore because she's dead. So, now I can tell anybody I want." He tightened his arm and pulled her against him. "I want to feel that again, to know that there's really life there, still alive, still breathing. I want you, Cecilia."

Alarm bells clanged in Jenny's head as he unbuttoned the back of her dress, keeping her firmly in his arms. The pink dress slid to the floor, leaving her wearing only her thin chemise. He dropped to his knees, shucked out of his coat and pressed an ear to her stomach. "I can hear you in there," he said, "little William. Are you turning somersaults and upsetting your mama's stomach?"

"Percy—" Jenny put her hands on his hair and fought the urge to shove him away.

Suddenly, he stood and snatched the chemise from her shoulders. She heard the thin batiste rip and the cold air close around her.

He looked at her for a long moment, allowing his gaze to slide up her naked body and back down to center on her stomach. Then, without taking his eyes off her, he quickly disrobed and stood before her naked.

"Cecilia, it's been so long."

She'd been called by other women's names before but never with the unearthliness that possessed Percy Sage's voice.

"You and William left me here alone and that was a bad thing to do, Cecilia. You know how I hate to be alone."

If she could just get him in bed, she could take control of the situation. From her experience, most men, once in the throes of passion, became more malleable. But the sight of him, throbbing before her, sent a wave of eeriness through her. She sensed no evil in him, just a detachment from reality that both repulsed her and evoked sympathy.

His hands were all over her, his mouth searching, tasting. He backed her toward the bed, lifted her onto the mattress, and joined her there, eagerly pushing her knees apart.

THE HEALING 35

"I'm frantic for you, Cecilia. Remember our first night?"

Jenny cooperated at first, allowing him to touch her intimately, enduring him. Perhaps he would get what he wanted and leave. A frantic worry for the baby spun through her, but she pushed it aside and concentrated on handling Percy. He scrambled over her, frantic in his quest to have her, trembling, shoving against her.

"Percy, stop. You're hurting me."

He paid her no heed, mumbling Cecilia's name, concentrating on burying himself in her as quickly as possible.

"Percy. Stop!" She scooted backwards, away from his groping, stopping only when the hard headboard pressed against her back.

But he pursued her still, hands smoothing her hair, knees gouging her sides as he clambered forward, all sense of the present lost.

"Percy, please. I'm not your Cecilia. You're going to hurt the baby." She fended off his hands that seemed to fly in all directions at once.

At that moment, Miss Lucille stuck her head in the door. "Is everything allri—" She stopped midsentence and her face blanched. "Thelma," she said softly. "Go to the post office across the street and get Constable Finnegan. I saw him bring in the mail this afternoon."

Lucille stood peering around the door, seemingly frozen in her tracks.

"Percy, why don't we play a game? You remember you used to like games," Jenny suggested, trying to keep her fear under control. She'd handled unruly men before. She only had to keep her wits about her.

He hesitated for an instant and raised his eyes to meet hers. "A game? You never liked games before, Cecilia."

And neither did Jenny. Too much time with a customer could result in some sort of attachment, so she'd always made it a rule never to dally in the performance of her job. "But you did, and I . . . feel guilty that I never played them with you."

He smiled slyly. "What are you up to, you vixen?"

She was buying time, hoping for some sane way out of this. Some way to preserve this poor man's sanity and her own safety.

"I paid good money for you." His eyes darkened. His mind had taken a leap out of the past and landed smack in the present. "I paid a ridiculous amount of money for this night and I'll have you, damn it, have you in any way I choose."

"I'm pregnant, Percy. You wouldn't want to hurt the baby, would you?" She slid off the bed and now had the four-poster between them.

"You're not pregnant. It's all part of Miss Lucille's plan. I asked for a pregnant whore, knowing all too well there is no such thing, is there? You girls know how to get rid of that sort of problem."

"Look at me. How can you say that?"

He glanced at her stomach. "I don't know how Miss Lucille accomplished that disguise, but . . ." He paused and frowned. "She's never failed to give me what I want. I don't care how she did it."

THE HEALING

He rounded the bed. "Why won't you come to me, Cecilia? Must I chase you around the room?" He smiled slyly. "Is that what you want?" He bent down and took a knife from his discarded pants.

Jenny's heart began to pound. Malice grew in his eyes as he advanced on her. Muted voices hummed outside the room and the door opened quietly. Over Percy's shoulder, Jenny watched a Mountie slip into the room and assess the situation with a glance. He took off his coat and hat and handed them to Miss Lucille. Then he rolled up his shirtsleeves to his elbows.

Thelma and Lucille's faces crowded the slight crack in the door. Other customers were just next door and across the hall. A semblance of normality must be kept at all times. Prostitution was illegal but rampant, and the already-overworked Mounted Police tolerated the practice as long as all established houses kept to a fringe area of town dubbed Lousetown and business was conducted quietly.

At Miss Lucille's request to fetch a constable, Jenny had expected an ugly scene with drawn revolvers and a room full of scarlet-suited rescuers—enough unwelcome attention to close down the house. But the man now approaching her walked with a deliberate nonchalance that masked the strength she felt emanating from him. Red hair topped an angular face and he walked with a slight limp. Small in stature, he rolled back his sleeves to reveal muscular forearms. Moving with an ambling gait, he picked up a quilt from the back of a chair and draped it over his arm.

"Mr. Sage?" His voice sang with a faint Irish lilt.

Percy pivoted. "Yes?" he answered, pasting on his business face, seemingly oblivious to the fact he was stark naked.

"Are you and Cecilia having some trouble here?"

Percy wrinkled his forehead and the intensity in his eyes faded. "No, no trouble."

"Cecilia looks cold. You know how pregnant women are." Without taking his eyes off Percy, the Mountie leaned across the bed and handed her the quilt which she quickly wrapped around her.

Percy smiled. "Yes, indeed, I know. Cecilia and I have been married for seven years and she was never cold-natured until she conceived my son."

How bizarre, Jenny thought, edging away from the bed. Constable Mike Finnegan, as Lucille had called him, didn't seem at all ruffled to be standing in the bedroom of a whorehouse with two naked people.

"Aye," Finnegan said, picking up another quilt from the foot of the bed. "My wife shivered her way through her first pregnancy. Thought she'd set the chimney on fire piling firewood in the fireplace." He draped the quilt around Percy's shoulders. "Now, Percy, you know this lady here isn't your Cecilia, don't you?"

Percy swung his gaze to Jenny as she sidled toward the foot of the bed. "Of course she is, aren't you, love?"

Finnegan caught Jenny's eye and shook his head slightly.

"No. My name is Jenny."

THE HEALING

"And she works here for Miss Lucille, don't you, Jenny?"

Percy frowned. "I paid a lot of money for tonight."

"Yes, you did." Finnegan eased himself down onto the edge of the bed and Percy followed, pulling the quilt around him, still clutching the knife. "But I don't think Miss Lucille allows knives here. That would be dangerous, wouldn't it? A man might get cut in the wrong place, wouldn't you say?"

Finnegan looked at Jenny and jerked his head toward the door. She began to sidestep across the space between the bed and the door.

Percy's eyes widened as he looked down at his hands. The knife clattered to the floor and he covered his face. "What have I done?"

Jenny bolted for the door, eased through the crack, then turned around to see Finnegan settle a hand on Percy's quivering shoulder.

"I'm going to jail, aren't I?" Percy asked softly.

"Well, let's go down to the office and talk about things first."

"I don't know what I was thinking, what I have been thinking since the night she died." He looked up, tears streaming down his cheeks. "I never visited a whorehouse before three months ago, never even dreaming of doing such a thing. But, the house ... It's so empty." He turned to face Finnegan. "I miss her so much. You know what I mean, don't you, Constable?"

Finnegan looked over Percy's bowed head. Jenny

met his eyes and felt a tingle and then a rush of embarrassment. There was such kindness in his face, compassion for the man beside him. She sensed from the moment he walked into the room that he'd passed no judgments, that he was a man well attuned to the flaws of mortals.

"Constable, help Mr. Sage with his clothes."

Jenny turned and stared into the wide-eyed face of a young constable whose Adam's apple bobbed up and down. He diverted his eyes from hers and brushed past.

"Are you all right, ma'am?" Finnegan had moved to her side and was guiding her into the hallway with a hand on her elbow.

"I'm fine. He didn't hurt me." She tugged the quilts closer, suddenly more ill at ease than she'd been with Percy. "What are you going to do with him?" She glanced past him to the room where Percy fumbled with his shirt, muttering to himself.

Finnegan followed her gaze, then returned his attention to her face. "Poor lad's lost his senses. Loss'll do that to a man sometimes. Do you want to press charges?"

"No. He's got enough problems." Jenny glanced away from Finnegan's face, garnering her suspicions around her, shaking awake all her cautionary voices. There was something about this man, something odd and unsettling. And familiar. As if they'd once met someplace, looking into each other's eyes for a second or brushed shoulders in a crowd.

Mike Finnegan was nothing like the men she'd been attracted to before. Surely she'd remember

THE HEALING

him if they'd ever spoken. In fact, if he'd been three feet high with a tall, green hat, she'd have thought for sure she was looking at a leprechaun. A riotous shade of red, his hair lay in disobedient curls. Eyes the color of a summer sky crinkled at the corners from years of laughter, Grandma would have said.

But leprechauns were devious and clever.

The man before her was downright dangerous.

Chapter Three

"Are you all right, lass?" Mike Finnegan touched her shoulder, his brows knitted together in concern.

His touch was gentle, undemanding. How she had often longed for a human caress that expected nothing in return. The skin on her shoulder flinched in anticipation and she pulled the quilt closer, suddenly aware of her nakedness, both physically and emotionally.

"What were you about, and you in this condition?" Finnegan lowered his gaze to her stomach, lingered there for a breath, then returned to her face.

"I'm a whore, Constable. What other reason do I need?"

The words, bitter and regrettable, spurted out of her mouth like snake's venom. She had no reason to hurt this man who'd probably saved her life and yet, some instinct bade her to put a wall between them. Perhaps it was a guilty conscience because he represented the law in the Yukon Territory and she knew all too well that the money that had brought her here was stained with blood.

He narrowed his gaze, unshaken by her bold comment. "I suspect you're more than that, lass, and too smart to get caught up in the likes of this without good reason."

She shrugged one shoulder. "Situations such as this happen from time to time in my business. Don't you encounter circumstances, Constable, where people act very differently than you would have supposed they would?"

"Aye," he said with a sly smile, "I do. I would have supposed a lass as smart as you would have found Mr. Sage's request more than a little odd. And Lucy, you should know better."

Lucille greeted his criticism with wide eyes. "He's one of our best customers, Mike," she said, dropping her voice to a whisper and stepping closer. "Heavens, he's building the new bank. I thought all he wanted was a little time with her and maybe a . . ." Lucille paused and swallowed, then stepped closer until her painted red lips nearly touched Finnegan's ear. "And now I'd like to get you and your very colorful jackets out of my house before everybody in town knows you're here."

"Take Mr. Sage out the back way, Constable," Finnegan said, jerking his head toward the stairs that led to the kitchen. "Miss—" He waited, expectantly.

"Hanson. Jenny Hanson."

"Miss Hanson and I'll be right along."

Jenny went to her room and quickly dressed. Returning to the quiet hallway, she found Finnegan waiting for her just inside the stairway.

"I thought waiting in the hall would make the customers nervous," he responded to her unasked question, holding the door open for her to brush past.

"You're awfully careful about offending the people you should be arresting." Holding up her skirts, Jenny picked her way down the dark, narrow steps.

Behind her she heard his disarming chuckle. "If I were to arrest every prostitute in this town, where would I put them all?"

They emerged in the alleyway that ran behind Miss Lucille's. The dank odor of urine and mold filled the moist night air as they moved quickly down the alley and across the street. A single lamp was lit in the post office and the young constable waited to open the door. With a furtive look down the street in both directions, Finnegan closed it behind them.

Sacks of mail were stacked in a lumpy mountain. Atop them, curled up in sleep, was Percy Sage, his cheek pillowed with one arm.

"I sat him down here and went to the back for the lamp. When I returned, he'd crawled up there and was sound asleep." The young constable shrugged his shoulders.

THE HEALING

"Chasing one's marbles makes a bloke tired, I'd imagine," Finnegan said with a wry smile. "Let him sleep. I'll take Miss Hanson back to the office and make out a report."

"I thought we weren't going to make this official," Jenny said as he led the way down a narrow hallway, a lamp throwing a halo of light in their path.

"No one'll see this except me and Constable Harper." He sat the lamp on a desk made of planks and two wooden crates. A quill sat in an empty whiskey bottle and a stack of papers lay scattered across the surface.

"While you were dressing, I talked to Lucy. She thinks Mr. Sage has family in Seattle. I'll send them a wire tomorrow and have somebody come and get the poor lad."

So he and Lucy were on a first-name basis. No one else called Lucille Lucy, as least none Jenny had heard. An unexplained edge of jealousy worked its way into her head like an embedded splinter.

"What exactly do you need with me, Constable? I believe that you saw everything you needed to see back at Miss Lucille's."

Finnegan looked up from the paper, a smile jerking at the corners of his mouth. "Should I put down, too, that the lady has a sassy tongue?"

"I don't care what you put down."

Finnegan laid the quill aside and leaned back, folding his arms across his chest. "Do you have some problem with authority, miss? You've been at me like a viper since I walked into your room. Then, I believe, you were at the disadvantage."

"I apologize," she said, chagrined at her behavior. The man had just rescued her and she couldn't even give him a civil answer. "Law enforcement and I don't usually mix well." If he only know just how true that statement was.

"Aye, I can see where that'd be a problem for you."

He paused, obviously waiting for her to say something else. When she didn't, he leaned forward over his work again. The scratch of his quill filled the silence.

"How long have you been a . . . working lady, Miss Hanson?"

The suddenness of his question startled her. "Since I was fifteen."

He paused in his writing, the only sign he'd heard her, then he continued. "Had you ever seen Mr. Sage before?"

"You mean 'seen' as seen on the street or 'seen' as in serviced him?"

He glanced up briefly with a wry smile. "At Lucille's."

"No. His favorite is Claudette."

"So, he was a frequent customer?"

"One of our best, according to Lucille. I haven't been . . . working, not like that, since Lucille hired me three months ago."

"What have you been doing?"

How on earth had she let the conversation drift

down this path? She hadn't meant to reveal her past to anyone, let alone this Mountie.

"I've been cleaning, doing odd jobs."

Finnegan raised his head to pin her with those eyes that could change from laughing to serious in a second.

"Most men don't want a pregnant whore, Constable. In fact, I'm a rarity—most whores get rid of unwanted pregnancies."

She'd meant to shock him into silence, but he didn't flinch, didn't react, keeping her wriggling beneath his gaze.

"But you want to keep this baby?"

"Yes."

She expected him to ask why and she had the it's-none-of-your-business answer waiting to fire, but he returned his attention to the paper before him.

"This report will go into my file. No one else will see it unless there's more trouble."

"May I leave?"

He sprinkled sand across the paper and dumped the excess to the floor. Then, he handed the document across the desk. "As soon as you sign your name here."

She accommodated with a flourish and handed it back. He picked it up and surveyed the paper.

"Surprised I can write?"

"No," he replied with a smile. "Just admiring your hand."

She rose and walked to the door.

"Miss Hanson." His voice stopped her in the doorway and she turned.

"You can tell me this is none of my business, but what do you intend to do once the baby's born?"

She put a hand on the door facing. "I intend to raise it, Constable, and give it the home I never had." Then, she slipped through the door without a backward look.

When she passed through the front room, Constable Harper lowered his feet to the floor from where he'd rested them on the desk. Percy was still asleep, curled in a ball, slumbering through his insanity. She allowed herself one memory of this evening, one image of the madness in his eyes, wrought by sorrow and loss and love. Then, she vowed never to think on it again.

A paper on the wall next to the door caught her eye and she turned for a closer look. It was a roughly sketched map of the area—gold fields, rivers, and streams were noted and named. A red line followed a crooked path from south to north with the words "mail route" sketched next to it.

"Constable Harper, what is this?" She tapped the paper with one finger.

Harper tilted back his head. "It's the mail route Constable Finnegan takes when he delivers mail to the gold fields. With all this," he gestured toward the mountain of canvas bags over his shoulder, "the Mounties'll be making regular runs now."

Tiny black boxes appeared at several points along the red line. "Matthews" was written next to one. "Anson" next to another. An unnamed box sat in the jut of land labeled "Cutter's Fork." "And these boxes with names. What are they?"

"They're the stopovers, ma'am. The police are paying folks along the route to take in our men on their runs. Going up and coming back."

"What's this one? This little one here with no name by it."

"That's an old trapper's cabin. Nobody lives there now. Was somebody there a while back, but they cleared out. Constable Finnegan's going up there in a day to two to find out whether or not it's fit for us to use."

Regular, steady money. A cabin along the route would produce income and provide a safe place for her to have and raise her baby. She traced a finger down the black-ink line until the Yukon River made a deep bend. She knew just the place and a gullible man that would sell it to her.

Sleep did not visit Mike Finnegan although he tried mightily to get some relief from the thoughts speeding through his head. But as he tangled his blankets into a fine mess, green eyes and rich chestnut hair chased away all thoughts of sleep. She was a beauty, skin like fine cream and a body built to pleasure a man. Pity she'd ended up in that way of life. He sat up on the side of his cot and ran his fingers through his hair. Fine one he was to admonish anybody for a life of excess.

The thick smell of overcooked coffee beckoned. He stood and headed for the stove. The dark liquid ran from the tin pot in a ribbon and one taste said it was worse than usual. Grimacing, Finnegan took another swallow.

He paced to the window and stared out at the clear night sky. Stars winked peacefully over the man-made chaos. No errant cloud drifting by would guess that the tiny creatures below complicated their lives in ever-amazingly intricate ways. And Jenny Hanson was complicating his.

Whore. The word grated on his nerves. Always had. Just the sound and the way the human mouth pronounced it, expelling the syllable in one swift breath, spoke of disgust and loathing. A woman who sold her body for profit. As opposed to brides who married rich husbands for the money. What was the difference? And yet society drew a neat line with a moral ruler, condemning one to shame and elevating the other to respect.

Niggling doubts haunted him. Something about Jenny Hanson reminded him of someone he'd once known. But the familiarity ended there. He could put no name or place on their meeting. If he'd once known her, even back in his alcohol-fogged days, he'd remember those eyes and her comely curves.

She was a worldly woman, no naive miss who could have innocently misjudged poor Percy Sage's intentions, he thought, shifting the direction of his musings. So why did she place herself in such peril? Did carrying the babe make her so desperate for money?

She'd laid herself a hard path, that was for sure. Once the child was born, she couldn't work in a

THE HEALING 51

brothel. Most madams frowned on girls who brought the baggage of children with them. And no respectable man would marry a woman of her ilk. Maybe she'd be lucky and some lonely miner would take her to wife. Then, she'd live a hard, if less lonely, existence, dependent on his futile and speculative scratching. And she'd bear him children from her beautiful, haunting body.

He closed his eyes and willed away the image of the terror in her eyes. At that moment, his attention had been on Percy and his madness, but his mind had recorded her image and now played it back with torturous repetition.

Lucy had sent for him because she knew he'd be discreet. If there was one thing he knew something about, it was houses of ill-repute. Many nights he'd awakened in the alleyway behind one, hung over and robbed. Then, there were other mornings when daylight poured across a rented bed to illuminate a snoring partner with little in common with the tempting vixen he'd taken to bed the night before. Funny how half a bottle of whiskey could make a man compromise.

Past is past, he thought, firmly shutting out those old, well-worn memories. Today he lived a new life. No whiskey. No women. No complications. He was a representative of justice, making the minutes of his existence count for something other than the passage of time.

He moved from the window and stared up at the spot on the mail sacks where Percy Sage had slept in oblivious repose. He'd sent him home and instructed Constable Harper to accompany him. Tomorrow he'd wire Sage's family in Seattle. By the end of the month, someone would come for poor Percy and take him away, another casualty of love and desire and life's twisted sense of humor.

Across the street, an intoxicated soul staggered out of Lucy's and paused by the hitching rail, as if getting his bearings. He misstepped off the sidewalk and tumbled into the muddy street. With awkward flounderings, the figure struggled to his feet, climbed back up on the sidewalk, and trudged away crookedly, his steps stiff and studied, trying to maintain some semblance of dignity. With every effort the shadowy figure made, Finnegan felt a corresponding twinge in his own body. The feel of wet, horse-trod mud slipping into his mouth; the jarring thud of meeting the ground face first; the overwhelming embarrassment at not being able to walk down the street without the last five hours of your life readable to everyone who passed.

Finnegan drained the cup and, leaving it on the stove, padded down the hall and back to the cot in his makeshift office. But even as he slipped between the blankets, he knew sleep would still be a stranger.

"How much do you want for it?" Jenny leaned forward, her heart pounding.

"Well . . ." Jules Winstead looked between the two women bending over him. "It's played out. Didn't find nothing there more'n a couple of nug-

THE HEALING

gets and a little dust. The real gold's further up the Yukon River."

"Then you oughta be willing to sell it real cheap." Thelma glowered at Jules across Loni's kitchen table.

"Well . . ." He paused again. "I reckon I can let it go for . . . say, seven hundred dollars."

"I wouldn't say that, Jules. No, I wouldn't say that at all." Thelma deepened her frown.

Jules again glanced between the two faces hovering near him. "Five hundred?"

Loni sliced an onion with a *thunk* and threw him one of her scolding looks.

"Four-fifty or I cut you off . . . permanently." Thelma crossed her arms over her ample bosom, drawing Jules's attention there.

"You wouldn't do that for a rickety old cabin and some thin ground, would you?" He looked pleadingly up at her.

"You oughta take three hundred, then, and consider yourself lucky."

"All right. All right, I reckon it's a deal, before you gals talk me into giving it to you."

Jenny counted out the gold with shaking hands and shoved a paper across the table. "Sign this bill of sale."

"I can't write," he complained.

"Then make your mark and I'll witness it," Thelma added.

"Wait a minute, I want it read to me first."

Thelma planted a fist on a cocked hip. "Now

Jules, if you can't read, how do you know I'm going to read it to you truthful?"

"I trust you, Thelma. Hell, I done asked you to be my wife five times now."

Thelma sent him a heated glance and snatched up the paper. Carefully, she read the terms of purchase. He pretended to listen while creeping a hand up her thigh.

All the while Jenny's heart hammered. Finally, she'd have her own place. Her own house, her own porch. Her yard and her kitchen. Bought and paid for. No one could ever take it away from her. It was on the mail route between Dawson and Forty Mile, equal distance between two other stops, if Jules was telling the truth. Now, she had to convince the Mounties to stop there.

"Satisfied?" Thelma asked, slapping the paper down in front of Jules.

He picked up the quill and carefully made an "X." "Not as satisfied as I'll be in about an hour. You owe me something special for this, Thelma."

Jenny snatched up the paper and scanned the careful lettering. Then, she folded it and put it into her apron pocket. "Thank you, Jules."

"I don't reckon I need the place anyhow." He gazed up at Thelma. "Not when my other claim's making enough to support two."

"You go on down to the claims office and file that. I know you don't want to do no prospecting, but just in case there's something on it Jules overlooked," Thelma urged. "You got everything right

THE HEALING 55

there you need. Go on, now." She turned to smile down at Jules. "I got a debt to pay."

Jenny stepped out of the claims office and suddenly the air smelled fresher. Weak sunshine seemed as bright as summer and the winter wind that swept down out of the mountains was colder, fresher.

The baby stirred and love for that tiny bit of life overwhelmed her, bringing quick tears to her eyes. She owned a home, a home for the two of them. She touched her swollen stomach, soothing a hand across the rough material of her dress. From the moment she knew she carried new life, she'd felt a sense of contentment, completion. Ridding herself of it had been unthinkable. Now, she was in command of her own future. Pulling her coat closer up around her neck, she set off down the street toward the office of the North West Mounted Police.

In front of the temporary office a dog team waited. Gray wolf-dogs sat on trembling haunches, their attention trained on the door of the tiny building. The door opened and they wagged their furry tails, making little sweeps in the snow. Mike Finnegan appeared, a large canvas sack thrown over his back like Santa Claus. He deposited the load in the sled and turned when she approached. A smile played at the edges of his mustache and his eyes crinkled. "Miss Hanson."

"I have a business proposition for the Mounted

Police, Constable Finnegan. Could we go inside and discuss it?"

Finnegan shifted his weight to one hip, crossed his arms over his chest, and smiled wider. "I was of the opinion last night that you held the police in none too high a regard."

He wasn't going to make this easy on her. An edge of anger crowded into her thoughts, but she chased it away. All she needed from him was an agreement. His friendship was unnecessary. *But*, a tiny voice whispered, *his friendship is something you'd very much like to have.*

"I apologize for my rudeness last night. I was upset."

He didn't look convinced and his smile deepened. "Somehow, lass, I don't think you'd have been any more agreeable if you hadn't been."

No comeback sprang to her lips and she stood there, marinating in his sarcasm.

"Come inside," he said finally, opening the door.

She brushed past, trying to keep the anger out of her eyes and her voice. Her future hinged on his answer. Pleasing men was something she did very well but something told her Mike Finnegan was a man not easily coerced.

She stopped in front of the map and placed a finger on the thin, red line that bisected it. "I've purchased a cabin here." She pointed at the bend in the river the claims officer had shown her. "I'd like to offer it to the Mounted Police as a stopover on the mail run for the fee of a hundred dollars a year."

Mike backed up against the desk, crossed his arms, and studied the map. "The old cabin at Cutter's Fork."

"Yes."

Beneath her practiced look of detachment, desperation swam in Jenny Hanson's eyes. Despite this haunting sense of *déjà vu* that seemed to float around her, there was something else only his policeman's instinct picked up on. Something about her just didn't ring true. Where had she gotten so much money? And what was she running from to hide herself and an unborn infant in the harshness of the Yukon?

She'd calculated well, whether she knew it or not. The bend of the river in which her cabin sat was a treacherous place where, even in frigid temperatures, the ice was unreliable and apt to break through. A stopover there could prove valuable, a fact he'd been about to pursue in the interest of the police himself.

He pushed away from the desk and stepped to her side. Pretending to examine the map, he watched her from the corner of his eye. "I think we can reach an agreement."

Relief flooded her face for an instant before she reapplied her mask of indifference. "I'm sure the arrangement will benefit both of us."

Only she knew the true depth of those words,

but Finnegan was sure it went deeper than a mere business deal. She turned to face him, her gray, oval eyes meeting his directly. "Thank you, Constable. May I ask a favor?"

She blinked and then swallowed, small signs that asking the impending question made her uncomfortable. "May I travel as far as my cabin with you on your return trip north?"

"A dogsled's a mighty bumpy ride for a lass in your condition."

Her expression never changed, but Finnegan sensed waves of panic rolling off her. When had he become so attuned to the thoughts of another? And if he was reading her thoughts, was she also reading his?

He took a step backwards and a slight frown crossed her face. "It's the only way I have of getting to my cabin, Constable."

"Are you going to live there alone? Just you and the wee one? Who'll deliver it when your time comes?"

"I'll do it myself."

Finnegan snorted and walked to the desk. "You're risking your life and that of the child. Stay here in Skagway until after the baby is born."

"I've seen babies born before. Do you know how many I've delivered, Constable?"

He turned and met her steady gaze.

"Ten. Twenty, maybe. When I worked in Seattle, we took the women in labor up to the attic so the customers wouldn't hear their screams. The mothers couldn't see their babies when they were

THE HEALING

born, of course, or they'd want to keep them. And then mother and child would be cast out onto the street to starve."

Riveted where he stood, Finnegan listened, trying to shut out the pictures her words evoked.

"So I'd wrap the baby in rags and sneak down the back steps."

The hair on the back of Finnegan's neck stood in anticipation of a horrific confession.

"Then, I'd take the baby and slip through town while everyone was asleep, down to the river."

Finnegan closed his eyes.

"Where I'd meet Father O'Hara and give him the child. He always found someone to love them." She studied his face and a slow smile tipped the corners of her mouth. "Did you think I was going to say I threw them in the river?"

She'd played his emotions like a fine instrument. Miss Hanson read people very well. "No, I—"

"You did think that." She slowly shook her head. "You must believe me a monster, indeed. Did you think, Constable Finnegan, there were never babies to be dealt with in a profession such as mine?"

"No, I would—"

"We are women before we are whores. We feel the same things as the women who hold their heads up when they walk down the street."

She whirled and walked to the door. "I can make other arrangements to get to my cabin." She stopped with her hand on the doorlatch. "But I intend to hold you to our agreement."

He nodded and started to say more, but she slipped through the door.

"Damn stubborn lass," he muttered to himself, feeling as though he'd just endured a windstorm.

Chapter Four

"I'm leaving tomorrow morning."

"Oh, dear God." Jenny gasped and dropped the bedpan she held, spattering a sickly yellow stain across the pristine snow. "Constable, you'd frighten a body to death."

Finnegan leaped the low, white picket fence that surrounded the backyard of Lucille's and hurried to her side. "I'm sorry. I thought you saw me come to the gate."

The cold had touched her cheeks and lips, reddening them against her creamy skin, and her green eyes sparkled with laughter. She was a different woman from the one oozing abstinence last night. Again, he felt the tug of familiarity.

Jenny grunted and bent to retrieve the pan, bumping her head against Finnegan's when he attempted the same. She straightened and laughed cheerfully, embellishing the winter-dulled garden.

"Many a man has leaped that fence, but usually to get *out*, not *in*." She smoothed back a strand of hair with a work-roughened hand and Finnegan's eyes traced the delicate line of her ear and the wispy sprigs of hair that defied obedience. "What can I do for you, Constable?"

"I'm leaving for Dawson City tomorrow. You're welcome to ride as far as your cabin."

She tipped her head, her expression suspicious. "Yesterday you were none too anxious to trouble yourself with a lass in my condition."

"You misunderstood me. I never said I wouldn't take you."

"No, you were too busy thinking me a monster."

Never had he met a more disagreeable woman . . . or a more enticing one. But enticing was her business and he was sure she did that very well.

"Sure and there's been many an unpleasant thing you've done because you had to. It's the same with all of us. Your story surprised me, that's all. I thought none the less of you because of it."

She glanced over her shoulder at the towering house faced with fading boards and he followed her gaze. She was reluctant, if only for an instant, to give up the known for the unknown. But inside that house waited a life of service and humiliation, no matter how Lucille dressed it up otherwise, and Jenny knew it. Mentally, he urged her not to go back on her plans, however dangerous and odd they had seemed before.

THE HEALING

"What time will you leave?" she asked, swinging her gaze back to him.

"About four in the morning."

She smiled, perhaps the only real smile he'd yet seen cross her lovely face. "I'll be there."

Four o'clock came cold and damp and dark. Finnegan loaded the last of the mail sacks into his sled, arranging them to leave a small space for Jenny, and wondered if he was out of his mind taking on the responsibility of transporting a pregnant—a very pregnant—woman a hundred miles in the dead of winter.

He'd made a run to the surrounding gold camps yesterday, giving himself time to think over her request. And now as he moved to the dog team, checking harnesses, he remembered her smile of freedom. He'd once felt the same, he thought, as he'd watched the coast of Ireland fade into the sea.

He looked down the street toward Lucille's. He should have offered to come for her, he chided himself. What was he thinking, allowing a woman in her condition to trudge through a dark, cold morning?

"Constable?"

She'd come up behind him, her fur-framed face made sallow by the yellow lamp that hung on the porch post.

"I was just thinking I should have come to get you."

"Nonsense," she said, swinging her arms for warmth, "a brisk walk never hurt anyone."

Someplace, she'd managed to scrounge a fur-lined coat, one with the fur turned inside to capture her body heat—a perfect garment for their journey.

"I'm afraid there's not much room." He gestured and glanced toward the crowded sled. When he looked back, she was smiling at him in a way that made cautioning bells go off in his head. "I'll be fine, Constable. Whatever room you can spare, I'll gladly take."

He glanced behind her and saw she'd brought nothing save a small satchel. "Where are your supplies?"

"I brought essentials. I was hoping I could impose on you and your men to bring things to me a little at a time." She frowned as doubt crossed his face. "I have money to pay you."

"I'm not worried about the money. I can't let you go there without adequate supplies. Flour. Sugar. Canned food. What are you going to eat?"

She produced a revolver from a pocket in her coat. "I intend to live off the land."

Frank Bentz eerily crossed his mind again as she expertly checked the chamber and re-pocketed the weapon as if she'd been born with an Enfield in her hand.

"I'll be fine until your return trip. You said yourself there isn't much room, certainly not enough for a load of supplies."

Debating with himself, Finnegan studied her and

calculated his own meager supplies. With luck and good weather, he could stretch his own until he arrived in Dawson City, leaving her the surplus. The alternative was to leave her here with Lucille. She might be angry and disappointed, but at least there'd be someone to help with the birth, someone to feed her, give her shelter.

"I can find other ways to reach my cabin," she reminded him. "But I prefer to go with you." She stared at him from inside her fur hood, reading his thoughts and interpreting his hesitation. Other men made the trip from Skagway to Dawson in winter. All sorts of men with all sorts of intentions upon their arrival. Again, he thought of the joy in her face yesterday when she realized she'd soon be leaving this life behind.

"All right. We'll work something out," his mouth muttered before his brain had time to countermand him.

She lowered herself into the sled, rejecting his offer of help. Nestled there amid the lumpy canvas bags, she would be anything but comfortable on their journey. Yet, she set about settling in without complaint.

Daylight came late and then it was weak, the sun a glowing disc that never ventured far above the horizon. They followed the river, sometimes traveling alongside it and sometimes gliding across the slick, frozen surface. Hours passed, whisked away by the wind that stole words and breath. The brief daylight faded back into a long night and they made camp in a protected bend of the river, sheltered from the wind.

Finnegan offered her a hand, which she accepted, and when she stepped out of the sled, her knees wobbled from their long-cramped position. He put his arm around her and pulled her against his hip until she'd moved forward a step or two and regained her balance.

"I'm fine, Constable," she said, stepping away from him. Above all, she didn't want him to think her a burden. He thought ill enough of her as it was. Usually, the opinion of others, particularly men, wasn't important. But consistently, she found herself eager to win this man's approval—something she'd never have, she reminded herself.

He let his arms drop back to his sides and began to set up camp. Jenny wanted to offer her help, but found that each way she thought of to offer that help, he'd already taken care of in his efficient way. So she sat down on a fallen log, shifted the bulk of her stomach, and watched her guardian.

He moved with a confidence and capability she admired. Beyond simple human kindness, he seemed to have no interest in her whatsoever, and that suited her just fine. She'd already had enough men to last her a lifetime. What a relief it was to look into Constable Finnegan's eyes and not see a glimmer of lust. Well, maybe just a little. Just enough to remind her she was still a woman despite the fact that she felt like a packhorse with a too-heavy load. She shifted on the log and repositioned the baby again.

"What's a good Irishman doing in the Yukon?"

He looked up from where he was slivering wood with an ax and laughed. "You're a nosy lass, aren't you?"

"Yes. Well?"

He stared at her a moment longer, smiling, then shook his head. "I came to Canada to seek my fortune."

"And you're going to stick with that story, I take it?"

"Yep."

"Don't you want to know about me?"

He split off a piece of spruce and stared down at the churned snow. "What's a woman like you doing in a whorehouse in Skagway?"

"I came to Canada to seek my fortune."

He laughed, never taking his eyes off the infant fire now smoking underneath his cupped palms. "Well, both of us are liars, at least."

"Since both of us are consummate liars, what do you say we make up a past—for both of us."

He bent down to blow on the bits of lichen and wood. "Isn't that a waste of time since we both already have pasts too horrid to discuss?"

"Mine's not horrible, just not . . . acceptable."

"And you were hoping mine was just as bad."

"Oh, at least as bad."

Finnegan chuckled and stood up. "Well, you go on and make yourself up an infamous past."

"Uh-uh. We have to make up each other's."

He shook his head and picked up his pack. "I'm

not much on games, Jenny. Never had the time nor the concentration for them."

"Come on, Constable—"

"Call me Finnegan." He looked up from rummaging in the canvas bag. "Just Finnegan."

"All right, Finnegan. We have to have some way to pass the time, don't we?"

"How about silence?"

She shook her head. "Too quiet."

"Do whatever suits you, lass." He pulled out a paper-wrapped parcel and handed her two strips of pemmican.

She turned the stiff, brown strips in her hand and wrinkled her nose. "Dear God, I'd hoped I'd never have to eat this again." She took a bite and chewed the tough meat concoction.

"I'll get a rabbit tomorrow." He squatted by the fire, the flat piece of pemmican held between his teeth as he coaxed the feeble flames into a blaze. He looked little like a Mountie in his furs, except for the two gold crowns pinned to his leather collar. She supposed it behooved them to move about incognito sometimes. Besides, furs were much warmer than serge.

"I think you left behind a string of broken hearts in Ireland. You were such a rake, some father threw you off the Emerald Isle at gunpoint."

Finnegan laughed, crinkling his eyes. "You have some imagination."

"You came to Canada a broken-hearted man, eager to lose your pain in the wilderness."

"Nothing so romantic as that."

THE HEALING

"You joined the Northwest Mounted Police and came to the Yukon hoping to find your fortune."

"I've already seen enough fortunes to know that I don't want one."

"What *do* you want, Constable?"

"Right at this moment? I want this snow not to put out our fire." Fine flakes began to fall, hissing and sizzling as they struck the glowing wood. He glanced over his shoulder. "We can move back into that spruce thicket if the snow worsens."

In an hour, the snow was falling thickly. They moved their camp back into the trees and Finnegan found a small clearing for the fire, but eventually the snowfall overpowered the flames and it died a sputtering death.

The dog team curled up in the snow, their tails wrapped over their noses. Finnegan moved the sled and their belongings underneath an ancient spruce whose spreading branches protected still-bare ground. Their backs against the tree, they sat on empty canvas mailbags and pulled furs over themselves for warmth.

"Are you warm enough?" Finnegan murmured, close by her side.

Jenny peeked out over the fur she held against her chest. His head thrown back against the tree trunk, he seemed oblivious to the cold.

"Yes, I'm fine."

"Let me know if you need anything." In seconds, he was snoring softly.

She should have been exhausted, but instead the quiet of the night stirred her to wakefulness. The snowfall provided its own light, covering everything with a dim, ghostly pallor. A gentle drawing tugged across her belly, not labor but a tightening she'd been told was normal. The baby shifted in response and suddenly, she had to relieve herself. Urgently.

Struggling to her feet, she heard the dogs stir behind her. She took a step and a hand closed around her arm.

"Where do you think you're going?"

"I have to go."

He stared at her sleepily, comprehension eluding him.

"I have to relieve myself."

"Now?"

"Right now." She shrugged as her face heated. "It goes with the pregnancy."

Finnegan stared out at the ever-deepening snow beyond their snug shelter. They had no source of light as the fire was long dead. She couldn't traipse around in the dark, stumbling over logs and sticks with her awkward balance. Under the tree was her only choice.

"Go around behind the tree," he said just as she arrived at the same conclusion.

"That would be the logical thing to do," she said, hating the embarrassment that crept over her. She, of all people, could lay no claim to modesty. So why did this particular situation bother her so much?

He caught her hand as she pulled off her gloves, holding onto her fingers for a moment. "I won't hear anything. I'll whistle."

THE HEALING

She laughed, partly at the absurdity of the situation and partly at his generous gesture. That bit of consideration would never cross the mind of any other man she'd ever met. "It's all right. I don't worry about that sort of thing," she lied.

She stepped to the back of the tree, struggled to untie her fur-lined pants and as she squatted down, she heard him softly whistling what might pass for a jaunty Irish jig.

By midday, they'd reached the wide, graceful bend of the Yukon River known as Cutter's Fork. In the dim sunlight, the river swung in a wide, icy arc to skirt a narrow jut of land. There, clinging to the abrupt land, sat a lonely, isolated cabin.

They'd been travelling for hours now on the ice-covered river, confident the plunging temperatures had safely thickened the ice. Fresh snow skittered across the frozen surface, driven by a restless wind and huddled into drifts. Finnegan stopped the team and stood surveying the river beyond.

"Why are we stopping?" Jenny asked, twisting to try and see him. She was so close to her dream, she could almost touch it. Home. Her home. All hers.

"This is a dangerous place. The ice here never freezes as thick as in other places."

"It's just over there. Can't we just swing in that direction?" She pointed toward the cabin about a hundred yards away, impatience sweeping away her caution.

Finnegan shook his head. "I don't like the way the ice looks. We'll have to backtrack, come back up alongside the river." He looked down into her face. "That'll take us about half a day extra."

Unexpected tears filled her eyes as she looked back toward the cabin. Before, the cold and discomfort hadn't mattered so much. At the end of her struggle would lie her prize, she'd comforted herself. Now, another half day seemed unbearable.

Finnegan stepped off the sled's runners and walked out onto the ice closer to shore. He looked down, poking the surface with his boot toe. He glanced back at her and she blinked to hide the silly tears. These days any- and everything brought tears. He stared at her a long moment, then returned to the sled.

"Haw. Easy," he commanded his team and they swung slowly toward shore, ears pricked forward. Finnegan stepped off the runners to walk alongside, his eyes trained on the ice ahead. A crack brought the team to an abrupt halt. The lead dog whined and began to back up, tangling his harness with the dog behind him. Soon, the whole team was in reverse, swiveling in their harnesses, scrambling back the way they'd come, their harnesses hopelessly twisted.

"Easy! Easy!" Finnegan called, one hand firmly on the sled handles.

Then the world fell out from under their feet. Jenny gasped as the wave of cold water took her breath and chunks of ice scraped around her arms and head. She was entangled in a maze of dogs, rope, and floating bags. For an instant she saw Finnegan under the water as he slashed harness lines with a knife to free his dogs.

Jenny shed her heavy coat and forced her way to the surface. The dogs were scrambling for shore, breaking off chunks of ice as they plunged ahead. Her arms were quickly growing numb and her thoughts fuzzy. Arm over arm she swam, keeping her eyes on the house waiting for her. Behind her she heard Finnegan shout encouragement to her and once his hand buoyed her up, cupped her backside and shoved her toward shore.

When she crawled ashore, she was showered with icy droplets as the dogs shook the water from their coats. She coughed up water, heaving and gagging until cold, biting air again filled her lungs. She struggled to her feet and looked back, but there was no sign of Finnegan. She stumbled to the edge of the water. A bag of mail floated to bump against her feet, then another.

She waded back in, up to her knees, shoving aside ice floes with her already numb hands. Then she caught a flash of brown floating beneath a chunk of ice. She plunged in an arm and pulled. Finnegan's head cleared the water's surface. His face was pale and his lips were blue.

Stumbling backwards, she hauled him with her. They both collapsed in the snow and she put an ear to his nose.

Nothing.

She rolled him to his stomach and pounded him between the shoulder blades. His body tensed, then he vomited water. Again he heaved and coughed. She heard the intake of breath and tears of relief coursed down her cheeks. Groaning, he rolled to his back and breathed deeply. One arm lay twisted at an odd angle.

"Are you all right?" he asked with his next breath.

"Yes," she managed between sobs. *Damn these worthless tears to hell.*

She lumbered to her feet, staggering against her own bulk and the heavy, wet fur pants. "Come on. We have to get inside."

He rolled to all fours, then staggered to his feet. She saw him quickly count the dogs, already warmed from their thick undercoat. Together, they pulled and pushed each other to the cabin. Inside, firewood waited, stacked beside the hearth. God bless whoever had been here last, she thought as she felt on the mantel, praying. Her fingers nudged a tiny metal box. With trembling hands she flipped it open and found precious matches.

Finnegan took a step toward the hearth, then collapsed in a heap on the cold, dusty floor. Trembling uncontrollably now, Jenny fumbled with the match, willing her numb fingers to cooperate. She struck the match once. It sputtered and the scent of sulfur wafted up. Concentrating on her hand, she struck it again. A tiny orange flame flared. Using both hands, she guided the match to the waiting kindling. Dry moss flared, sizzled, and caught the wood. A puff of wind rattled the door and increased the draft in the chimney. The

THE HEALING

flames leaped in response, and soon the fire was blazing merrily.

Shedding her heavy fur pants, Jenny stood shivering in only her shirt and pantalets. She longed to hold her hands over the flames and feel her fingers again, but Finnegan lay in a cold puddle. She rolled him over, pulled off his clothes down to a red union suit, and managed to drag him closer to the fire. Then she sat down on a rickety stool and buried her face in her hands to sob out the inevitable flow of tears before he regained consciousness.

Finnegan awoke with a mouthful of dog fur. He sputtered and coughed then slid away from the musky scent. But movement brought searing pain to his left arm resting on his hip. He groaned and shut his eyes against the wave of nausea that rose to torment him.

A hand touched his shoulder. "You've got a broken arm, but outside of that, as far as I can tell, you're all right. So are your dogs." Her voice was steady and reassuring. He cracked open an eye. She knelt over him, a man's shirt opening down to the swell of her breasts. Lace-edged pantalets peeked out from underneath. Her hair hung long and wet across her shoulder and her eyes were filled with concern.

His dogs lay all around him, some curled up against his back, already panting from the heat in the cabin. "They wanted to come in and I thought they might help you warm up. Seems they had the same idea."

He looked up into her face and tried to arrange his scattered thoughts. Had she pulled him to shore? In her condition? "Are you sure you're all right?"

"I'm fine," she repeated with a pat to his shoulder. "When I get my pants dry," she pointed to where her pants were spread over a three-legged stool by the fire, "I'll go out and get wood for a splint."

Finnegan pushed up on one elbow and the world spun. Nausea rose again and he slumped to the floor. "Wait. I'll go."

"Nonsense," she replied as she picked up the pants from their place close by the fire and felt them. "There's nothing wrong with me that these warm pants won't fix." She stepped into them and tied the leather thong around her swollen middle, then tucked the voluminous shirt into the waistband. "I'm going to try and find my coat, too. Your clothes are over there, drying."

Finnegan took her word for it, afraid to raise his head lest the nausea return. A soft hand felt his forehead and slid down the side of his face. "You had me worried. You vomited again and I was afraid you'd choke."

He moaned in response and lay perfectly still. If she'd set her mind to swim across the river, there was little he could have done about it at the moment. The door closed with a swoosh and he

THE HEALING

listened, hoping if he heard a shout he'd be able to get to his feet.

Despite his efforts at vigilance, sleep claimed him. He awakened when she opened the door and softly shooed his dogs outside. He attempted to roll over onto his back, but his arm screamed in protest. Then her hands were on his face again, feeling for fever, tracing down his cheeks. "Your arm's badly broken, maybe in two places," she said through the curtain of hair that teased his chest. "We've got to set it before it swells too much."

He opened his eyes and looked into her face. Her skin was pale and drawn, and fatigue haunted eyes were nonetheless clear and alert. He reached up with his good arm and touched her cheek. "How's the baby?"

She smiled. "The baby's fine. They're tough little creatures. Now, see if you can wriggle up against that wall."

Summoning his strength, he sat up, waited for his head to stop spinning, then pushed backwards until he felt the log wall firmly against his back. She laid two green sticks on the floor. Then, with a grunt, settled herself beside them. She braced her bare feet against his thigh and took his hand and wrist in her hands. "I'm going to give it a good yank and then we'll splint it."

"Do you know what you're doing here? I've had broken arms before, but none that hurt like this."

"I've set plenty of arms before and yours is broken in more than one place." Her fingers crept up the soft knit of his union suit and gently probed an area above his elbow. "There." He winced and she moved down his arm to a point halfway to his wrist. "And there."

She clamped a strip of cloth between her teeth and got a better grip on his arm. "Ready?"

He nodded and she gave a hard yank. Something popped and the whole world turned red in front of his eyes. Darkness circled him, but he fought it off. She expertly laid the sticks along his arm and wrapped them securely in place with the strips of torn cloth. She tied the last knot, tightening it with her teeth and fingers, then slipped a sling over his head that looked suspiciously like women's underwear.

He looked down at the delicate lace edging, then back up at her.

"I had one extra pair," she said with a mischievous grin. "Doesn't matter. Won't be able to get them on soon, anyway." She rolled to her feet, wearing nothing save her *only* pair of pantalets and the loose shirt. Finnegan closed his eyes and let his head drop back against the log wall.

From the quick look he'd gotten at the room, it appeared she'd managed to fish out almost all their belongings, including several sacks of mail which lay drying all around the room. His clothes hung over two chairs by the fire and she padded about as if she were in complete command of the situation. She *was* in complete command. Jenny Hanson was never caught unprepared, he'd guess. Except for that night in Lucille's when she'd been scared and vulnerable, her dark eyes huge in fright. He'd been there when her well-built defenses crumbled, something he'd bet money almost never happened. And in that moment an unwelcome bond had taken root and begun to grow.

Chapter Five

The wee hours of morning crept by on silent footfalls until a dark dawn arrived. Finnegan awoke with a throbbing head, his thoughts disjointed and fuzzy. Swiping a parched tongue around the inside of his mouth, he wished for a drink of water, but thirst was quickly consumed by pain as he leaned forward. With a deep, rumbling groan he laid his head back on the doubled-over mail sack and waited for the pain to subside and cognizant thought to return.

He was burning up, too close to the lazy fire, now more embers than flames. Gathering his willpower, he slid his hips backwards and gritted his teeth while he maneuvered his shoulders to follow, careful to keep his broken arm immobile. When he had wiggled to a cooler space, he glanced around the room. Jenny slept in a far corner, another mail sack for a pillow. She lay on her side, the bulk of her stomach sagging to the floor, pulling her skin uncomfortably tight across her ribs, no doubt.

She flinched in her sleep, her fingers flexing, grasping. Tiny sounds of protest came from her lips, moans and murmurs of disapproval. Somewhere within her had to dwell a chorus of demons, spawned by crushed dreams and disillusionment. Were they loose tonight? Tormenting her already exhausted sleep? He wished he could crawl to her side and shake her awake, but all he could do was lie with his arm like a damned stick of firewood and watch the evidence of her nightmares.

Time came and went in mysterious patterns. When he awoke later, hours later if the fire was any measure, he knew he had a fever. A high fever. The room danced in slow contortion, twisting and stretching. Deep thirst nagged at him, but he couldn't think nor form the words to wake Jenny.

Had he slept again? He blinked as a cool, soft hand slipped beneath his cheek.

"Dear God, what a fever," she murmured as she put the wonderful water to his lips. He lunged for the cup, intent on drinking it down to the last drop, but she pulled it away after he'd only gotten one sip. "If you drink too much, you'll throw it back up." She let his head slide gently to the floor and he was only vaguely aware that she'd slipped a furry coat underneath his cheek.

Panic edged its way into her carefully controlled thoughts. He was burning up with fever. With so much damage to his arm he could die of infection. She walked to the window and looked outside to clear her thoughts and get control of the fear threatening to overtake her.

What would Grandma have done? She smiled at her own dark reflection in the dusty glass. How many years had it been since she'd thought of her childhood? And of the woman who'd raised her? The woman whose heart she'd broken the day she left home. Of all the sins she'd committed, that was the only one she truly regretted.

Closing her eyes, she could shut out the quivering, reflected firelight and the dirty, meager surroundings and again run barefooted in the warm prairie sunshine. Chickens clucked around her feet and down by the creek Grandma navigated the narrow bank, dusty dress hem tucked up into her belt exposing spindly, white legs as she swung on a willow branch.

Willow bark. Grandma boiled willow bark for fevers.

Jenny snapped open her eyes and reality returned. Grabbing Finnegan's sheathed knife from the floor beside him, she shrugged one shoulder into her now-dry coat and slipped outside into the cold starlight. The dogs, sleeping against the door, rose stiffly and ambled a short distance away before lying back down with an "oof."

She picked her way across the snow-covered yard to the edge of the river. The crushed surface they'd churned and broken in their escape from the riv-

THE HEALING

er's hold had refrozen, healed, leaving only long, white scars in the ice as evidence.

Down by the river's edge a group of willows clung to the water-gnawed bank, their bare-knuckled roots clawing for a hold in the dark soil. Grotesque in the starlight, she could imagine that in summer the delicate branches would quiver with teetering birds warbling their songs in the short, warm season.

Grandma used to reach up into the willow's higher branches, Jenny remembered, closing her eyes and again going back in time. Perched on a bottom limb like a tough little sparrow, she'd strain to reach the top branches, severing them into sharp canes that she clamped in her teeth until she could scamper back down to earth. Jenny glanced down at her burgeoning stomach, then back at the tree, and cut some of the branches closer to the ground, hoping they would do.

Back inside, she slivered off chips of bark and brewed the mix in an old tin can over the fire. A sharp, bitter odor rose as the water hissed and boiled and she strained the dark liquid through a piece of her last petticoat.

She knelt at Finnegan's side. His skin was dry and hot as she cupped his grizzled cheek in her hand and raised his face.

"Drink this, Finnegan," she said, hoping her demanding tone would work through the stupor that held him.

Miraculously, he opened his mouth and she poured the mixture in. She braced, expecting him to sputter and cough, maybe even throw the tea back up. Instead, his throat worked convulsively and he softly sighed without opening his eyes.

Jenny sat down on the floor and crossed her legs, cradling his cheek on the muscle of her calf. Little by little, she coaxed the remaining liquid into him. Then, she cupped a palm across his forehead. All she could do now was wait. Helplessness descended.

The long winter days had little meaning in terms of sunrise and sunset. Midday, a lightening of the sky was all that reminded mortals that somewhere the sun still ruled the sky, some mystical place just below the elusive horizon. Here in the Yukon, winter's day and night could only be marked by one's inner clock and many a soul went mad in the effort. Jenny looked down at Finnegan's quiet face, elusively peaceful in his illness. Sprigs of auburn hair teased the tips of his ears and a long, white scar etched a path from behind his ear to a point on his cheek. An old wound, it was now nearly gone, but had surely once been gaping and painful. A knife wound—she'd bet anything, she thought as she traced the straight, clean path with a fingertip.

So many men had come and gone, vague shadows in her life and in her mind, faceless visitors set on their own satisfaction. She was a device to them, a receptacle for their lust and nothing else, bought and paid for like a glass of whiskey or passage to the gold fields. They hadn't seen her as a woman, but as some being in between. And why should she complain? She'd been no bit of fluff driven by the wind of circumstance. She'd con-

THE HEALING

sciously chosen this life over a lifetime of wind and dust and babies on some barren prairie homestead. Quilting and apple preserve recipes had never held the fascination for her they had for her sister.

Had it been happenstance or some quirk in God's sense of humor that had brought Dave Marcus to her door that brilliant October day? Ready with a smile and an eye for an eager woman, he'd been the answer to her longings. With hands as talented in cards as in love, he'd quickly broken down her feeble resistance and when he left town, his pockets lined with easy money, she'd willingly followed, leaving behind perhaps the last honest and true thing she remembered.

Grandma had stood in the edge of the yard and watched her leave, her feet bare in the fine, dusty soil. There was no condemnation in her eyes nor her countenance, only a deep disappointment and a silent and prophetic promise that one day Jenny would regret her actions. And now she did. For now she was a murderess. No matter that Frank deserved what he'd gotten. For the rest of her life, she'd look over her shoulder and live another day with her baby. Ironically, it seemed Frank had gotten the last word after all.

The fire popped softly and Finnegan stirred, scrubbing the remains of his beard against her leg. She was needed—a wry twist, she thought. Perhaps the only time she'd ever been needed in her life. And now two lives depended on her. Their circumstances were dire, meager, and dangerous. And yet, here with life narrowed to basics—fire, warmth, compassion—she felt for the first time in years, content.

Finnegan awoke to a gentle lethargy that beckoned him to stretch lazily toward the fire like one of his dogs. Something soft pillowed his head and for the first time in hours, his arm didn't stab with pain. He moved his head and felt his cheek chafe against skin. Beneath his jaw he could feel the surge of a heartbeat.

The pulse was steady and even. Her hand rested on his chest. She was asleep, propped in the corner, cradling his head in her lap. As the fog of sleep receded, he concentrated on clearing his mind, sorting through the images and memories of the last hours. A day had passed. No, more like two. He'd be long overdue in Dawson City and someone would be coming soon to find him.

He hunched a shoulder to raise himself and she stirred softly against his back. The sensation shot straight to his soul.

Human touch. Warmth. Trust.

Trust, the most dangerous weakness of all.

And yet here he lay, at her mercy—or the lack of it if she so chose—content.

The fire popped and he turned his attention back to the pulse beneath his cheek, focusing on that bit of skin where their bodies met. Thump, thump, a beat as steady and dependable as she, a woman far more dangerous to a man's future than a bit of flirting fluff. Here was a woman to build a life with, to tame a wilderness and raise a family. More dangerous than a vixen mistress, she would be a companion and a soulmate to some fortunate man. But not he. He had no place in his life any longer for a woman and all the comforts she might bring.

He shook away the errant thoughts, attributing them to pain. Shifting, he raised his head and pushed up on his good hand. The room spun for a moment, then righted itself. He heard her stir behind him and cool fingers found his forehead.

"How are you feeling?"

He sat up, bracing against the wall, cradling his now-aching arm, and turned to look at her. "Better, I think. How about you?"

She smiled, crinkling tired eyes. "I'm fine."

Fatigue lined her face and a gray pallor shadowed her eyes but there was no sign of defeat there, even in their circumstances. In fact, she did indeed look satisfied and for a brief moment his thoughts drifted back to Lucille's and the way soft light had danced off her bare skin.

"Are you hungry?" she asked, scrambling to her feet.

"My stomach's willing, but the thoughts of chewing pemmican right now . . ."

"Oh, I have more than pemmican," she replied with a twinkle in her eye and moved to the fireplace. She pulled a pot out of the embers and a wisp of steam hurried away, carrying the distinctive odor of fish. "Fish soup."

Astonished, Finnegan could only gaze up at her. "And how did you trick a fish into that can?"

She grinned and reached down to pick up her coat. A small square area had been hacked from the sleeve. "I broke the ice at the edge of the river. Then, I cut the skin into little pieces. When the fishes came to eat it, I scooped them out of the water with that." She pointed to an old, ragged snowshoe propped by the fireplace.

If a man had related the same tale, Finnegan would have called him a liar to his face. But the proof was there, floating temptingly in the rich broth.

She poured a generous portion into their one cup and moved it toward his lips, but he covered her hand with his and gently took the cup away from her. Their eyes met as she surrendered control and she looked surprised.

"I can do that for myself, lass."

She backed away as a commotion began outside. Baying and barking, the scuffle of dog paws scrambled across the porch. The door swept open and a man stepped inside, swathed head to toe in furs, yanking off beaver-skin gloves.

"We thought you were a lost man, Finnegan," he said in a rolling Scottish brogue as his gaze flitted around the room, a slight frown forming between his eyes.

"I almost was if Miss Hanson here hadn't fished me out of the Yukon River," Finnegan replied, sipping his soup.

The man took off his wide Stetson and ran a

THE HEALING

beefy hand through his dark hair. "Ma'am," he said with a nod in her direction. "When you didn't show up for Sam's dinner two nights ago, she sent me to look for you, Finnegan."

"And did Superintendent Steele have anything to do with sending you out into the wilderness?" Finnegan asked with a grin.

"Not as much as facing the wrath of my wife."

"Jenny Hanson, this is Inspector Duncan McLeod. And a more irritating man God never made." Despite the light tone between them, Finnegan knew Duncan was taking in every detail of their situation with a practiced eye.

"What happened?" Duncan asked, his face sobering.

"We broke through the ice out there off the point. The whole sled went down, mail and all. I cut the dogs loose and they swam to shore. Miss Hanson got herself out of the water and then came back for me. Oh, and she fished most of the mail out, too."

Duncan ran an assessing eye over Jenny, then turned his attention back to Finnegan. "And you weren't good for much in the whole operation, I take it?"

Finnegan smiled and shook his head. "Not much except to twist my arm nearly off."

"Miss Hanson, the Mounted Police are grateful to you for rescuing one of our best," he said with a twinkling eye, "and for saving the mail, no thanks to Finnegan here."

Duncan cast a dubious glance at the tin can

tightly grasped in Finnegan's hand. "As enticing as that smells, I've got better in the sled."

Finnegan peered down into the oily soup floating in the cup, then up at Jenny. She watched him with dark eyes, a hesitant trace of expectation brimming in them. "I think I'll just finish this first."

"We'll start for Dawson City in the morning," Duncan said, stretching his feet toward the fire. "It'll be slow going with both of you in the sled, and a tight fit. Might take a few days longer to get there."

"I'm not going, Constable."

Finnegan winced and glanced at Duncan's surprised expression.

"I appreciate your concern, Constable McLeod, but this is my home now. I intend to stay right here." Jenny stepped between them and the fireplace, folding one of the blankets Duncan had brought inside.

Duncan threw Finnegan an incredulous look. "Well, lass, I understand your attachment for these fine surroundings, but—"

"There's no but to it, Constable. I bought this place. I own it free and clear. It's my home and I intend to raise my baby here."

Duncan glanced around the sparse room. "Miss Hanson—"

"It's Jenny."

"Jenny. I can't very well go off and—"

"You certainly can, Constable. You can go off

THE HEALING

and leave me here in peace. I've made an arrangement with Constable Finnegan. All your mail carriers will stop over here on their way to and from Dawson City and Skagway. I'm hoping that I can convince you to bring me supplies now and then. I'll pay, of course. That way you can all satisfy the obligation you feel to look after me."

"Jenny—" he replied again.

"What do you propose to do, Constable? Tie me hand and foot and force me from my home?"

"Well . . . no, but I can't in good conscience leave you here to give birth alone. Come back with us to Dawson City. After the baby's born—"

"The baby will be born here. I'm sorry, Inspector McLeod. My mind is made up."

Duncan looked expectantly at Finnegan. "Leave her be," Finnegan said with a shake of his head.

Duncan frowned. "Don't tell me she's convinced you to throw in with this insane idea?"

Finnegan looked into Jenny's calm, steady expression, eyes that watched him and waited to see if her trust in him was well-founded. To her, freedom was more important than safety, than comfort. And he supposed he'd feel the same— had felt the same. "She knows what she's doing," he answered finally. "She's earned the right to have the say."

Hands braced on the porch railing, Duncan stared off across the snow, his pipe clamped between his teeth, a wreath of smoke circling his head. "It goes against everything I know is right."

"We can't make her go," Finnegan answered, one hip propped against the railing.

"The hell we can't. We're the police here." Duncan shoved away from the railing to stride to the other side of the porch and lean against the wall.

"This is all she has, Duncan, the only home she's ever known," Finnegan said, grunting as he shifted his arm in the sling.

Duncan took his pipe from his mouth and squinted through the smoke. "So what's the rest of the story here? Where'd you find her?" He gestured toward the cabin door with the end of his pipe.

"She was working at Lucille's, changing chamber pots."

"She's a prostitute?"

"Was. She'd saved some money and talked somebody into selling her this place. She asked me to bring her here when I left Skagway."

Duncan folded his arms over his chest. "So you were going to leave her here with no supplies and due to deliver any day? Did you leave your good sense in the river? What's gotten into you, lad?"

Finnegan squirmed inwardly under Duncan's gaze. How could he explain desperation so deep that one would abandon all that seemed logical to focus on one chance at salvation? Could he explain the reasons that would make a young man, without clothes or money and a string of constables on his

THE HEALING

tail, leap aboard a ship pulling away from the Irish shoreline bound for places unknown?

"If I hadn't brought her, she'd have found someone else to. She's determined to settle in before the baby's born."

"What sort of deal did you make with her?"

"She'll provide a stopover for the mail route in return for a fee. Good place, here, with the river like it is. Good chance for the men to rest their teams and her to earn a living."

"Hmmm," Duncan said around his pipe.

"I'm going to send supplies back with the next mail run in a day or two. Until then, she's a resourceful woman."

"Aye, she is, but then her judgment's questionable if she fished your sorry hide out of the Yukon River. Are you going to confess to that tale in the barracks?"

Finnegan gazed across the snow to the sleeping river. "And grateful I am that she did. Else I'd be fish food come spring." He glanced back at Duncan. "This was her only chance to escape her former life. I couldn't deny her that."

Duncan's chest rose and fell in a silent sigh as he gazed off toward the snowy woods. "No, I don't suppose you could."

"She's a grown woman with her own mind. It's not our place to interfere."

"Don't suppose it is." Duncan put his pipe back in his mouth and puffed another smoke ring.

Finnegan pushed away from the wall. "She was safer with me and safer here than in Lucille's."

Duncan's eyes twinkled and he grinned around the pipe stem. "Are you trying to convince me or you, lad?"

Finnegan grunted as his arm pulsed a stab of pain. "I don't like leaving her here any better than you. People have told her what to do most of her life. I won't add my name to that list."

Duncan studied him a moment longer through narrowed eyes. "I'll leave her all the supplies I brought, all the blankets. The next mail run goes out in a day or two. They'll stop by and see to her." Duncan moved toward the door and the sparse warmth within. He paused with a hand on the door latch and turned back to face Finnegan. "But you won't be able to leave it at that, will you, lad?"

Finnegan met Duncan's eyes. "I mean to come back in a week or two."

Duncan studied him from beneath his brooding eyebrows and after years of service together, Finnegan knew exactly what the big␁Scotsman was thinking. "There's nothing between the two of us." Oh, but there was. Something as new and as fragile as the dewy spiderwebs that sparkled in morning sun. Something that begged definition and yet would not bear close examination. Not yet and not now.

"I'll be back in a week or two. Until then, the carriers will stop every week with supplies and your payment."

They stood alone in the middle of the cabin,

THE HEALING 95

minutes hurrying by like seconds. Outside, Duncan readied the dog team for the trip back to Dawson City. Jenny nodded solemnly, her eyes large and moist. From fear or regret, Finnegan couldn't tell nor could he decide which he wished it was. He swallowed, hesitated over an impulse, then brushed back a strand of hair that teased her upper lip, reveling in the chance to touch her. Was his reluctance to go guilt over leaving her here alone or was it something else? He took a deep breath and saved the contemplation for the long trip ahead.

"I'll be fine. Don't worry about me." She blinked, a new resolution in her eyes, the brief vulnerability gone.

"Frettin's in the Irish soul," Finnegan said with a grin he didn't feel.

"Still and all, don't worry. This is what I want and I'll be fine." Her voice held a resolution he wished he felt at leaving her here alone.

"I might not be standing here if you hadn't fished me out of the drink."

She shrugged one shoulder and smiled. "Couldn't have you fouling my drinking water."

Involuntarily, he glanced down at her bulging stomach. They hadn't discussed her pregnancy beyond those few cautionary remarks back in Skagway before they left. She'd never offered a why or when and he hadn't asked. Until now. "When are you due?"

Wariness crept into her expression. "In about a month, near as I can figure." She tipped her head to one side. "Don't try to guess the time and come back here. I know what I'm doing, Mike."

His name, so common and seldom used, rolled exotically off her tongue.

"I'm a big girl and I'm not a fool. I know exactly the chance I'm taking. But when one is left with few choices, one has to make the best of what's at hand." She took his hand, her flesh soft and warm against his. "You're a good man, Mike Finnegan."

The sweet honey of desire slid smoothly into his veins, heating his blood, redirecting his thoughts, much like every other man who had ever touched her, he imagined. He leaned forward and she didn't draw away but met his gaze with honest eyes. She knew exactly what he was thinking, knew that the desire to kiss her had suddenly taken over his mind and his body. There was no resistance in her expression, but no invitation either.

And so he followed instinct. She didn't pull away as his lips touched hers. The kiss was brief and sweet, more a peck between friends. Her fingers fumbled against his pant leg, found his hand, and entwined their fingers. His heart didn't race with unchecked passion and his blood didn't throb in his ears. But the gentle touch of her mouth, the tiny flick of her tongue against his, started a slow warmth deep inside his chest, a fire sure to burn long and sweet.

Chapter Six

Superintendent Sam Steele shifted to one side in his desk chair and worried a pencil between his fingers, seemingly intent on the papers before him.

"You wanted to see me, sir?" Finnegan sat down in a chair across the desk, balanced his hat on his knee, and frowned as a sense of foreboding crept through him.

Steele spun the pencil another rotation, then raised his eyes. "How's your arm mending?"

Finnegan flexed the fingers that protruded from the sling around his neck. "Better than it was two weeks ago. It aches when it rains and most times in between, but it's healing, I suppose. Did you ask me here to talk about my arm?"

"No," Steele said firmly. "I did not." He pulled forward the documents he'd been studying. "You made a report on a preliminary investigation you did some months ago at the request of a bar owner in Eldorado. He told you a gambler named Frank Bentz was missing, according to people who knew him."

Finnegan nodded. "I found nothing solid as evidence they were right. As I said in the report, I did find a cabin, belongings tossed about, like somebody left in a hurry."

"And you noted you saw a pile of rocks that could have been a grave."

"There was no body, not as near as I could tell. Wolves had been digging at the rocks, but beyond that, nothing."

Steele rose from his chair and walked to the window. "I'd like you and Inspector McLeod to return to Eldorado and investigate this further."

"Has a body been found?" Finnegan questioned, remembering the cold chill that had crept up his back as he'd knelt beside the pile of stones at the deserted cabin.

Steele shook his head. "No body. No sign of him at all."

"Well, sir, why are you pursuing it as a murder investigation?"

Steele turned. "Because yesterday afternoon his wife walked into my office and announced that her husband had been murdered by the whore that was traveling with him."

Finnegan blinked the shock from his expression as his thoughts flew to Jenny, to her past and the lover she didn't talk about. She'd made no mention of how long she'd been at Lucille's or if she'd traveled in the company of a man. Instantly, he pushed the thought away—and then the guilt that followed. Jenny couldn't have had a part in this. There were hundreds of prostitutes in the Yukon and tens of couples just like Frank Bentz and the woman his wife said he'd been living with.

So, the elusive and infamous Frank Bentz had a wife. One willing to travel all the way to the Yukon to look for him. Was she sincere in her concern, or did gold and money figure into this? After all, what kind of life must a woman like that lead, waiting for a man who makes his living on chance and others' misfortunes, counting her days by the drips and bits of money he might have sent home? Did she have some other motive? Gold? Revenge? Or did she just want to make sure he was dead?

"Is she still here in town?"

Steele nodded to the wintry sky beyond the window glass. "She's staying at the Nugget Hotel. I've told her to expect you."

If Frank Bentz had kept on the move, he had good reason, Finnegan concluded, as he stared into Harriet Bentz's pinched face.

"Would you like another pastry, Constable Finnegan?" She lifted the delicate china plate and poked it at him as if refusing could be grounds for a stern tongue-lashing he was sure she was capable of doling out.

"No, thank you."

She pursed her lips and frowned slightly before

deliberately setting the plate back on the table, disapproval in every move. Pausing over the task, she carefully rearranged her narrow face into a proper mask of disappointment.

"When did you last see your husband, Mrs. Bentz?" He wanted to get this information and get out of this woman's presence.

She folded her hands demurely in her lap. "About a year ago. He kissed me good-bye in the doorway of our little house in Seattle and promised to come back to me a rich man." She lifted a hand and delicately wiped at the corner of her eye. Despite the demure facade she was so aptly feigning, Finnegan sensed a deep insincerity about her that permeated everything she said and did.

"Hmmm." Finnegan scrawled left-handed, nearly unreadable notes on a paper propped against his knee. "So you knew he was coming to the Yukon?"

"Oh, yes, Frankie told me everything and he shared with me his desire to become a gold field gambler."

"Gold field gambler," Finnegan repeated in a mumble.

"Those are his words. Frankie was so clever with words."

"Yes, ma'am. Now, why did you tell Commander Steele that you believed your husband had been murdered?"

She widened her eyes and pushed her bottom lip out into a halfhearted pout that rankled Finnegan like the squeal of chalk against chalkboard. "Because Frankie would have come back to me no matter what." She leaned forward conspiratorially. "There've been rumors he was seen in the company of a whore. But I can forgive him that. Men like my Frankie have strong desires and in my absence—" She leaned back, a delicate blush staining her cheeks.

He was in the company of a consummate con artist, Finnegan surmised. Maybe even better at it than gambling, whoring Frankie. And the feeling that he was being played like an upright piano made him struggle to remain civil.

"Have you considered the possibility that your husband might have just . . . intentionally disappeared?"

True horror filled her face. Her lips quivered with just the right amount of emotion and she touched a lace handkerchief to her eye. "How could you be so cruel, Constable, as to suggest that my husband would . . . leave me? No, I know that something terrible has befallen my Frankie or else he'd have come home to me as soon as he could."

Finnegan leaned back in the chair and studied the woman. What was it about her that made the hair on his neck stand on end? Was it the excessive posturing and preening that seemed to occupy so much of her time? Or was it her air of insincerity? Pausing, he sorted through his perceptions, trying to separate his personal views from his policeman's instincts.

"I have to pursue all angles, Mrs. Bentz," he said finally.

Her expression hardened and her narrow eyes

glittered with anger. "I can assure you, Constable Finnegan, that my Frankie did not wander off with some harlot. My Frankie is dead. I can sense the absence of his spirit in my soul. And I expect you to do your job, to find out who did it and bring Frankie's body back to me so I can bury him properly." She sobbed with a loud, gulping sound and pressed the handkerchief to her face. "I'm afraid I can't continue, Constable."

Finnegan rose and walked to the door of her hotel room. Pausing for one last assessment, he glanced back over his shoulder. She sat where he'd left her, covering her face with the handkerchief, her shoulders shaking. Quietly, he slipped out the door and felt cleansed when he emerged into the cold morning sun. Glancing down at the sparse notes in his hand, he wondered how he could put into his report the unfounded suspicions circling in his mind.

A swirl of dust rose from the plank floor, swirled briefly, then settled on the floor again. Jenny leaned on her makeshift broom and put a hand to her aching back. Thorough cleaning would have to wait until summer when the dirt could be sluiced out the door with a bucket of hot water. She glanced out the window at the gray day and wondered if Christmas had passed her by.

She sat down in a chair she'd patched with some nails she found in a rusty can using a piece of firewood as a hammer. Back at Lucille's, if it was

THE HEALING

indeed Christmas, there'd be eggnog made with fresh eggs from Loni's carefully guarded hens. Mistletoe would dangle from the crystal chandeliers and strains of carols would drift through the house when Maria played the pedal organ. A warm fire would burn in every room and a buffet would be laid for the guests on Christmas Eve.

Tears burned her eyes as the first tendrils of regret worked their way into her thoughts. She wiped them away with the heel of her hand and a shake of her head. No, she wouldn't look back. There, she'd be changing bedpans and mopping floors, answering to the beck and call of everyone. Here, despite sparse circumstances, she was in her own home, answerable to no one save the life growing within her. She glanced around the room, noting the cobwebs that hung from the windows and the rags stuffed into the broken window panes. Someone had once built this cabin with love and care, as was evidenced by the skill of construction that had allowed the house to withstand winter winds and heavy snow. She'd make it a home again. Somehow.

The baby stirred, its tiny feet moving beneath her skin. She ran a hand across her swollen stomach and the baby moved in response. She wanted this baby like she'd wanted little else in life. From the moment she found she carried a child, she'd known she couldn't rid herself of it. Even though Frank insisted—demanded, even—that she drink a potion to end its brief life. When she'd refused, there'd been a fight. He'd struck her, knocked her to her knees. And there, on her knees, she'd defied him still.

Frank had succumbed to her wishes too easily. She saw that now and should have realized that his quick and complete reversal of position meant nothing but ill for her. She'd known what he was all along, known his appetite for money and women and his dream of becoming rich in the gold fields. And yet she'd abandoned her logic and followed him to the Yukon where his dreams fizzled and his desperation grew. And when his scheming backfired, he'd demanded more abandonment of her morals, more than she was willing to do. Her refusal lead to violence as he vented his frustration on her. And so she'd killed him. Before he killed her. Before he killed the baby she bore.

A shudder passed through her as the image of Frank's surprised expression quavered before her—eyes wide, mouth open, bright, red blood spreading across his shirt, as red as the room in which they'd conceived their child. She closed her eyes, but the image grew more vivid and the horror returned.

A ruckus outside interrupted her reminiscence. Feet scraped on the porch. She glanced up at the strip of hide fastened to the wall bearing five scratch marks. Five days had passed since the last Mounted Police mail carrier passed through. It was too early for another run. She stood and moved away from the window to the pallet she'd spread on the floor. Reaching underneath, she pulled out her revolver and checked the chamber. It was loaded.

"Who's there?" she called, pointing the gun toward the center of the door.

No answer. Only more scraping of feet and a thump as something heavy was set on the porch.

She moved forward a few steps, her hands quivering from the weight of the gun. "I said, who's there?"

"Mike Finnegan," came the familiar voice.

With a sigh, she hurried to the door and swung it open wide. Finnegan stood on the porch with a canvas bag at his side. Covering the bottom half of his face was a scraggly, homemade beard, constructed out of shredded white cloth. Beyond, Inspector McLeod examined the dog team's harnesses, shaking his head as he cast a wry glance in Finnegan's direction.

For an instant, Jenny contemplated leaping into Finnegan's arms, but she quickly quelled that ridiculous impulse when the image of her knocking him backwards into the snow filled her mind's eye. She hadn't known loneliness could be so complete.

"This is a surprise," was the response she settled for instead. "What's that on your face?"

Finnegan grinned at her with a twinkle in his eyes and his arm securely bound in a sling. "Sure an' I'm Santa Claus. Don't you recognize the red suit and the beard, lass?

She laughed, surprised at how good it made her feel. "Come inside," she said, standing to the side and motioning her hand toward Inspector

McLeod. Once they were all in the cabin, Finnegan pinned the bag between his feet and hauled out a package wrapped in cheerful paper. "Merry Christmas."

Emotion clogged Jenny's throat as she took the package. She couldn't remember the last time someone had given her a present. Especially one wrapped and tied with a ribbon. "Is today Christmas?"

His expression softened. "Tomorrow. Tomorrow is Christmas."

She glanced over her shoulder to the hearth where a wrapped packet of pemmican and steaming fish stew waited. Poor fare for a holiday celebration, especially with company. She swung her gaze back to Finnegan, but not before he'd read her mind. He reached into the bag a second time and hauled out two freshly killed rabbits.

"And what Christmas dinner would be complete without rabbit to roast?"

Her mouth watered so at the mention of the delicacy, she nearly drooled. "Where on earth did you get it?"

"Duncan there shot and killed them on the trail."

"How can I thank you for your kindness?" she said to the dark-haired Scotsman just closing the door.

He waved a gloved hand at her. "No thanks necessary. I was in the right place at the right time."

"You're both too kind." She settled her gaze

THE HEALING

back on Finnegan and an odd stirring in her chest heated her cheeks.

"Open your package." He stared at the gift in her hands, his enthusiasm evident.

Curiosity piqued, she sat down in her chair and pulled off ribbon and paper, careful to preserve both. A dress lay folded in layers of paper, a soft pink dress with tiny lace around a collar. And nestled next to it was a tiny gown, edged in matching lace and fancy stitchery.

Tears, controllable before, now flowed down her cheeks. She'd never received a more heartfelt gift. Frank had bought her gowns and lacy underwear, but more for his own pleasure at peeling them off than any attempt to make her happy.

"Ah, now I've made you cry." Finnegan squatted at her side, his silly beard yanked down underneath his chin. "Should I take it back? Did I get the wrong size? I'll return it." He reached for the box.

She turned to answer "no" and saw that his eyes twinkled with mirth. "No. They're perfect."

Finnegan stood, grunting as his knees popped loudly. "Then, there's no time for crying when there's eating to be done."

"I'll be going along now," Duncan said with his hand on the door latch.

Jenny glanced between the two men. "You're not staying?"

"His wife threatened to skin off that thick Scottish hide if he missed their first Christmas together," Finnegan answered. "There'll be a mail carrier by day after tomorrow. I'll ride back to Dawson with him."

"You came here just for me?"

His smile softened from teasing to tender. "Aye. Just to have Christmas with you."

She glanced up at Inspector McLeod, but his face held no disapproval.

"Are you sure this is a good idea?"

Finnegan glanced at Duncan, then back down at her. "What do you mean, lass?"

"I'm a whore. You're choosing to spend two days here alone with me. You're a policeman." She shrugged, some of the joy subsiding as saying the plain facts made them even more unsavory.

He smiled at her. "I was here longer than two days before, just you and me."

"That was different. Your arm was broken."

He waggled his fingers at her from his sling. "My arm's still broken. And you're still expecting. I doubt either of us is a threat to the other and our reputations, such as they are, are safe. No one's going to give us a care, lass."

She glanced up at Duncan, expecting some admonition from him as Finnegan's superior. But Duncan only winked, mirth lurking in his dark eyes.

"Merry Christmas to the three of you." With that, he slipped out the door.

Jenny had almost forgotten what it was like to be sated. She leaned back in the chair and stared across the remains of supper at Finnegan. Elbows on the table and fingers steepled beneath his chin, he watched her with a hint of a sly smile playing about his lips.

"That was good," she said and his smile widened into a grin.

"The way you were going after that rabbit, I thought maybe I should hide me fingers in me sling."

A furious blush heated her cheeks as his soft laughter wound around her. "I couldn't resist teasing you just a bit," he added.

"The rabbit was very good."

"Rabbit is my specialty." His face sobered. "But I owe you more than rabbits and dresses."

"You don't owe me anything."

"You saved my life. Sure an' without you, I'd have drowned."

"And without you, I'd never have made it here to my cabin. No one else would have bothered with me."

"Then, I'd say we're either even or eternally in each other's debt."

Something in his eyes quelled the flippant answer that rose to her lips. And set internal alarm bells to clanging.

She rose abruptly, jarring the already unstable table into a nervous dance that rattled the tin cups and plates. Finnegan grabbed for his coffee cup while she swept up her own dishes and headed for the hearth. "I'll see to these in the morning," she said, placing them on the stones by the fire. "I think I'll go to bed now."

Behind her, she heard the scrape of a chair as Finnegan rose and the metal clink as he gathered up the remaining dishes and utensils. His arm brushed past her as he leaned down and placed the dishes next to hers on the hearth.

"I think I will, too," he said softly.

For the first time in years, a flutter of true desire rose within her, beating gossamer wings against her insides. She swallowed and concentrated on not looking at him, chiding herself for the foolishness running through her head. She'd long ago packed away real emotion where love and lovemaking were concerned, quickly learning to separate her body from her mind when in a man's arms, to give him the part of her he lusted after and keep the rest for herself. Except for Frank. She'd foolishly broken that rule for Frank. And lived to regret it.

He moved away toward the bedroll propped in the corner, then leaned down and unrolled the blankets with his one good hand.

"Do you want some help?" she asked, slanting him a glance.

"No, I'll get them arranged someway," he answered, an edge of irritation in his voice. Mike Finnegan was a man unaccustomed to needing anyone's help. And a man unlikely to ask for it unless dire circumstance dictated. She felt much

THE HEALING

the same herself. Reliance on other people had never brought anything but unhappiness and sorrow to her life.

She turned toward her own pile of tumbled blankets in the opposite corner. His eyes followed her, his gaze warming her back as she stifled a grunt, dropped to her knees, then lay down. The hardness of the floor bit into her already-aching back and she turned onto her side facing him, allowing the weight of her child to rest on a bunched-up blanket.

Finnegan struggled out of his coat, releasing his arm from the sling and wincing softly as the fabric slid over the still-sore limb. Then he crawled into his own blankets and turned on his left side to tuck his right arm securely against his chest.

They lay facing each other across the firelit room, encroaching shadows hiding their faces. Wind sighed against the side of the cabin and the fireplace popped an ember onto the stone hearth. Things unspoken seemed to quiver on the air and Jenny wondered, as the baby moved low in her abdomen, why Finnegan had come back. Did he feel such an overwhelming sense of responsibility? Or was it better defined as guilt at leaving her here alone? Did she dare hope it was more?

No, she told herself with a mental shake. She wouldn't allow such thoughts, even as idle musings. Not even for a man as kind and gentle as Finnegan. She'd not involve another man in her life. She had a home now, and soon would have a baby. Her life was complete and she needed nothing more.

Outside the window's one unbroken pane, two stars twinkled in a still, clear sky, reminding her this was Christmas Eve. She closed her eyes and sank back into her memories. Grandma's voice rose sweet and quivering as she read the Christmas story from a thumb-worn Bible. Jenny could almost smell the orange Grandma would have given her and taste the gingersnap cookies they'd have worked on for two days.

Sharp tears of regret burned her eyes. Grandma wanted so much more for her than the life she'd chosen. She smiled to herself, amazed that after all these years and all the sins she'd committed, Grandma's teachings could still haunt her conscience. The odd, bent little woman who'd opened her heart and her home to two orphaned little girls had more in common with the beasts of the forest than folks in town. And yet, she'd raised them with a quick wit and a firm hand. Sarah had taken to that raising, adapting quickly to life among the civilized and the righteous. But Jenny had gone in the other direction, absorbing Grandma's appetite for the odd and flamboyant, leaving her wanting more from life than a husband and babies.

Jenny smiled at the irony. For all her elaborate dreams, she was spending Christmas in a lonely cabin, pregnant and with nothing to her name save a rickety table and chairs and a few borrowed blankets. But, as Grandma would have reminded her, she had her baby, a tiny soul eternally linked to hers.

Most folks are lucky if they get one thing they want in

life, Grandma would have said. *Be smart enough to recognize it when it comes along.*

She glanced toward the corner where Finnegan's breathing had evened out into peaceful slumber. Could she possibly have two things?

Chapter Seven

The velvety stillness of deep night surrounded Jenny when she awoke abruptly. Foggy consciousness addled her mind for a few seconds as she struggled out of the web of dreams that held her thoughts captive. Except for the wind that dragged itself around the cabin, no sound disturbed the quietness. What, then, had awakened her?

She focused her attention on the baby inside her. It lay still, no movement, no kicking. Listening to her instincts, she decided the babe was well and turned her attention to her surroundings.

Someone crouched at her side, blocking the fire's dancing shadows. Her heart lunged into a pounding beat and she started up, but a hand pressed against her shoulder, urging her to lie back down.

"It's all right, lass. It's only me."

"Finnegan." She took a deep breath to still her pounding heart. "What's wrong?"

"You were thrashing about in your sleep."

Jenny touched a hand to her face and wiped a thin layer of perspiration from her forehead. Her thoughts spun backwards and erratic bits of memories swirled about in a kaleidoscope of nonsense, making no clear picture in her mind. She remembered only being afraid—terrified—and the sharp crack of a pistol. Unnerved that what she tried to blank from her conscious mind would creep in to haunt her dreams, she took a deep breath and tried to erase the evidence of concern from her eyes.

She looked up into his face, softly shadowed by the firelight. "It must have been a nightmare."

He studied her face, his eyes the color of wild blueberries.

"Is the baby all right?"

Her hand went to her stomach, bulging beneath the blanket. "Yes, we're both fine." She pushed herself to her elbows. "My back aches. Maybe that's what woke me." She put a hand to the small of her back where a brief, annoying pain had evolved into a deep ache.

He stood and held out his hand. "Come here."

His fingers closed firmly over her hand and he hauled her to her feet.

"Sit down there." He pointed at a stool and she eased her swollen body onto the seat, wondering what he was up to. He moved behind her, out of her line of vision. One hand came to rest on her shoulder and began to knead the muscle there.

"Finnegan, I don't know. Your arm." Could she bear his hands on her in so intimate a fashion when just seconds before she'd fought down a growing attraction to him, one she wanted to avoid at all costs? But the promise of a backrub, warm, strong hands soothing away the deep ache, lured her from her caution and she closed her eyes and submitted.

"Like that, do you?" His voice held a note of laughter, but she didn't care. His touch felt too good to contemplate what demons it might conjure up.

His hand moved lower, across the back of her shoulder blades, stroking and kneading, down toward her lower back.

"Lean forward," he said and she obeyed as far as her swollen belly would allow.

His fingers found the ache in the small of her back and kneaded the pain into submission, smoothing the tight flesh, easing the tension with the heat of his hand.

"When I was a boy, my sister had a baby. 'Twas my job to rub her back." His voice was almost a whisper, throaty and soft.

"Were you born in Ireland?"

He hesitated for an instant. "Yes."

"Do you miss your family there?"

Again, his touch paused, piquing her curiosity. "I haven't seen them in a long time."

"Do you ever think about going back?"

"No," came his answer, quick and firm.

THE HEALING

Jenny wanted to ask more, but something in his voice warned her away.

"Doesn't that hurt your hand?"

"No. My hands are strong."

Indeed they were. Where else would those hands be oh-so-strong and capable?

No, she told herself. She would not think of Constable Finnegan in that manner. *You simply will not fall into a trap made of your own desires, Jenny Hanson.*

"Better?"

His touch slowed and then stopped and she knew her moment of splendor was over. "Yes, much. Thank you." She rose from the stool and he moved away. "Would you like some coffee?"

He smiled a slow smile. "Do I want to know what you're using as coffee?"

She walked to the fireplace. "I would imagine it's now Christmas morning. This is my Christmas present to you." She picked up a small packet from the mantel, walked over to him, and held it under his nose. He inhaled, then looked down at her in wonderment. "Where did you get real coffee?"

"Lucille sent it along by Constable Posten when he came from Skagway last week." She walked back to the hearth, shook some of the contents into a battered coffee pot, poured in water, then placed the pot on the embers in the fireplace. "She said everybody should have good coffee to go with their Christmas dinner."

"And did she send the Christmas dinner as well?"

"No, but she sent some more ammunition for my revolver."

"And you shot something?"

She glanced at him over her shoulder, then threw another log onto the fire. "You sound like you don't think I could."

"Nothing you do would amaze me." He rose from the chair, stretched, then padded in socked feet to the window. "Just for curiosity, what did you shoot?"

"A deer."

He laughed and turned toward her. "With a revolver?"

"Yes."

"The bullet's not a large enough caliber to kill an animal the size of a deer."

"Well, the bullet didn't actually kill it."

He turned full around and waited.

"I shot it all right, but it ran into a tree and, I suppose, broke its neck."

Finnegan laughed outright then. "You're the most amazing lass I've ever met." His face sobered. "Truly the most amazing."

She turned back to the fireplace, suddenly embarrassed at his exuberant praise. No, she wasn't amazing. Blessed with pure, dumb luck in some instances maybe. But, no. Mike Finnegan's definition of an amazing woman did not include someone like her. Of that she was sure. And just as sure that she wished it did.

* * *

Morning woke her with tentative light. A rough rustling, accompanied by an off-tune whistling, worked its way into her sleep. She opened her eyes to dim light. Finnegan's bedroll was empty. The fireplace had been stoked again and the rustling came from outside.

Rolling to her feet, she walked to the window and looked out onto the porch. Finnegan sat in one of the two chairs, a willow branch clamped tightly between his knees, strips of willow bark scattered around his feet. A pile of young, supple willow limbs lay at his side, waiting to be stripped. A half-finished frame of lashed-together willow branches leaned against the porch railing. She stood in the curtainless window and watched while her heart turned an unpleasant flip-flop. Whatever he was intent on, it was for her, another kindness she didn't know how to repay or acknowledge. Unexpected and unfounded anger rose within her. As if a silent message had passed between them through the dirty glass, he looked up and smiled, then motioned for her to come outside.

She stepped out into the frigid air, the coldness of it making her lungs hurt as she inhaled and wrapped her arms around herself. "What are you making?"

"A bed frame."

"How have you managed with one hand?"

He wriggled the fingers of his broken arm, now out of his sling. "I can use them some."

The task looked impossible to her, but he'd managed nonetheless and even seemed to be enjoying the job, apparently ignoring the cold that was already making her tremble. Why would he go to so much trouble for her? Unless he expected she would return his kindness in some form. Did he expect sex in return? If that's what was in his mind, he was out of luck for the moment, she thought with an inner smile. And then the smile faded as that dark thought grew and took control of her thoughts.

"Don't you want to do that inside?"

He shook his head. "Makes too much mess."

"You don't have to do that for me. I'll be fine on the floor until spring; then I'll figure out something."

"I know you will, but I figured you'd be more comfortable in a bed."

"You've done too much for me already."

He looked up, honest surprise on his face.

"I appreciate all you've done, but I can look after myself."

The pause between them lingered. "Knowing when to graciously accept help is as valuable as knowing how to look after yourself."

Her cheeks flamed. Why hadn't she just kept her mouth shut and accepted his kindness? But long-held suspicions and an illogical anger rose and overshadowed anything he might say. She'd fallen in love with him and, dammit, that was the last thing on earth she'd wanted to do. "Men don't usually do things for whores for nothing."

Incredulity filled his eyes as his face reddened and the branch he was stripping dropped to the porch. "You think I want something in return?"

She shrugged one shoulder as sickening guilt filled her. Now, why on earth had she said that? "Why else would you offer to rub my back like you did?"

His face reddened until it nearly matched his hair. He stood, sending shavings and strips of bark fluttering to the porch floor. Fury snapped in his eyes and his jaw worked, tightening the skin across his cheek. "You were in pain. I thought it might help."

No firm logic rose in her thoughts to substantiate what she was saying, but she plunged ahead, deriving a perverse pleasure from his growing anger toward her. Unleashed, all her insecurities and doubts poured out in acidic words. "Nobody ever does anything for nothing."

He fought making a sudden response. She could tell by the way his jaw twitched. His chest rose in a breath and she stepped backwards, instinctually expecting him to slap her. Her recoil didn't go unnoticed. The anger faded from his eyes, replaced by sorrow.

"Not every kindness comes with a price, Jenny," he said softly, his voice barely a whisper. "And not every encounter with a man is a business arrangement." With that, he stalked off the porch toward the frozen river, leaving a trail of shavings behind him.

She was beyond a doubt the most infuriating and confusing woman he'd ever met.

Finnegan leaned his good arm against the trunk of a bending willow and gazed out across the darkened river surface, breathing deeply to dispel the remains of his anger. She trusted no one, didn't want to trust anyone, preferring instead to remain foolishly, stubbornly independent rather than accept a kindness. But that wasn't what had made him so angry. Despite his best efforts, despite all the cautions whispering in his head, he feared he was falling in love.

Finnegan looked down and toed at a clump of hard snow. He'd warned himself time and again that the compassion he felt for this damaged woman could easily develop into more, fueled by a loneliness he hadn't realized before. His heart, and not his concern, had drawn him back here to spend Christmas. Even Duncan had cautioned him in carefully measured words against becoming too deeply involved. Any other woman, any other time, his common sense and natural caution would have steered him away. But not this woman. This woman disabled all his warning systems and drew him to her like a moth to a glass lamp chimney, leaving him as frustrated and bewildered as the battered moth.

Thoughts of her here, alone and vulnerable, had

tortured him through the many painful, sleepless nights since he'd left her. Impulse had dictated that he drag her back to Dawson City, physically if necessary, and install her there until the baby was born. More than once, in his capacity as constable in the North West Mounted Police, he'd sent some prospector back over Chilkoot Pass for having too few supplies or not enough money to make it through the winter in the Yukon. Interfering in the lives of others for their own good was sometimes part of his duties. But Jenny made all that different. He'd not damage the fragile respect she'd slowly built for herself. Not even to impose his opinions on her. And so, he was left to watch and wait and pray.

Cold seeped into his damaged arm and an ache spread from the fractured bone to his shoulder and finally to his head. He turned back toward the cabin and saw her waiting on the porch, arms crossed over her expanding stomach, coatless. He trudged back through the snow, formulating an apology for his hasty words, fortifying himself against her unfounded suspicions.

"I'm so sorry," she said as soon as his foot touched the bottom step. "I was rude and ungrateful. Please forgive me."

His anger drained away. He looked into her eyes, large and sorrowful, further hamstringing his resolution not to fall in love with her.

"You were right. I don't know how to accept help."

"I don't expect anything in return for what I've done for you."

She met his gaze unwaveringly. "I know. It was arrogant of me to assume you would. I don't know what got into me."

"Truce?"

She smiled. "Truce," then backed away a step. "Would you mind helping me with the venison?"

Together, despite Finnegan's stiffening fingers, they speared a partially frozen venison roast onto a stick and arranged it over the fireplace flames.

"What did you do with the rest of the meat?" he asked, intrigued by her cleverness.

She swept the hair off her forehead with the back of her hand, her face reddened by the heat of the fire. "Whoever once owned this lovely cabin left behind quite a collection of debris. I found a large, metal box out back. I cleaned it out and put the meat inside, wrapped in some of those empty mailbags you left."

"Here I worried you were starving and lonely and you were feasting on roasted venison."

She straightened to meet his gaze. "Did you really worry about me?"

She asked the question with a childlike innocence, as if the thought that someone would care enough to lose sleep over her was a novel idea. And the idea that she thought no one would was enough to wrench his heart.

"I was afraid you'd bitten off more than you expected," he explained evenly.

"Part of your job, I guess, to recognize these things."

Was there a note of bitterness there? As if she wanted his thoughts to be more than simple devotion to duty?

"Not just my job. I care about you. As one person should care for another," he quickly added.

She nodded slowly, then turned away to tend the roast, leaving the conversation hanging between them.

By nightfall, rich drippings fed the fire that crackled and hissed and the aroma of roasting meat filled the cabin. Finnegan brought in the sections of the bed frame he'd lashed together from willow and rope and, with her help, assembled them into a bed. He folded and placed her blankets on the rope latticework woven to hold them.

"Go ahead. Try it," he said.

Jenny sat on the edge, then lay down. The woven ropes gave gently beneath her weight. "This is wonderful." She turned toward him. "Thank you again."

"You're very welcome. See? That wasn't so hard, now was it?"

She rolled to her side to get up and Finnegan offered her a hand. She clasped his fingers and pulled herself to her feet, but he didn't let go once she stood at his side.

So small and warm in his grasp, her hand seemed to fit inside his perfectly. Tempting fate, he squeezed her fingers and waited to see what she would do.

She looked away at first, then raised her eyes to meet his gaze and held it, unwavering. Would she bolt if he kissed her? Would all his words of this afternoon be for naught if he tasted her lips just once?

He lowered his head and she raised her face. "What are we doing?" he whispered.

"I don't know."

"Do you want me to stop?"

"No."

Their lips met, hers practiced and passionate beneath his. The slow fire of desire ignited and poured through him. She stepped closer until her swollen belly pressed against his belt. He slid an arm around her waist, his fingers spread against the skin he'd caressed this morning. She drew him closer, deeper into the kiss with arms around his neck. Long out of practice, his body responded with frightening intensity. Embarrassed, he made a minute move to step away, but she held him firm in the embrace until her lips had thoroughly seduced him into mindlessness.

She released him slowly, flicking the tip of her tongue against his teeth before pulling away, desire softening her eyes. "Merry Christmas, Mike."

"How perfectly dreadful for you, my dear. How ever have you borne up under this sorrow?" Edith Cornell hovered over Harriet Bentz, bobbing corkscrew curls accentuating her enthusiastic comforting.

"I have made it my mission to find out what happened to my husband. We have no family—we were everything to each other." Harriet's voice drifted across the crowded mess hall, barely audible over the out-of-tune strains of Christmas carols and tapping feet. She dabbed at the corner of her eye with a lace handkerchief and Edith put an arm around her shoulder, cooing her sympathy and drawing the attention of other matrons until Harriet was surrounded by a circle of women, all oozing their compassion.

His back against the refreshment table, uncomfortable in ceremonial dress, Finnegan watched Harriet Bentz's performance while he sipped a glass of terrible punch.

"What do you think?" Duncan asked, sliding in beside him and nodding in the direction of the women.

Finnegan slid Duncan a glance. "How'd you get away from Sam?"

"I just walked out of the house. I couldn't stand her another minute."

Finnegan laughed. "Now even I know that's not the truth."

"Sadly, lad, it is. If the baby's not born soon, I'm going to move in with the horses."

Finnegan chuckled again. Nothing swayed the calm demeanor of Duncan McLeod. They'd served in the Mounted Police together for better than ten years and until Duncan met Samantha Wilder, the big Scotsman had never encountered a situation he couldn't control. And then along had come

Sam, as impetuous and unpredictable as Duncan was conservative and steady. The attraction had been instantaneous. After a whirlwind courtship, they'd married, taken in Duncan's two grown daughters, and now expected their first child at any moment.

"She took that bunch in hand smoothly, don't you think?" Finnegan nodded toward Harriet and her circle of supporters, an island of femininity amid a sea of scarlet-clad men.

Duncan nodded slowly and took a sip of his punch. "I never saw a better performance."

"Something about the lovely Mrs. Bentz doesn't seem quite right, does it?"

Duncan turned to the young constable manning the refreshment table. "Lad, would you have some tea back there? Something fit to drink?" he asked, handing the young man his cup of punch.

"Yes, Inspector McLeod. Coming right up," the young man answered with a crooked grin. "I have a collection of abandoned punch glasses back here."

"Thank you, lad. You've made my evening." Duncan turned and crossed his arms over his chest. "I wouldn't go so far as to say she's up to something, but I'd bet my new pouch of pipe tobacco she's not what she seems."

Harriet cast a glance in Finnegan's direction, catching his eye for a moment and then looking away with a tiny smile. The exchange didn't escape Duncan's notice and he chuckled softly. "I believe the lovely Mrs. Bentz is flirting with you, Irishman."

As if affirming Duncan's words, Harriet excused

herself from her companions and began to weave her way through the crowd.

"Good evening, Constable Finnegan," she said when she reached him. "Inspector McLeod."

"Mrs. Bentz," Duncan replied with a nod.

"Have you discovered any more information about my husband's whereabouts, Constable?" The question was asked softly, her voice vulnerable with a slight emotional quiver. But as he looked down into her face, her eyes were hard and alert. Calculating.

"No, ma'am, I'm sorry to say I haven't."

"I know little of these sorts of things, but I would think that the sooner this is pursued the easier it would be to obtain information." The barb was nicely sheathed in her velvety voice, but her meaning was clear.

"Any additional information you could give us on your husband would help our investigation."

She smiled slowly, her expression guarded. "What additional sort of information do you think I could provide, Constable?"

"There's no record of your husband having filed a claim here in the Territory."

"That's because he's a gambler, not a miner, so naturally, there would be no claim."

Her answer was given smoothly, without evidence his request had taken her by surprise.

"You had said before you thought he came here to claim land."

"I could be wrong."

"Perhaps you could provide us with a little more

information as to your husband's pursuits while he was here."

She glanced between the two men, her face molded into a demure, feminine mask. "I've told you all I know," she responded with a feeble lift of one shoulder. "Every day when I arise, I hang all my hopes and dreams on the fact that he loved me deeply and if he could, he would have returned to my side by now. He has not, so I know he is dead."

Finnegan shook his head. Feminine logic had always eluded him and now even more so. In both Harriet Bentz and Jenny Hanson, alone on this dreary New Year's Eve. "Have you ever considered the possibility, Mrs. Bentz, that your husband might have chosen to shirk his responsibilities to you and just left?"

She looked genuinely shocked and her lips formed a round "O" of astonishment, as if the thought had never entered her mind. "Of course not. Frank was devoted to me."

So devoted a husband, in fact, that he'd left behind a colorful reputation with the whores of the Yukon Territory, Finnegan mused.

"I may, however, have some information for you, Constable. Perhaps you should begin your investigation with a woman of ill repute named Jenny Hanson."

Chapter Eight

The cold, sharp ice pellets bit into Jenny's knees as she sank into the snow. Gripping her abdomen, she sat back on her heels and breathed deeply. Cold air hurt her lungs and anticipation warred with fear as the pain rippled through her, subsiding in tiny, relenting waves. Memories of other births performed in dark rooms and whispered tones haunted her now, but she rallied her courage and remembered that this was the baby she'd longed for and had committed murder to keep.

When the pain finally eased, she struggled to her feet, churning the snow to reveal the dark soil below, and waded toward the cabin, praying to make it before another contraction gripped her. The cold metal handle of the water bucket bit into her gloveless palm as she lugged it, filled with snow, toward the porch.

Labor had begun this morning, just as the rising sun lightened the sky. Over the last few days, she'd torn rags into usable pieces, collected willow bark in case of a fever, and cut a stout willow branch to bite on during her pain. The preparations had helped keep her mind off her fear and her loneliness.

The hand railing on the steps wobbled as she threw her weight against it, using it to pull herself up onto the porch. Strangely, her legs seemed stiff and hard to move—full strides were becoming impossible. She placed the bucket of snow on the hearth to melt and checked the supply of wood in the corner, gathered in anticipation of the birth.

She stopped and listened to the silence around her. For all the days she'd spent here, only now did the loneliness seem real and palpable, almost as if it were an embodied being standing at her side, reminding her with a soft tap on the shoulder that she was the only human for hundreds of miles. Right or wrong, she now had only herself to rely upon. During those days spent in whorehouses, catering to others, she'd wished for independence, dreamed of a time when she only had to please herself. Now the truth of that wish was about to be tested.

Another pain arced across her stomach and she thought of the child struggling to get out. Once-well-corralled fear now slammed into her. Would the baby be all right, born with all the necessary parts? Would she survive the birth or die and leave

THE HEALING 133

her baby doomed? Suddenly her well-thought-out plan seemed foolish and selfish.

She gripped the back of a chair as the next pain moved lower. They were getting closer together and harder. The birth couldn't be far off. She'd gathered up all the blankets Finnegan and Duncan had left her and laid them by the bed. Others she'd spread across the bed, topping them with the single smooth sheet graciously sent by Inspector McLeod's wife so her child's first touch would be soft cotton instead of coarse wool.

In between pains, she stoked up the fire and hauled the end of the bed around until she was closer to the heat. Preparations finished and daylight waning, she stripped off her clothes and lay down on the bed to await her child.

A ghostly specter cut across Finnegan's path. Silent, wings spread, the snowy owl skimmed the surface of the trail, then soared up and into a nearby spruce, sending down a shower of snow and neatly avoiding a collision. Finnegan scolded the team that had shied, eyes wide in surprise, and they quickly corrected their path and continued to race through the dark, snowy forest.

Urgency made him irritable and short with his team. He was anxious to reach Jenny's cabin. He'd tried to stay away as she'd asked, tried to honor her wishes to have this baby alone. But, no woman should face that task by herself.

Duncan and Sam had stuffed supplies into the

sled until Finnegan had warned it might become too heavy for the dogs to pull. If Sam hadn't also been due soon, he believed she'd have hopped into the sled along with the mail sacks.

He reached the clearing as the moon took domination of the night sky. Except for an occasional drifting cloud, the sky was filled with flirting stars, elegant and cold. The dim glow of firelight lit the windows, casting a yellow shading on the snow. Surely it was far past midnight and Jenny should be long asleep. His sense of urgency grew.

He stepped off the sled runners and bade the dogs to stay. They lay down at his command and watched as he waded through the snow to the porch. A deep, faint groan cut the silence of the night. Disregarding the instinct to barge into the house with gun drawn, he cautiously pushed open the door a crack and peered in.

Soft firelight caressed her naked skin. The bed was parallel to the fireplace and the curves of her body lay in silhouette against the flames. Hands limp on her swollen belly, Jenny had obviously been in labor for some time.

"Jenny?" He stepped inside, but she was oblivious to his presence. She moaned then, bent her knees and made a feeble effort to arch her back. Her fingers scratched at her belly, leaving long, red marks on her skin, discernible even in the dim light. She trembled with the futile effort, then fell back against her makeshift pillow, finally spent.

His knowledge of childbirth was nonexistent, but even he knew something was terribly wrong.

THE HEALING

Finnegan took off his coat and ripped his sling off over his head. He rolled up his sleeves and moved to the end of the bed. He'd never delivered a baby, and had been present at only one, but he'd assisted in the birthing of colts and calves. Women couldn't be so different. Could they?

He stoked the fire, lit the lamp, and dragged the table to the end of the bed. Light flooded the room, but Jenny responded neither to him nor the added light.

"Jenny, lass." He touched her bare knee, but she didn't even flinch. Brushing aside a reluctance to violate her privacy, he pushed apart her limp knees. The crown of a baby's head showed, complete with a circle of dark hair.

Jenny stirred, moaning faintly, her back arching again. "Push, lass. Push your baby out."

The circle of hair widened, revealing part of the baby's face. But Jenny's stamina faded and the baby receded back into her body.

Finnegan dipped a readied cloth into a pan of the water she'd left warming by the hearth, moved to her head, and wiped her face. "Jenny. Look at me, lass."

She cracked open her eyes a slit. "Finnegan?"

"Your baby's ready to come. You have to push him out."

"It's been so long. He won't come. I think he's dead." A tear ran out of the corner of her eye. "I should have listened to you and gone to Dawson City." Her words drifted off, replaced by another groan.

Finnegan sat the pan down on the floor and hurried to the end of the bed. The baby's head emerged again, a little more this time. Finnegan grasped the small head, shoved aside propriety, and pushed two of his fingers between the baby and Jenny's flesh.

"Help me, Jenny." He tugged on the baby and the whole head popped out. But its shoulders seemed stuck. Jenny's body trembled uncontrollably with the effort.

"He's coming."

She tensed again, arching her back off the bed. The baby began to rotate, its face turning downward. Finnegan turned the baby in the direction it seemed headed.

Suddenly, Jenny tensed, screamed and bore down with a grunt. The baby slid out into Finnegan's hands, accompanied by a gush of water that splattered the front of his shirt.

His hands trembling, Finnegan fought to hold onto the slippery infant until he could lay the baby, cord attached, on the soft, drenched sheet. "You've got a son, Jenny. A fine boy. And he's perfect."

"You have to cut the cord," she said, fishing a ball of string and a knife from underneath her pillow. "Tie this around it near the baby and another time about an inch away. Cut in between."

Finnegan did as asked, wincing as the knife sliced through the thick tissue, freeing the baby.

"Hold him upside down and slap him on his bottom," she instructed.

Finnegan did as she asked, trusting her judgment. A thin stream of liquid ran out of the baby's mouth, then he took a deep breath and squalled.

"And a fine set of lungs, too."

The baby stopped crying and cooed as Finnegan wrapped him in a cloth and cradled him in the crook of his arm. What a small miracle he held. Perfect in every way, the baby squinted from the unaccustomed light. Once, long ago, Finnegan had looked forward to doing this to his own son. Once, there had been a place in his life for a woman and children. But he had abandoned that notion when he abandoned everything else. Now, he was a different man, one with nothing to offer a family.

He looked down at the baby and offered him a finger. The baby grasped it tightly—an instinctive action, Finnegan assumed, but disarming nonetheless.

He walked to her side, bent, and tucked the baby in beside Jenny. She opened the cloth and touched the baby's forehead, then looked up at Finnegan. "The afterbirth will come soon."

Finnegan nodded.

"I'm sorry you have to do this."

He stroked back her hair. "No need to apologize."

Seconds passed and then the last pain struck. Amazed that a woman's body could hold what hers had held, then so easily discard it, Finnegan quickly wrapped the afterbirth with trembling hands and moved it away from the bed.

He covered both mother and child with a blanket, gazing down on them with a twinge of envy.

Before he could straighten, she stopped him with a hand clamped around his elbow. "Thank you."

Finnegan looked into her face, hair plastered to her forehead, cheeks flushed, and marveled at her strength and her courage.

"You did all the work. I arrived late for the party."

"We'd have died without you."

The thought of having arrived too late and finding her and the baby dead shook him down to the soles of his much-patched boots. "But you didn't."

"No, we didn't."

Her expression seemed soft and angelic in the firelight, almost ethereal, something not to be touched by mere mortals. Women had always mystified him. They were friends, mothers, lovers; giving life to their children, pleasure and comfort to their men. And to Finnegan, all such pleasures, except the most base and emotionless, seemed an unattainable goal.

"You always seem to be finding me without my clothes on," she said with a mischievous smile, breaking his contemplation.

Finnegan chuckled. "We have a unique way of meeting, that's a fact."

She peeled away the rag that swaddled her baby and examined every finger and toe, touching his soft skin and his hair. "Isn't he beautiful?"

"That he is. What are you going to name him?"

She looked up into his face. "Would you mind terribly if I named him Michael?"

A lump in his throat suddenly forced down words

and set tears to stinging behind his lids. "No, of course not."

"Michael it is, then." She smiled down at the baby, then looked up into Finnegan's face. "Touch him."

"What?"

She grasped Finnegan's wrist and moved his hand toward the baby. "Touch him."

She guided his hand to the baby's bare chest. His fingers slid across new skin, soft and supple, like the finest velvet. Such a wonder, babies. Conceived in pleasure, born in pain. A longing he didn't often acknowledge rose as he stroked the soft skin. Another man's seed. Another man's moment of pleasure with her. The importance of any of that faded as he stared down at the bit of humanity in her arms. And that tiny bit of life staring up at him with squinted eyes burrowed a little closer to his heart.

He often envied Duncan and Sam McLeod. The love that circulated through their home drew him back there again and again, like some insatiable voyeur obsessed with another's pleasure. In each other they'd found lifelong friends, lovers, confidantes—an extension of themselves. Finnegan had spent his life avoiding such entanglements, telling himself the life he'd chosen didn't leave room for such pleasures. But he knew better. He'd watched Adam McPhail and now Duncan find and commit to a woman and a family. The only barrier now was himself. He stiffened and made a feeble effort to pull away.

Jenny chuckled softly, a deep, throaty laugh. "He won't break, Mike. Babies are tough. Just think what he had to go through to get here."

She was enjoying his obvious discomfort immensely.

Finnegan straightened with a grunt born of a long night and a brutal ride in the cold. "I'll see to the things that need to be done."

She reached up and caught his hand before he could move away, her face serious. "Thank you again. I should be doing all this for myself."

"You were a foolish lass to think that you could."

She moved her hand back to the baby's head then, undaunted by Finnegan's presence, turned back the blanket, and offered the baby her breast. He eagerly accepted, his tiny mouth hungrily seeking the nipple, his hands grasping for her soft flesh. Finnegan turned away, the intimacy of that action unnerving and threatening to his resolve not to love this woman.

He gathered up the soiled blankets and hurried outside into the dark loneliness he understood best.

Sunlight had returned when she awoke, stirred from sleep by the baby's contented nursing. One tiny hand kneaded the flesh of her breast, the other grasped rhythmically at the sheet. She offered him a finger and he clutched it tightly. Watching him nurse, her tortured body supplying comfort to his, she marveled that he was so perfect, so innocent.

THE HEALING

Not yet aware of the harshness in the world. For now, all he knew was love and contentment. How fortunate that everyone knew such peace, if even for the fleeting hours of infancy.

She looked around the room, suddenly remembering Finnegan. Or had the nightmarish struggle been a dream? He was asleep in a chair by the fire, his booted feet propped on the hearth. Head thrown back, arms crossed over his chest, he slept, snoring softly. She watched him for a moment, the fire sprinkling auburn highlights through his hair. He must be exhausted. Surely he'd driven all night to get here. What kind of man was he to so easily move about in a person's life without asking something for himself? Was she just another assignment or was there something more there?

She stretched and her skin pulled tight. Looking down, she realized she was covered with dried blood, now cracked and peeling. So was the baby. Carefully wrapping him against the cold room and placing him securely in the center of the bed, she rose stiffly, caught the blanket around her, and wobbled on unsteady legs for a moment before padding across to the fireplace.

The logs of last night had burned down to glowing embers waiting to be fed. With a glance at Finnegan, Jenny laid on small wood and flames burst to life. She added more wood until the fire was leaping, pouring heat into the cold room.

Dabbling a finger into the water in the bucket, she was surprised to find it lukewarm, not cold. She poured some into a pan and glanced at Finnegan again. He snored softly, his chest rising and falling regularly in sleep. Quickly, she dropped the blanket to the floor and washed away the blood, leaving the pan balanced on the hearth. Then she padded her flow of blood, donned her clothes of yesterday, and turned to the baby. She'd bent to pick him up when a hand touched her arm.

"Go back to your bed. I'll wash the baby."

She turned around to stare into Finnegan's sleepy blue eyes. How long had he been awake?

"I've washed many a babe. Not in a while, mind you, but I haven't forgotten the knack."

The weakness in her knees growing, she relented and climbed back into her bed. Finnegan prepared a fresh pan of water, then lifted the baby from her side, crooning nonsense as he laid him on the table. He peeled away the blood-stained rags, tore a piece off a fresh one and began to wipe away the signs of his birth.

Although her eyelids drooped, she wouldn't have missed the picture the two of them made for all the luxurious sleep in the world. Arms and legs flailing, the baby cooed and chortled as Finnegan spun some ridiculous story about pots of gold and little men. He was a natural father, at ease with a baby in his hands. Maybe more at ease with a baby than a woman.

"Do you have any children, Finnegan?"

He glanced up briefly, laughed, and shook his head. "No, not me."

"You do that very well. Where'd you learn?"

"My older sister had a whole brood. Eight of

them. After her husband was killed, they came to live with us. I've washed and changed my share of babies."

"Do you ever want any of your own?"

He shook his head, keeping his attention on the flailing arm he was attempting to dry. "Not much in my life I could offer a wife or a family."

"You have more than you know."

He glanced at her, his expression dark and closed. "Leave it alone, Jenny." His words were nearly a whisper, shaking her confidence and piquing her curiosity.

A cold rain soaked Harriet Bentz's clothes, even through her borrowed oilskins. The mule stumbled on the steep incline, pitching Harriet forward against wet, smelly mule hair. Sputtering, she clung to the saddle and cursed.

The mining town of Eldorado appeared as she topped the ridge. Scattered buildings filled the small valley and drifted up the hillsides like spreading mushrooms. Partially melted snow clung to roofs and lay in piles, gray and dirty under the relentless rain. A thin layer of fog clung to the ground and wisps of clouds floated by like disembodied spirits. A fitting place for Frank Bentz to die, she thought, punching the mule in the sides to urge her down the hill.

The Dead Horse Saloon provided the only color along the main street. Painted a cheerful red and yellow, it stood out obscenely on the conservative row of graying buildings. Churned the consistency of cake batter, the muddy street held quivering puddles and deep ruts. Harriet slipped to the ground and immediately mired to her ankles. After looping her reins over the hitching rail, she slogged to the sidewalk and knocked thick, sticky mud off her boots before stepping up onto the rain-slick boards.

The glass paneled doors of the Dead Horse swung open silently and the scent of liquor and the unwashed surged out to greet her. Closing the door behind her, she stepped inside and paused, pulling off her gloves and allowing her eyes to adjust to the dim light.

"Can I help you?"

She turned toward the voice. A man wearing a dingy apron wiped at a tabletop in the corner.

"I'm looking for George Hastings."

He straightened, a slight frown furrowing his brow. "Who's asking?"

"Mrs. Frank Bentz."

His face paled but his gaze never wavered. "I'm George."

"Then you're the man I need to see." She pulled off the heavy, wet coat, smugly aware that his gaze ran over her appreciatively when she revealed she wore a man's shirt and pants.

"Can I get you something to warm you up? Coffee? Tea?" he offered.

"I came here for information."

His expression hardened. "What kind of information?"

THE HEALING

"I'm looking for my husband."

"Frank?"

"So, you know him?"

George stepped around the bar, rearranged some liquor bottles, then reached underneath and set a teacup on the polished bar top. "I knew him."

"Do you think my Frank's dead, Mr. Hastings?"

George braced both hands on the bar, his face absent of the surprise she'd expected. "Yes ma'am, I do. I haven't seen Frank in here for weeks and he was a regular customer. Besides that," he paused for a moment, "Frank had some enemies."

"What sort of enemies?" Harriet leaned forward. Now he was getting to what she wanted to know.

"The kind that wouldn't have hesitated to put a bullet through his head if they got the chance."

She managed to coax to life a few tears to moisten her eyes, a difficult task when all she wanted to do was pursue Hastings's comments. But his sympathy might be more valuable later.

"Mrs. Bentz, do you have a place to stay? I could take you down to the hotel and see to it that you got settled in." He frowned, compassion in his eyes. Tears would work every time, she noted, and tucked the information away.

"No, thank you, Mr. Hastings. I can see to that myself. In fact, I plan to be in town for however long it takes me to find out what happened to my Frank."

A soft, sultry giggle drifted down from above. Harriet looked up. A buxom, dark-haired woman hung over the railing of the upper floor. "You looking for Frankie?" she asked, her voice smooth and thick.

"Yes, I'm his wife."

The woman laughed, throaty and taunting. "Well, you're arriving a little late, honey. He's dead."

"Everyone keeps telling me that, but no one has any proof."

"Well, I ain't got your proof, but I can tell you what happened. Come on up."

"Mrs. Bentz, don't pay Flora any mind. You got no business up there," George whispered urgently.

Harriet walked to the foot of the steps. "Watch my coat, would you, Mr. Hastings?"

She climbed the rickety stairs into the realm of sin and satisfaction. Bedchambers lined one side of the hall, some open doors revealing unmade beds and scattered pillows.

The woman stood in the hall, holding out a hand to indicate her room. Harriet walked past and into a neat room decorated in pink drapes and white bed coverings. The woman closed the door behind them and then opened the drapes to flood the room with dim light. "It took you long enough to get here."

Harriet sat down on the bed. "I didn't get your letter until six weeks ago. Damned mail service. It's piled up in Dawson City and Skagway. You got a cigar?"

Flora Miller moved to the dresser and picked up a pack of long, slim cheroots, slid one out, and handed it to Harriet, who leaned over, raised the lamp chimney, and lit the end. She closed her eyes

THE HEALING

and inhaled the rich smoke, savoring the forbidden flavor.

"So, what do you know?" Harriet leaned back on her hands, cigar clamped in her teeth, and watched the smoke spiral over her head.

"About a year ago, Frankie said he'd found something better than making a living at the gambling tables. I thought he was bringing somebody new in on our deal here, but he had something else in the works. Every now and then he'd turn up here in Eldorado with his pockets full of gold dust. Now, you know Frankie ain't gonna go mining for no gold dust, so I asked him once where he got it." Flora sat down in a chair by the table.

"He wouldn't say nothing, just smiled. Pretty soon, he stopped gambling at all in the saloons and the money dried up. He took up with a whore on one of his trips to Skagway, then he disappeared and that's when I wrote you."

Harriet took the cheroot out of her mouth and examined the glowing end. "Where was he living with this whore?"

"They had a cabin over behind Chandler's Ridge, down by Gold Creek."

"Is she still around?"

Flora shook her head. "Word is she went back down to Skagway and started working in one of the houses there not long after Frankie disappeared."

"Which house?"

"Lucille's, as I hear it."

Thoughts spinning, Harriet leaned forward. "Do you know if she's still there?"

Flora shook her head. "Maudie Baker and some of Lucille's girls were here a month or so ago for a fling. Seems Frankie's whore left Skagway with a Mountie."

"A Mountie?"

Flora nodded.

"Well, they're men, too, and just as susceptible to getting horny as the rest of us, I guess."

Flora shook her head. "It ain't like that, I heard. She hired him to take her to her cabin she bought, out there in the bend of the Yukon River they call Cutter's Fork."

"Dammit, don't make me drag it all out of you, Flora."

"Well, story is Mike Finnegan—"

"Mike Finnegan?"

Flora blinked slowly and nodded. "Yes."

"Hell, I know him. I was at a party with him Christmas night. Go on."

"Well, he took her on the mail sled from Skagway and dropped her off at her cabin, then he come on to Dawson City. But," Flora's eyes twinkled as she leaned closer, "word is he's been back there more than once since then."

"Probably screwing her on his way past with the mail."

"Oh, not lately, I wouldn't imagine." Flora shook her head with raised eyebrows.

"Well, don't just bob your head. What?"

"She's knocked up—not long 'til she delivers, I hear."

Angry heat washed over Harriet, cleansing her

THE HEALING

of every decent thought she might have had about Frank and this whore. Damn Frank and his wandering morals. She could overlook an indiscretion or two as long as the money kept coming in and Frank didn't bring home any evidence. But once upon a time he'd promised her a better life, a little house, children, a place in San Francisco society guaranteed by his father's money. He'd run through his inheritance in record time, then he'd taken to gambling to raise quick, easy money.

She looked up into Flora's over-painted face. How could a woman weathered and worn from use compete with what she had to offer a man? Unless this Jenny Hanson had money or knew where to get it. "How far away is this cabin they shared?"

Chapter Nine

A howling storm tore at Harriet's clothes with icy fingers, flinging her scarf across her face with the force of a whip.

"Ma'am, we oughta turn back. This 'uns gonna be bad," Billy Mitchell shouted from behind her. Ahead, the bouncing tails of the dog team was all that was visible through the swirling snow.

"There it is," she said as the cabin came into view. Deserted and dilapidated, the porch hung at an odd angle, threatening to pull away from the rest of the house.

"The real snow ain't got started yet. Ifen we were to turn back now, we might make it to town before the hard blow starts," he added, his own trepidation obvious.

She ignored his cautions and climbed out of the sled without assistance. All seemed quiet. Eerily so, she thought as she stepped up on the groaning porch boards. The door hung open and a collection of sticks and spruce needles made a small mound just beyond the reach of the wind. She skidded the debris out of the way with the door and stepped inside.

The musky odor of a long-dead fire soured the air. Soft, gray dust covered everything, save the swirling patterns made by a sneaky breath of wind and the mouse tracks that crisscrossed the floor. Discarded clothes lay scattered about. Underneath the dust on the floor, the dark mark of blood was unmistakable. Harriet knelt and spread her hand across the width. So much blood.

She followed the dark trail to the porch and halfway across before it was lost in the quickly thickening snowfall.

"You thinkin' somebody killed Mr. Frank, Mrs. Bentz?"

"Yes, Billy. That's exactly what I think." She narrowed her eyes at him. Billy Mitchell wasn't the brightest star in the sky but he was the only person who knew the area and was greedy enough to agree to come with her—for the right price, of course—in the face of an approaching storm.

"Well, ifen that's the case, there's a pile of rocks just over there always looked mighty suspicious to me."

Harriet stood and followed his pointing finger toward the tree line. There, just visible in the thickening snow, was the gray surface of windswept granite.

"You've been here before?"

"Yes, ma'am, lots of times. Running my trap line."

She trudged through the snow, Billy on her heels, and knelt by the rocks. With gloved hands, she began to rake away the leaves, snow, and dirt.

"Wolves been digging here," Billy muttered. "Might not like what you find," he finished with an unsure voice.

Her hands numb and her feet freezing, Harriet had all but given up when she uncovered what looked to be a scrap of material. She rolled a rock out of the way, brushed aside the dirt, and gasped. A human face—or what was left of it—lay frozen and dirty. From the looks of it, he'd taken a gun blast at point-blank range. Extensive damage made it unrecognizable. Steeling herself, she leaned closer. Was it Frank? Some instinct said no, else she'd feel an odd twist of loss in her heart, wouldn't she? Shouldn't she?

She moved another rock, revealing more of the mangled face. The hair was a dark shade of brown, but not nearly dark enough to be Frank's. She rocked back on her heels. If this wasn't Frank buried here where he should rightfully be, by all accounts, then where was he? And where was the gold he'd promised?

Billy had backed away until he stood nearly halfway to the sled, looking as though he might decide to forget the hundred dollars she'd offered him and go back to town without her.

"Don't you leave me, Billy. I'll hunt you down

and cut off parts of you you can't replace," she called over her shoulder.

"No, ma'am. That thought never entered my mind."

The clothes on the corpse were plain, devoid of any distinguishing markings. She poked further but found nothing. A gust of wind buffeted her, nearly knocking her over into the snow. She'd found what she came after. Frank had been here, all right. Those were his clothes hanging forgotten and dusty in the cabin. Something bloody had lain on the floor, then been dragged across the porch. Somebody was buried in this shallow grave.

She returned to the cabin and searched the two rooms. When that yielded nothing, she ripped up floor boards with a pry bar she'd brought and wiggled the hearthstones, hoping for a loose one. By the time evening arrived, Harriet had exhausted every idea and every suspicion, leaving her only one assumption: if Frank's gold was still around, Jenny Hanson had it.

"Ooh. There he is! There he is! Don't let him get away!"

Finnegan threw Jenny a chastising glance as she danced from foot to foot behind him. "Be quiet or I'll not catch a thing," he whispered and watched the hole in the ice. The surface of the water stirred in swirls and a fish nibbled at the surface.

"Just a little closer," Finnegan said softly, intent

on the fishing line and the frozen bait just below the surface. The line went taut and Finnegan set the hook with a yank, then reeled in the fish, retrieving the line hand over gloved hand.

"You caught him!" Jenny slapped his shoulder and laughed, her voice echoing back from the thick forest.

"You'd think you'd never seen a fish before," he said as he dragged it onto land and removed the hook from its mouth. "And a nice one it is, too."

"He's large enough to roast. No fish soup for him." She glanced over her shoulder to the cabin a short distance away. "I should check on the baby."

"Go ahead. I'll clean supper before I come in." Hooking a thumb in the fish's mouth, he strode toward the back of the house, bundled in his heavy fur coat.

Jenny waded through the snow, grateful for a few moments alone outside. Finnegan had left for Skagway two days after the birth and only then did she realize the true meaning of loneliness. Colicky and fretful, little Michael had cried nearly all of every day and night for two weeks now. Never had she been so glad to see anyone as she had been to see Finnegan drive his team into her yard this afternoon. Any other pair of adult hands would have done nicely, but his nicer than most, she thought with a secret smile.

She stepped up on the porch and heard the baby fretting from where she'd left him in the center of her bed. Contemplating turning around and

THE HEALING 155

marching straight back down to the river's edge for a second or two, she lifted the door latch and went inside with a sigh.

Nothing seemed to appease him. Not walking or back rubs or feeding. On and on through the long, dark night he cried, tensing his body, his face red with the effort. At first she'd been terrified and had convinced herself he was deathly ill and she'd have to walk all the way to Dawson for help. But after the first wave of panic passed, she remembered Grandma helping neighboring families with fussy babies. Only time and love would help, she'd said, and a pinch or two of catnip. Which Jenny didn't have.

She picked him up, his body stiff and unyielding as she put him to her shoulder for their nightly ritual of walking the floor and crying.

"What's all this howling in here?" Finnegan asked as he came through the door, stamping his feet. He walked to the hearth and laid the large fish on the stones there.

"Colic," Jenny said over the din as little Michael reached the apex of his performance—and his volume.

Finnegan shed his coat, draped it over a chair, rolled up his sleeves, and held out his arms. "Give him to me."

"You're cold from the outdoors and your hands are fishy."

Finnegan motioned with his outstretched arms and Jenny handed over the baby and his yowling.

"You're testing your mama's patience," he said

as he expertly braced the baby's neck and put him onto his shoulder.

Michael wailed another minute or two, then subsided into sobs as Finnegan walked to the window and looked out at the night, murmuring softly, a broad hand against the tiny back.

Jenny sat down on her bed and sighed, the silence ringing loud and grateful around her. "What on earth did you do?"

"Don't know. I used to do this with Maureen's babies. I never knew just what I did. But, whatever it was, it worked."

"Maybe you could stay around for, say, the next six months or so."

He turned and smiled. "I'll not be a kept man, Miss Hanson."

"You'd not be kept at all, Constable Finnegan. You'd work for your keep."

He raised his eyebrows, his eyes twinkling. "And what would be my duties?"

Warming to the game, she followed his lead, curious about this sudden playful turn of nature. "Your namesake there would be duty enough, I'd think."

"He's no trouble at all. His mama feeds him well and all else he asks is clean pants and an occasional back rub. Surely you can think of other duties I might do?"

Where on earth was he going with this and why? She studied his eyes for a hint to the point of this banter but all she saw was a glint of mischief.

"Now that you've mentioned it, I could use a back rub now and again, too," she said.

"And I'd be glad to oblige." He watched her for a moment longer, then turned his attention back to the baby, now fast asleep on his shoulder. "But as much as I'd love to be your nanny, I have to be back in Dawson day after tomorrow."

"Oh."

"Come back with me, Jenny."

She shook her head, his suggestion more appealing than he should know. "No, this is my home. I'll manage." She hoped he heard more conviction in her words than she did.

Finnegan laid the baby on the bed beside her, covering him with a blanket before he straightened and met her eyes. "You've proven yourself, Jenny. Done what you set out to do. This will always be yours if you decide to return someday. Come with me now to Dawson where there's a doctor and help with the little one here."

"And what would you have me do to earn my keep in Dawson City? Whore at the local saloon? Or let everyone wonder if I am?"

He met her eyes, riveting her with his gaze. "I wasn't suggesting whoring as an occupation. You chose that path, Jenny, and now you've chosen differently. You can't spend the rest of your life hiding from what you were."

She shivered under his directness. "I don't have any shame for what I did to feed myself, Constable. It's everybody else who seems to have a problem with it. I made my mistake in leaving home in the first place. Since then, I've acted in self-defense."

She wished she could call back the words the moment they left her lips. Her blood turned cold and the room spun. She tried to keep her expression noncommittal as she stared into Finnegan's eyes.

He crossed his arms over his chest. "Then why do you insist on living in seclusion? Some day little Michael there will want children to play with, a school to attend."

She gazed down at the milky-faced baby, now sound asleep. "Because by living alone I can make my own destiny. I'll worry about the rest when the time comes."

"I'll buy the cabin from you. You can take the money and buy a house closer to town."

She shook her head. "And have everybody know his mother's a whore?"

"I thought you said you didn't care about that."

"I don't care for me. I do care for him. How long before some group of self-righteous matrons shows up on your doorstep, Constable, and demands that you run me out of town? What would you do then?"

He shifted his weight to his other hip. "I guess I'd have to run you out of town," he said with a smirk.

"Well, I'll save you the trouble of all that. I'll stay in my cabin."

"In a town like Dawson City, nearly everybody's got a sin, secret or public. I doubt that by the time

THE HEALING

he's five or six anybody would remember how you and he came to be."

"People's memories are long and cruel."

"Not everyone's."

"And where would I live? Would you fit Michael into your footlocker in the barracks?"

"And have you sleep in my bed?"

No answer sprang to her lips, shocked as she was at his reply.

"You could stay with the McLeods," he continued. "Sam's baby's due any day. Duncan and I are gone for weeks at a time on patrol. You'd be company for each other."

"What about their other daughters?"

"They're visiting their aunt in Edmonton and won't be back until spring."

She shook her head. "That would be too much like charity. Somebody help the poor, unemployed whore." The whine of self-pity in her words shocked even her. Dear God, that had sounded awful. Apparently Finnegan thought so, too, because his eyes were snapping with fury. She turned to walk away from him, to put distance between them. Just his standing next to her addled her thoughts.

His hand clamped around her elbow and yanked her to face him. "You're smarter than that, Jenny, and it makes me furious to hear you belittle yourself."

"Then don't listen."

His grip on her arm softened. His arm slid around her waist and drew her close. Her breasts ached against the hardness of his chest. She thought for a moment he would kiss her, but his other hand cupped the back of her head and pressed her cheek against his shoulder. "What did he do to you, Jenny?"

She paused in her answer, listening to the rhythm of his body, wanting to tell and hesitating to trust. "More than I'll ever tell you."

The thump of his heart was comforting beneath her ear. She shoved aside intruding thoughts of tomorrow and next week and concentrated instead on all the places his body touched hers, tucked the memory away to take out and remember on long, lonely nights.

He released her suddenly and walked to the fireplace, where their supper lay oozing blood onto the hearthstones. He squatted down, speared the fish with a stick, and propped it above the embers to cook. "I fight a battle every day with my past sins," he said softly. "Some days I win, some days the past does. But I never stop trying. I can't go back and undo the things I've done. Neither can you."

The acrid scent of smoke worked its way into Finnegan's troubled sleep. He sniffed and cracked open an eye. The fire had burned out long ago, reduced now to a pile of glowing embers. No backdraft teased flames to life or scattered ashes across the floor.

He sat up and looked around the shadowy room.

THE HEALING 161

Something was wrong. Rising, he padded to Jenny's bed and looked down where she slept peacefully, the baby tucked in her arms. He smiled and longed to stroke their heads for reassurance. But she got precious little sleep as it was. Better not to awaken her.

A soft crackling caught his attention. Steady and growing in volume, the sound came from above, not the fireplace. Finnegan glanced at the window. The outside was softly illuminated in quivering light.

Dear God. "Jenny! Wake up!" He shook her shoulder. "The cabin's on fire!"

"What?" She struggled to her elbows even as Finnegan snatched up the baby and grabbed her wrist.

"We have to get out." He yanked her to her feet. "Get your clothes on quickly."

He shrugged into his coat with one arm, his thoughts reeling. There was no chance of putting out the fire. Jenny was dressed and hauling her satchel from under the bed as Finnegan grabbed extra blankets, his rifle and Jenny's revolver from the mantel. He flung open the door and the crackling sound grew deafening.

Tongues of flame licked from the porch roof, showering the floor with hungry sparks from where it had already burned through the boards overhead.

"Jenny!"

"I'm coming."

He handed her the baby and guided her toward the steps with a hand to her back.

"I have to move the sled," he shouted over the roar of the fire.

She nodded. He threw the things into his sled and wrestled it away from the house. Jenny hurried toward him, her arms full. He took her satchel and more blankets from her arms as she looked back over her shoulder at the leaping flames.

"Come on." Finnegan took the baby from her and pulled her across the yard, half dragging her toward the sled and team waiting yards away.

"My house. I have to go back inside."

"No, you don't," he said, tightening his grip on her wrist.

"Yes, I do." She wrenched free and ran toward the cabin, now engulfed in flames.

"Damn it," Finnegan muttered, looking for someplace safe to lay the baby so he could go after her. "Jenny, come back here!"

She paid him no heed and disappeared into the smoke now rolling out the front door. Afraid to leave the baby alone with the dogs, he started after her, clutching Michael in his arms.

He'd gone halfway across the yard when she emerged from the house, coughing and stumbling, her face blackened. He rushed to meet her and caught her arm to steady her.

"That was a damned stupid thing to do."

"I had to go back after my money," she said between coughs.

"Money wouldn't have done you much good if

THE HEALING 163

that roof had caved in on you." At that moment, as if he'd ordered it, the cabin collapsed, sending a cloud of smoke and thousands of sparks to abrupt deaths in the snow.

Jenny turned to him, tears cutting paths through the soot on her face. "It's all gone. Everything."

He looked over her head to the pile of burning, smoking logs, now bearing little semblance to the home it once had been. Suspicions began to form. The house had burned far too quickly. Mixed with the smoke and soot filling the air was the faint odor of lamp oil. He glanced down at Jenny, clutching a leather drawstring bag to her chest, sobbing as she watched the last wall collapse. Again, Harriet Bentz's accusations rose to hiss doubts into his ear.

He put an arm around Jenny's shoulder and pulled her close, comforting her sobs with a hand tangled in her hair. "Well, this answers the question of whether or not you'll come to Dawson City with me."

Chapter Ten

Bits of snow stung her face, invisible assailants thrown up from the churning paws of the dog team as they raced through the night. All she'd saved for, hoped for, gone in minutes, now only black, charred remains. She had nothing save her son, warmly tucked into her arms, and the tenuous friendship of the man at her back. Once again, her existence would have to be gleaned from tomorrow's opportunities.

She glanced at the woods racing past, tree trunks dark sentinels illuminated only by reflections from the snow. They'd been on the trail for two days and were fast approaching Dawson City. Despair seemed her constant predator, coiled, waiting to strike. Could the fire have been an accident? Something within her said no and she thought of the bag of gold dust tucked between her breasts. Did

THE HEALING 165

one of Frank's victims know she'd salvaged the gold from their stormy relationship? And were they intent on regaining what Frank had stolen from them?

A dozen possibilities flew through her mind, all rejected as absurd. Her thoughts turned again to survival. What would an ex-whore do in a town teetering on the brink of hard-won respectability? Law and order had followed close on the heels of lawlessness. The Mounted Police dispensed justice and punishment. Wives had followed their men to the gold fields and established homes and families along the banks of gold-bearing streams. Raucous Dawson City was becoming a gentled, if not tamed, town.

"We'll be at the McLeods' soon," Finnegan yelled in her ear as the first lights of town twinkled into view.

The sled slid to a stop in front of a newly built cabin, the logs still yellow and fresh. Finnegan stepped off the runners and took the baby from her arms as Jenny clambered out of the sled and stumbled forward on half-asleep legs.

The door opened, spreading a carpet of welcome light down the snowy steps.

"What the hell happened to the two of you?"

Jenny squinted, blinded for a second by the light, then realized that Duncan stood at the top of the steps, his pipe firmly clenched in his teeth.

"The cabin burned," Finnegan answered and took her elbow to guide her up the slippery steps.

"Come inside." Duncan held the door open with his back.

They struggled up the steps, each nearly too tired to make the final climb. Once inside, the odor of burnt wood swirled around them and they exchanged glances. They both reeked.

"What happened?" Duncan asked, taking Jenny's coat.

Finnegan shrugged. "I woke up and the cabin was on fire. Burned to the ground."

Jenny didn't miss the look that passed between the two men but at the moment, she was just too tired to care.

A pregnant young woman waddled into view, one hand cupping her burgeoning belly, the other waving in front of her nose. "Jesus, the two of you stink."

"Jenny Hanson, my wife Sam McLeod, the queen of hospitality," Duncan said with a raised eyebrow.

The petite blonde shot her husband a sassy look and Jenny liked her immediately. "I'm pleased to meet you."

Sam spied the baby and hurried closer. "You poor dear." She pulled aside the ragged, smoke-smudged blanket. "He's beautiful."

"Could Jenny stay with the two of you for a few days? Just until she figures out what to do?"

"Of course she can," Sam replied, Michael now securely in her grasp.

"I'm going down to the fort to file a report and see to the team." Finnegan moved toward the door and Duncan reached for his coat to follow.

"Duncan, would you pour water into the tub before you go with Finnegan?" Sam asked. "I'll bet Jenny would like a bath."

Jenny closed her eyes and inhaled the steamy, rose-scented air. Warm water lapped around her shoulders, tempting her to drift off into luxurious sleep while immersed in the copper tub.

"Do you know what caused the fire?" Sam asked as she peeled aside Michael's blankets and dropped the first layer to the floor.

"No. Finnegan thinks it's suspicious, though," Jenny responded without opening her eyes, preferring to remain suspended in her world of darkness and comfort, if only for a few moments.

"Really?" Sam threw her a curious glance. "What makes him think it's suspicious?"

Caution worked its way into Jenny's bath-lulled mind. She shouldn't have confessed their suspicions. "I can't imagine." She laid her head against the edge of the tub and sighed with contentment. The water felt too good to worry. At least for now. "I suppose he wouldn't be a good Mountie unless he always wonders if things are really the way they appear."

"I suppose," Sam mumbled, her attention now completely captured by the baby.

"When is your baby due?" Jenny changed the subject, not feeling up to the challenge of avoiding direct questions about her past.

"Any day. Can't be too soon for me." Sam picked

up the naked, wriggling baby and rubbed her nose against his.

"Is this your first child?"

Sam nodded and eased Michael into a pan of water on the kitchen table. "My first, Duncan's third. He has two grown daughters. They live with us, but they're visiting their aunt in Edmonton for the winter. But you'd never know it the way he frets and worries." Sam glanced over her shoulder. "So how was it?"

"Childbirth?"

Sam nodded.

Should she tell her the truth or romanticize the experience? She opted for the romantic version. "It was amazing." And terrifying and humiliating when your best friend, at the moment, literally yanks your child from your body.

"Well, amazing or not, I can't wait to get this child out of my body and into my arms. I'm not sure Duncan will survive another day. He hovers and worries and asks me a dozen questions until I'm almost glad to see him leave on patrol."

"You don't mean that."

"No, I don't. I miss him awfully when he's gone for weeks at a time."

"He's just concerned. Enjoy the attention." Jenny trailed a hand in the cooling water and shoved away a tickle of jealousy.

"Did you deliver your baby yourself?"

Jenny sensed no purpose in Sam's questions other than simple curiosity, but years of avoidance

THE HEALING

dictated caution and she found herself carefully measuring her responses.

"No, Finnegan did."

Sam hooted with laughter. "Mike delivered your baby? Mike Finnegan?"

Jenny looked up, puzzled. "I probably would have died if he hadn't come along when he did." Instantly, she regretted the words when a shadow crossed Sam's face. "But once he was there, Michael was born just fine," she hurried to add.

"You like this warm water, don't you?" Sam asked the baby and giggled when he cooed in response. "Somehow I can't see Mike delivering a baby. He usually steers clear of anything smacking of family life or intimacy—except my Sunday dinners, that is."

"I'm afraid I didn't give him much choice in the matter. He was there and Michael was on the way."

"You named him Michael? After Mike?"

Jenny nodded.

"Really?" Sam said with a raised eyebrow.

"It was arson. I'd bet money on it." Finnegan swished his straight razor in the pan of soapy water, wiped it on a towel, and positioned the blade to shave his other cheek.

"What makes you so sure?" Duncan asked, one hip propped on a nearby table.

Finnegan leaned closer to the cracked oval mirror in the bathroom built into the Fort Herchmer barracks and adjusted the lamp at his side for better light. He slid the sharp blade down his cheek, slicing away three days of stubbly growth. "Well, it burned too quickly, for one reason. And outside I smelled lamp oil and a lot of it."

"Could have been her lamps."

Finnegan shook his head and rinsed the razor again. "She only had one. No, this was in the air. Call it a gut feeling if you like."

"Can't begin an investigation based on gut feelings."

Finnegan slid his fingers down his shaved cheek. "I don't intend to, at least not officially."

Duncan slid off the table and tossed another stick of firewood into the fireplace. Small tables lined one wall of the room, mirrors over each, designed to offer sparse comfort to the men assigned there. A small hip tub sat in one corner, now filled with cold, soapy water.

"Do you want to tell me what you're thinking?" Duncan asked.

"No, not yet."

"Has this got anything to do with Harriet Bentz?"

Finnegan's strokes slowed and he turned to face Duncan.

"I've had the same thoughts," Duncan said.

Finnegan took a towel and wiped the remaining soap from his face. "I haven't said anything to Jenny."

"And well you shouldn't until you're sure."

"I'm not sure. Not sure at all, but the suspicion won't leave me alone."

Duncan returned to his seat on the table. "If

THE HEALING

Jenny dispatched old Frank, she probably had good reason, from what I've heard."

Finnegan wiped the dribbles of water from his bare chest and pulled his knit undershirt over his head. "You've been looking into this?" He snapped his suspenders onto his shoulders and turned.

Duncan shrugged. "I asked a few questions when I was in Eldorado last week. Seems Frank liked to knock women around. You won't get the women to complain, though. He paid his whores well."

Finnegan cringed at the word, but hid his reaction. "What else did you find out?"

"Word is he was suspected of stealing gold from sluice boxes. George Hastings thinks that's where he got his money. A little here, a little there. It all added up to a tidy sum after a while. Nobody could catch him at it, though."

Finnegan remembered Jenny's leather sack, the one she'd risked her life to retrieve, and wondered what was inside—or should he wonder *how much?*

"Long patrol, this, all the way to Whitehorse," Duncan said, more to himself than out loud.

Worry was evident on Duncan's usually tranquil face. He knew that in the days ahead, while he was miles and days away, his wife would give birth. She would do so without him at her side and he wouldn't know the outcome until he returned.

Finnegan buttoned his shirt while Duncan stared at the floor. Odd, Finnegan mused, that he would now be in the position to understand that concern. "I could take Harper. Leave you here with Sam." Finnegan leaned down and picked up his gunbelt.

Duncan shook his head. "She's forbidden me to change my duties. Says she'll prove 'em wrong yet about men in the Force marrying."

"Ah, well. Not many men marry the likes of Sam McLeod, do they?" Finnegan settled the belt on his hips and checked the chamber of his revolver.

"I wouldn't imagine much would throw Sam *or* Jenny. Together, heaven help the man that runs afoul of 'em." Duncan folded his arms over his chest.

Finnegan glanced up. "Meaning me."

"Meaning that you're in deep, lad. I hope you've got your wading boots in good shape."

Finnegan shook his head. "She's just a friend."

"And how long before you stop believing that load of blarney?"

Finnegan jerked his head up, a sudden and unexplainable flush of anger flaming through him.

"Hit a nerve, did I?" Duncan said with a smirk.

Finnegan took a deep breath. "She needed help and I was there."

"And you've been back again and again." Duncan slid off the table to stand in front of him.

"That's my concern and none of yours."

Duncan's expression softened. "I've only got your best interest at heart. I like the lass. She's a strong woman, but if she's mixed up in this—"

"She isn't."

"You're losing your objectivity."

"Don't tell me how to do my job."

Duncan studied him a moment. "All right, lad. I'll drop the subject."

THE HEALING

As the sickening aftermath of anger poured through him, Finnegan grudgingly acknowledged Duncan's cautions. He was in too deep. In fact, he was caught and wrapped in Jenny's web as securely as any spider's supper.

"I care about her but I'm not in love with her." He looked up to meet Duncan's even expression. "She needed help and I had the means to offer it."

"You've no need to explain it to me. I said I'd drop it."

"I know you better than that. Dropping the subject isn't an option with you . . . or Sam." Snatching up his fur-lined coat, Finnegan strode to the door and shoved it open. Breathtakingly cold air swept away the warm, moist heat.

"Sam only wants to see you happy. You know Sam. Since we've been married, she thinks the whole world should be."

"I'm happy the way I am. Alone." Shoving his hands into his pockets, he strode down the snowy path to the shelter where their dog teams were kept.

Duncan matched his strides. "I thought that myself once."

"You were meant to have a wife and a house full of children. Not me."

Finnegan swung open the door to the shed. Wagging tails and lolling tongues met him at the door. "Are you lads ready to go?" he asked, dispensing pats to wiggling gray-and-white dogs.

Duncan and Finnegan dropped their conversation and concentrated on hitching their teams. The patrol would be long and hard, with no room for an argument between them. Done, they swung their teams back toward Dawson City to pick up sacks of mail and to say good-byes.

Smoke curled from the chimney of Duncan's cabin at the edge of town, a poignant reminder of what they were leaving behind, Finnegan mused. Worry and regret furrowed Duncan's usually placid expression as they left their teams in front of the house and trudged up the steps to the porch.

Sam met them at the door and held out Duncan's pack. She looked miserable and tired, but summoned a smile. "No long good-byes," she said. "You'll be back in a week or two and the baby and I will be waiting for you."

Duncan's hand trembled almost imperceivably as he took the battered pack from her. "You'll take care?"

"You found me buried in an avalanche, Duncan McLeod. I can handle a simple birth."

He leaned forward and kissed her. When they separated, her eyes were misty, but her smile was still firmly in place.

"You'll see to her?" Duncan said to Jenny, standing close behind Sam.

Jenny nodded solemnly.

Duncan turned and walked down the steps without looking back. Her smile fading, Sam ducked back into the house, leaving Jenny and Finnegan on the snowy porch.

"We'll be back in two or three weeks."

THE HEALING

She nodded her answer.

"You'll be here?" Unasked, the question would have haunted him every snowy mile.

She smiled slowly. "That sounded hopeful, Constable."

"Maybe it was."

She studied his face and seemed to see a little too much. "I'll be here. Sam's already convinced me we should throw our lots in together until Duncan and you return."

"What about the birth?"

"Nothing to it," she said with a shrug of her shoulders. "You should know."

They laughed together, but he felt no humor at the parting he was about to make. "Good-bye." He hesitated for a moment, then leaned forward and kissed her cheek.

She watched him withdraw with large, soft eyes. "Keep safe, Mike Finnegan. And come back to me."

Shaken by the sincerity of her words, Finnegan turned and walked down the steps. He looked back once and regretted it before he stepped onto the runners of his sled. "Hike!"

The team surged forward, made a wide arc in the street, and headed toward the outskirts of the settlement.

"Whatever splinter you've got stuck in your soul, Finnegan lad, one day it's going to fester up and slip out, bringing the corruption with it," Duncan said to Finnegan's back as the last buildings of Dawson City sped by in a snowy blur.

* * *

Swish. Swish.

A soft noise woke Jenny. She rolled to her back and stared at the quivering shadows on the ceiling, trying to remember where she was and how she'd gotten here.

She pushed her hair out of her face and sat up.

Swish. Swish.

The noise was out of place. She rolled to her side and looked over the edge of the mattress. Tucked in his dresser-drawer bed, little Michael slept peacefully. She swung her legs over the side of the bed, gathered up her too-long gown and walked toward the soft light coming from the other room.

Sam rocked back and forth in front of the fireplace.

"What's wrong?" Jenny asked, moving around in front of her.

Sam looked up, tears shining in her eyes. "I'm in labor. Duncan missed it by a few hours."

Jenny squatted by her side and smoothed the hair off her forehead. "How far along are you?"

"Pretty far. The pains are getting closer together."

"We should get you into bed." Jenny stood and reached down to help Sam, but she ignored the outstretched hand and shook her head.

"I've already tried that. I want to stay on my feet."

While Jenny readied water and cloths, Sam

walked the floor, pausing often by the wide front window that looked out on sleeping Dawson City hoping, Jenny knew, to see Duncan and his dog team come around the curve at the end of the street.

A tingle of jealousy ran through her for the love Sam and Duncan shared. They were united across the distance, each one's hopes centered on the child now struggling to be born. She followed Sam's gaze to the quiet dawn just lightening the sky beyond their wavy reflections and wished, for a dangerous moment, that her own path had been different, that Michael had been born into a home filled with love and commitment. That Frank had been more of a man and less of a bastard. Quickly, she shook off the thought. She'd promised herself she'd never think of Frank again, never think of what she'd done and why she'd done it.

"I wonder where Duncan is," Sam murmured.

"They're safe wherever they are," Jenny reassured.

Sam turned to her, her face pale and damp with perspiration. "Were you afraid?"

"Yes."

"Did you think you might die?"

"Yes. But I knew I couldn't. But Michael would have no one except me once he was born. I had to survive for him."

"I can't imagine doing this alone. What did you do in all those hours of labor?"

Jenny looked back out the window. "Waited.

Made preparations. Prayed I'd have the courage and the wisdom to do what had to be done."

Jenny felt Sam tense beside her. When she looked, Sam's face had blanched as another contraction gripped her. "It's time," she announced, trembling.

Jenny helped Sam to her generous four-poster bed and before the sun was full up, Skye McLeod slid into the world.

Chapter Eleven

The odor of smoldering pipe tobacco became part of Finnegan's dream, the sweet-sharp aroma winding itself around Jenny as she stood before him, gloriously naked, her skin glowing in the soft light. Lips, red and eager, sought his and kissed him, sweet and erotic. His body strained, raging with desire for the vision just beyond his reach. He stretched toward her, aching with need. His fingers brushed something cold and hard. He opened his eyes and stared at the lashings on his sled.

His body still responding to the dream as it quickly dissipated, he lay still and tried to call back the images, to tuck them away in his mind. Behind him he heard Duncan stir. They'd spent the night in their sleds under the lee of a huge hemlock tree, protected from the wind by its graceful branches. The time must be somewhere near dawn. Finnegan wondered if Duncan had slept at all.

"Have you been awake all night?" he asked.

"Most of it," Duncan replied and tapped his pipe on the hollow-sounding frame of his sled. "She's all right. Jenny's with her and she's delivered babies before."

"Aye," he said, reverting to his native brogue. "But I still wish I was there."

Duncan rarely spoke of his own feelings or thoughts. And the fact that he did now revealed a trust between the two of them they'd never spoken of. To do so seemed ... unmanly, somehow.

"We'll be home tonight."

"Aye, and the knowing of it is what's tormenting me."

Finnegan turned over and shoved himself into a sitting position. His lead dog stood and looked over his shoulder. Moonlight reflected off the snow, providing soft illumination, even beneath the gently sagging branches.

"Not yet, Buck."

After a moment's hesitation, Buck lay back down and tucked his tail securely around his nose, his black eyes blinking above the gray fur.

"Why don't you get out of the Force when your time's up?" Finnegan asked. "You've a family now."

Duncan shook his head. "Sam and I had an agreement when we married that we'd not try to change each other. That includes, according to Sam, my work."

"Life with the Force's hard on a woman. McPhail nearly lost Lauren. If he hadn't followed her to Regina and brought her back, they'd not be together today."

Duncan smiled and tapped the remaining ashes out of his pipe. "I think Fate would have intervened in the McPhail case. I've never seen any two more besotted with each other than Adam and Lauren." He wrested a leather pouch from his coat and filled his pipe. "And so, old man, that leaves only you unwed."

"And I intend to stay that way."

"Do you now?" Duncan struck a match on the side of the sled and lit the pipe's bowl. He drew in and then expelled the smoke in a hazy ring over his head.

"A week ago you were warning me away from Jenny."

"I've not said a word about Miss Hanson."

Neatly caught in Duncan's trap, Finnegan felt the color creep up his face, gratefully hidden by the half-light.

"Look, lad, I know you've got somethin' eatin' at you, have had since I've known you. I've never asked any questions and I won't now. Don't let it empty you out, whatever it is."

Finnegan had never felt the need to unburden himself and he didn't now. His sins were his sins. But Duncan had been a good and true friend for many years. Perhaps he deserved an explanation to put to rest his concerns. "I haven't always been a decent man," Finnegan began.

Duncan chuckled. "Has any of us?"

"I left some things behind in Ireland . . . I can't go back."

Duncan took his pipe out of his mouth and studied the orange glow of the bowl. "What are you wanted for?"

"Suspicion of murder."

Duncan raised his face, his eyes dark. "Are you guilty?"

Finnegan shook his head. "I don't know. I was drunk, on my hands and knees in the alley vomiting up my guts. Somebody grabbed me from behind. I had a knife and I used it. After that, I don't remember much until somebody told me Red O'Leery was dead. Stabbed."

Duncan returned to studying his pipe. "How old were you?"

"Fifteen."

"Just a lad."

"No. I'd been on my own since my mum died. Pa died first. My sister took her brood and moved away. I took to the streets of Dublin, earning my living any way I could. I discovered whiskey and women early."

"How long before you discovered the two don't mix?"

Finnegan laughed. "Quickly."

"Have you told the lass this?"

"Jenny? No. And I don't intend to. You're the first person I've told in fifteen years. And the last."

"If you love her—"

"I don't."

Duncan threw aside the blankets and climbed out of the sled. He stretched his arms over his head as his team stood, tails wagging in anticipation.

"I'm no expert in love, but I'm fast becoming one on women—out of self-defense, mind you. You may not love her, but she's in love with you, if I'm any judge. And if you're going to break her heart, lad, you at least owe her the truth."

The fire had worried itself down to embers that warmed the cozy room with an orange glow. Outside, an angry wind buffeted the house and shards of ice tinkled against the glass windows.

"Don't you worry about Duncan on a night like this?" Jenny shifted Michael to cradle him in the bend of her other knee as she sat cross-legged on the McLeods' hearth rug. The rocking chair beside her swished softly and little Skye made loud gulping noises as she nursed at Sam's breast. No one could have guessed that Sam McLeod had given birth only a week ago.

"Yes, but I know he knows what he's doing. He's been in the Force for more than ten years. You get used to it after a while." Sam looked down at her, one delicate eyebrow raised. "Do you worry about Finnegan?"

"He and I are just friends."

"I swear, the two of you have that line down pat. I didn't ask you if you were friends. I asked you if you worried about him."

She looked up at Sam and smiled at the mischief in her expression. "Sometimes."

Sam raised both eyebrows.

"All right, more than sometimes. When a storm's blowing, I wonder where he is, if he's warm and safe."

"And how long has this non-worrying been going on?"

Jenny chucked Michael's chin and was rewarded with a smile. "Practically since the first time I saw him. I don't think the worry is returned, though."

"My dear, you're dead wrong there. You're all he talks about."

"Truly?"

"Well, mostly he's cursing, but I think that could be filed under the heading of 'talking about'."

"No, I guess we don't get on very well together. He thinks I'm stubborn and I think he . . . fusses."

Sam hooted with laughter until Skye whimpered in fear. "Oh, baby, I didn't mean to frighten you." She put the baby to her shoulder and soothed her with a hand on her back.

"Despite the fact, Duncan adores him. Maybe *adores* isn't a good word for men. Maybe *admires* is better. Anyway, Duncan and Finnegan have been inseparable for years. And despite that, Finnegan still doesn't talk about himself. We don't know anything about his past, why he joined the Mounties, nothing. We didn't know about you until Duncan came home one night, stomping around, cursing Finnegan for leaving a stubborn woman in

THE HEALING 185

a cabin down at Cutter's Fork. Took me a day or two to pick the whole story out of him."

"What did Duncan tell you?" she asked cautiously.

"Only that you were expecting a child, had bought the cabin, and intended to live there alone."

"Nothing else?"

"No."

Sam rocked for a few minutes and repositioned the baby. Jenny knew Sam was burning with questions about her and Finnegan, but how much could she safely divulge?

"Where did the two of you meet?"

Jenny smiled, remembering. "In Skagway. I'm afraid the details might shock you."

Sam picked up her daughter and placed her on her shoulder. "Nothing shocks me. I used to be a newspaper reporter. I'm a Mountie's wife. I'm raising two stepdaughters, one of whom is getting married in the spring. The other has just discovered men. I repeat, nothing shocks me. Besides, I'll bet this is too good to pass up."

Jenny related the incident in Lucille's while Sam listened with wide eyes.

"I was right. That was too good to pass up. How dreadful for you. Weren't you scared to death?"

"It doesn't shock you what I was doing?"

Sam shrugged and patted her daughter on the back. "We all do what we have to. I came to the Yukon over the Chilkoot Pass, posing as my best friend Oscar's wife. I was dead set to prove the police were stealing gold dust. And Duncan was my prime suspect."

"And was he guilty?"

Sam rolled her eyes. "Heavens, no. Duncan McLeod guilty of a crime? He won't even play cards for matchsticks. No, it turned out to be someone else. But not before I had made his life miserable. Luckily, he was in love with me all along," she said with a smug smile.

What would it feel like to be so confident of a man's affections?

"No, I wasn't scared after Finnegan got there. He didn't pass judgment on me or poor Percy. He just stepped in and handled the situation."

"That's our Finnegan. Mysterious. Capable. Polite. Just once, I'd like to see him lose his temper and throw things. Or people."

Jenny laughed, basking in the gentle camaraderie. Over the years, she'd called a few other women *friends*. But in their business, nothing was for long. Girls came and went, died or were killed. She quickly learned to keep relationships on a shallow level and not become attached too deeply to anyone. Most especially not to men.

Sam rose and padded to the bedroom, motioning for Jenny to follow. She laid her sleeping daughter in one end of the cradle and took Michael from Jenny before she could protest and laid him in the other. "See, I told you they'd both fit." She leaned down and adjusted their shared blanket. "Come out to the kitchen. I'll make some tea."

Jenny closed the door and followed Sam to the

kitchen. Sam waved her to a chair, stirred up the coals, and added wood to the firebox until orange flames flickered through the grates.

"It's nice having someone here while Duncan's gone. The nights get awfully long sometimes." Sam bent down and shoved in another stick of firewood. She set a kettle on the stove eye and joined Jenny at the table, easing gingerly into the chair. "What was it like there? In the whorehouses."

Startled, Jenny stared at her while a dozen images raced through her mind.

"I'm sorry. You don't have to answer that. It's just my reporter's curiosity, I suppose."

Jenny twirled the cup Sam had put in front of her, staring down into its white, smooth inside. "Not always bad. Some of the houses were very clean and well run. We were well cared for. Others," she shrugged a shoulder, "not so good. Lucille's was the best, though."

"How did you do . . . what you did . . . without becoming involved with the men?"

"It's a job. Like any other you don't particularly like, I suppose. You learn to shut yourself off from what you're really doing. Treat it as business and nothing else."

"I'm going to pry again. You've had fair warning. Deal?"

"Deal."

"Was there ever anyone special, who made you forget it should be business?"

"Once."

"The baby's father?" Sam's eyes widened. "Oh, heavens. Finnegan's not the father, is he?"

Jenny laughed and blushed. "No, no. There's nothing like that between us. Michael's father was a terrible mistake. He left me when he found out I was pregnant." She was treading on dangerous ground here, she realized. "I never saw him again and I just assumed he must have been married."

"He left you with nothing?" Sam propped her chin on her fist and stared, wide-eyed.

"Just Michael. And the desire to give him a better life than I had at that moment."

Sam rose and retrieved the protesting kettle from the stove. She sprinkled tea into each cup and poured in steaming water.

"Where's your family?" she asked as she set the kettle back on the stove eye.

Jenny shook her head. "Grandma raised my sister and me until I left home at fifteen. I haven't seen either of them since."

"Have you tried to write to them?"

Jenny stirred the tea and shook her head. "I doubt anyone cares, the way I left."

"Hearts are forgiving," Sam said, easing back into her seat. "You should write and see what happens."

They drank their tea in companionable silence with only the snap of the fire and the moan of the wind for company. Jenny wondered about Finnegan, somewhere out in the howling storm with Duncan. How lonely the nights must be for Sam McLeod, eternally waiting for her husband to come home. She glanced across the table at Sam, who smiled distractedly into her swirling tea leaves. Perhaps, for Sam, the wait was worth it.

A patchwork pattern of yellow light shone across the snow, reflecting from the paned glass windows. Duncan drew his team to a halt and Finnegan's team trotted to a stop behind him. A stiff, cold wind buffeted them from behind as they stared at the once-abandoned cabin, Frank Bentz's last suspected residence.

"What do you make of that?" Duncan said, nodding toward the cabin, the fur on his hood fluttering in the wind.

"Looks like somebody's moved in," Finnegan answered.

They urged their dog teams closer and stepped off the runners into the new snowfall. Stomping their feet, they walked up onto the porch and rapped on the door.

"Why, good evening, gentlemen."

Harriet Bentz stood in the doorway, clutching a silky wrapper—and wearing little else.

"Mrs. Bentz," Duncan said. "We didn't expect to find anyone here." He glanced at Finnegan.

"Please, come in." She moved aside and held the door open. "You can take your coats off by the fire."

The cabin had been transformed from a dusty, dirty hovel to a gleaming, cozy home. Finnegan's hopes fell. Any evidence still around was now thrown out with the mop water.

They took off their fur-lined coats and hung them by the cheery fire. Newly upholstered chairs faced the hearth and a hooked rug covered the clean floor. Finnegan wondered if the bloodstain still lay beneath the blue-and-gold loops of cloth. But he wondered more how she'd brought such luxuries here, deep in the Yukon wilderness, without attracting undue attention.

"What a pleasant surprise to have two such handsome visitors on a cold winter's night." She moved toward them, her hips swaying gently beneath the thin fabric that left little to the imagination. "I apologize for my attire. I hadn't expected company." She looked genuinely flustered, as if they'd intruded. "If you'll excuse me." She turned and sauntered to the blanket that separated the room into two parts. With a final smile, she eased the curtain closed.

Duncan raised his eyebrows and Finnegan shook his head. This was nothing like the grieving widow who had attempted to pin him down about her errant husband's whereabouts. Harriet Bentz was now playing the part of seductress. But why? He glanced around the room. There was no sign of a man's presence anywhere. Was she living out here alone?

A few minutes later she emerged, more appropriately attired in a modest green dress. "Now, gentlemen, what can I do for you?"

"We were doing more investigation into the disappearance of your husband and had hoped to look over the cabin again," Duncan said. "I can see you've rearranged things a bit."

"And I messed up your plans, didn't I?" she cooed.

Duncan threw Finnegan a glance. "I'm afraid you did."

"Well, when I cleaned this place out, I didn't find anything of much interest. A few clothes, mostly my husband's."

"You're sure they were his?" Duncan asked.

"Oh, yes. They were my Frankie's. I embroidered my name in each and every garment I made or bought him. Do you want to see?" She moved toward the curtain again, disappeared behind it, then reemerged carrying a man's shirt. She held it out for them to see. Sure enough, stitched on the inside of the collar was "HJB with love."

"I made this shirt." She ran a hand down the sleeve. "I stitched on it during the evenings of last winter when Frankie was gone. Then I mailed it to him. As you can see, he adored the things I made him."

"And why is that, ma'am?" Duncan asked.

She raised her eyes to meet his. "Why, because he kept it even though it had a tiny hole in it." She ran a finger underneath the tattered fabric, a small hole over the left shoulder. "It was uncommonly dirty, though. Frankie never gets his clothes dirty. But, I washed it with lye soap and finally it all came out."

Finnegan took the garment from her and studied

the frayed edges. Telltale rusty marks stained the end of the torn fibers.

"And a fine shirt it is. I'm sure he treasured it."

She stared up at Finnegan. "Do you have any further information on my husband's whereabouts, Constable?"

"No, ma'am. Maybe in the spring, when the snow melts and we can move around better, maybe then we'll find out something more."

"I am still determined to find my Frankie and I sometimes believe he's alive somewhere."

"Life's rugged living out here alone. Wouldn't you be more comfortable in town? You're a good twenty miles from Dawson City."

"Oh, no, Constable. This was Frankie's cabin. The deed is registered at the land agent's office. And now it's mine, all I have left of him. I wouldn't dream of living anyplace else."

She moved to the fireplace, bent down, and threw a piece of wood onto the fire. "Would you gentlemen like to stay for the night?"

"No," they chorused.

"We have a patrol to run and should be on our way. We'll be back by in a few days and we'll check in on you then." Duncan snared his coat off the chair by the fireplace and began to inch toward the door. Finnegan headed toward the hearth, but Harriet cut across his path.

"I'll look forward to speaking with you again, Constable, on this matter." She reached up and turned one of the gold crowns pinned to his collar.

THE HEALING

"Perhaps together we can come up with a new plan to look for Frankie."

Finnegan stared down into her face and she dropped an eyelid in a sultry wink. He picked up his coat and started for the door.

"I'll look forward to your visit when you come back."

Finnegan stepped outside the door, closed it behind him, and heaved a sigh of relief.

"Two women, fifty miles apart. You're going to be a busy man," Duncan said with an evil grin.

Finnegan laughed and shook his head. "Not me. What do you make of all that?"

"Seem to you that we interrupted something?"

Finnegan glanced back at the cabin as he stepped up on his sled runners. "Could be. But where was he?"

Duncan shook his head. "I don't know, but I can't get Sam to wear things like that when we're home alone. I doubt she'd even wear something like that when she's by herself. Should we circle around behind?"

Finnegan shook his head. "Let's not tip our hand. We'll be back this way in a few days. We'll stop back by and see."

Harriet braced her hand on the cabin door and heaved a sigh of relief. Trembling, she inhaled and let out a slow breath. "You can come out now."

Frank Bentz crawled out from beneath the bed, straightened, and brushed at the dirt on his neatly creased black pants. "Nice little performance you put on there."

She turned toward him and smiled. "I always told you I should be an actress."

"Come over here and give me some of the attention you were paying to that Mountie."

Harriet sauntered toward him, noting the way his eyes followed the sway of her hips. "I just wanted to rattle him a little."

"You rattled me."

"Good." She stopped in front of him and snaked both arms around his neck. "I like you when you're rattled."

He buried his face in her neck and rolled the tender skin between his teeth. "Sweet Harriet."

"Sweet Harriet indeed." She shoved him away and stepped back. "If I'm so sweet, why did you take up with that harlot and get her with a bastard?"

"You were far away, my dear, and I . . . well, a man has certain needs that must be dealt with . . . and often."

She rolled her bottom lip out in a gesture she knew threw the momentum of any argument to her side. True to form, his eyes were immediately drawn to her mouth.

"Well, perhaps I could forgive you if you were to gift me with my heart's desires."

He moved toward her and clasped her shoulders. "I have more gold than you can imagine, my sweet. You can have whatever you want."

"You've never told me how you fooled your harlot into believing she'd killed you." Harriet moved

THE HEALING

to a chair and sat down, prolonging his agony by delaying what he wanted most.

"She shot me, all right. Nearly point-blank. The blast knocked me out, but the bullet only caught me in the shoulder. Poor bitch shut her eyes when she pulled the trigger. I came to while she was dragging me through the snow. So, I let her. She couldn't dig a hole in the hard ground, so she tried to cover me with rocks. I waited there until she was gone, then I got up. Simple."

"But who was the body I found there?"

"A prospector that happened by a day or two later. I needed a body in case she went to the Mounties. One blast to his face and he became Frank Bentz."

Harriet stood and Frank moved toward her. "I wish you hadn't shown them the shirt, though."

"Why not?" she asked as he pulled her into his arms.

"Because that's the one I was wearing when she shot me."

Harriet leaned back. "Is that what that hole was?"

Frank nipped at her neck. "They won't be smart enough to figure that out, so don't worry. Concentrate on me, sweet."

With talented fingers, Frank unbuttoned her dress and slid it to the floor. He made quick work of her chemise and corset and then stripped her of her drawers. Fingers splayed, he ran his hands over her breasts, down to her waist, and over her hips. He dropped to his knees in front of her and kissed places that allowed her to tangle her fingers in his hair.

He swept her into his arms and deposited her on their narrow bed. After disrobing quickly, he wasted little time finding the part of her he desired most. He sank into her deeply, shoving her against the head of the bed with a gasp. Then he rocked against her harder, harder until the bed screeched its objection.

Harriet wildly joined his rhythm, too long without a man, too long without release. They came together, crying out in unison, then lay spent upon each other.

"Remember, Harriet, that only I can do this for you," Frankie said, his face pressed against her breast.

"Sure, Frankie. Only you." Harriet twisted a strand of his hair in her fingers and smiled.

Chapter Twelve

The wind and snow swept the sky clear. Lazy arcs of clouds lay in the east and reflected tinted ribbons of a midday sunrise. Jenny pushed aside the lacy curtain at the guest room window and stared out at the birth of the new day. Daylight only lasted a few hours and was a faint imitation of its summer companion. Despite the early morning beauty, the lethargy of the day matched Jenny's mood.

She dropped the curtain in place and crawled back into the warm, soft bed. Pictures of ladies' fashions stared at her from every wall. Upswept hair and bustled fannies dominated the elaborate pictures, crookedly scissored from fashion magazines.

After a day or two in Lizzy McLeod's bedroom, Jenny had quickly surmised that Lizzy's interest in fashion went beyond a girlish fascination. She'd drawn some of the pictures and done them with great insight and care. Obviously, she was very talented.

Jenny sat up in the bed and focused on one pencil drawing plastered against the opposite wall. A model with a long, slim neck sported a frilly blouse tucked into the narrow waistband of an elegantly draped skirt. A small train on the back elongated and feminized the entire outfit. With a ridge of tiny stitches there, she mused, and another there, the blouse could be made of thinnest batiste and still be proper for afternoon wear.

In the corner of her borrowed room stood a dress form draped with a shimmering blue fabric— Lizzy McLeod's half-finished wedding dress. Flipping back the covers, Jenny rose and padded to the dress form. She touched the fabric and found that it slid smoothly beneath her fingers. It was finely warped, close-woven and yet delicate. She rubbed an edge between her fingers. Soft and supple, it would drape nicely across a woman's figure and move gracefully when she walked. An excellent choice for a wedding gown.

Envy sank its talons in her again as she imagined an adoring groom, blushing bride, friends and family gathered on a sunny summer day. She jerked her hand away from the fabric and shook her head. She had to find something profitable to occupy her time and her mind.

The baby stirred in his dresser-drawer bed as she stepped closer to the pictures on the walls. *Godey's Ladies' Book* was the name in the corner of the page.

The volumes of fashion plates and advice had been a highly prized commodity in Lucille's and The Velvet Rose, coveted to the point of provoking near-fistfights among the girls. More than once she'd been called upon to stitch together a copy of a garment, altered to showcase the wearer's assets, of course. She'd found then that she had a surprising aptitude for the task.

She wandered to a small desk, apparently another of Duncan's contributions to the furnishing of his home. Papers lay scattered across the top, the upper sheet lines of figures addressing the price and number of bolts of fabric. She glanced around the room again as Michael whimpered. Was Lizzy McLeod contemplating the same venture as she?

The bag of gold dust lay sewn into her carpetbag, hundreds of dollars ill-gotten but waiting to be put to use. She could finance the initial purchases, rent a building, and pay for advertising. She and Lizzy could run the business together. Fending off a voice that chided that the whole idea was a silly notion, she picked up the baby and changed him, fabrics and designs floating through her thoughts as she went to find Sam.

"Lizzy's room is lovely," Jenny said, bending to put her baby into the cradle in Sam's room.

"She's got those darned fashion pages everywhere," Sam said, doing the same with her daughter.

Jenny straightened. "Do you think she wants her own shop?"

"That's all she talks about." Sam flipped up the quilt on her bed and straightened the pillows. "She's gotten the notion into her head that she wants to go into this marriage a financially stable woman." Sam smiled. "Duncan says he can't imagine where she got such a notion."

"Is that what you did?"

"Oscar and I had a photography shop on Main Street. When he and his wife moved to Edmonton, I kept the shop and hired a young man to run it for me when I found out I was carrying Skye. Didn't want to have her around the chemicals. Fate took an ironic turn and that young man will soon be my son-in-law."

Jenny ran a hand over the smooth rungs of the foot of the bed. "Do you suppose she'd want a partner?"

Sam stopped folding diapers and looked at Jenny. "Are you interested?"

Jenny sat down on the bed. "I need a job, now that the cabin is gone. Michael and I have to find a place of our own or else rebuild the cabin. And, I've realized that Finnegan is probably right, as much as I hate to admit it. I've no business living so isolated with the baby. And, I'm developing a fine case of feeling sorry for myself. I saw her figures and the pictures. I'm a good seamstress and . . . I have some money I could invest."

Sam dropped the square of cloth and caught both of Jenny's hands in hers. "Oh, Jenny. Lizzy'd be delighted, I'm sure. That would be the answer to her prayers. And Finnegan's. And mine."

THE HEALING 201

Jenny looked up into Sam's sparkling eyes. "Truly and honestly, Sam, there's nothing between Finnegan and me. Not that I wouldn't like there to be—"

"Uh-huh, the truth finally comes out."

"But he is what he is and I am what I am. The Mountie and the whore. It'll never be."

Sam planted her hands on her hips and grinned. "Well, we'll just see about that."

"Duncan!"

Sam's cry brought Jenny out of the bed. She hurried to the living room to find Sam clasped in Duncan's bear hug, snow-covered coat and all. Her feet dangling inches above the floor, Sam's bright laugh rang out, Duncan's deep chuckle supplying harmony.

"Put me down, Duncan, I've just had a baby," she protested none too seriously, her giggle giving away her pleasure.

Finnegan stood by the door, watching the reunion, an odd expression on his face. Jenny returned to the bedroom to fetch her wrapper off the bed and when she turned, Finnegan stood in the door.

"How's the baby?" he asked, his coat leaking little drops of water onto the wooden floor.

Jenny slid her arms into the garment and pulled it around her, self-conscious about wearing only the thin nightgown despite the fact he'd already seen her naked twice. She smiled to herself when his eyes followed her motions.

"Michael's fine. Sam and Duncan have a beautiful daughter."

"Where's my girl?" they heard Duncan ask.

"Do you want some tea?" she asked and Finnegan nodded.

She stepped past him to lead the way to the kitchen. He paused by the fireplace to hang his coat over the back of a chair to dry.

They walked past the McLeods' bedroom on their way to the kitchen. Duncan was on his knees at the bedside, one arm across Sam, one hand on his daughter. His broad shoulders shook as he buried his face in Sam's neck. Jenny quietly pulled the door shut.

She stoked the fire and put the kettle on the stove eye, all the while conscious that Finnegan watched her from the doorway, one shoulder leaned against the jam, his arms crossed over his chest.

"Why are you watching me like that?" she finally asked without turning around.

When he didn't answer, she turned.

"I was surprised to find you still here."

"Where did you think I'd be? I have no place else to go." Despite her efforts, a peevishness had crept into her voice. Apparently, Finnegan noticed it, too. A frown flickered across his face, but before he could say what he thought, Michael began to cry. Jenny started toward the bedroom, but Finnegan crossed her path and reached the baby first. He

THE HEALING

scooped him up into the crook of his arm, tickled his stomach, and was rewarded with a yawn and a puzzled look.

"You handle him like you're an old hand at that," Jenny said from the doorway.

Finnegan looked up. "No, but he and I have an agreement. I won't drop him and he won't leave any surprises on my uniform."

She took the baby from him. Finnegan turned his back, walked to the window, and put his hands on his hips as she opened her dress to allow the baby to nurse.

"Are you going to stay in Dawson City?"

"For the time being."

"And after that?"

"I don't know."

He stood profiled in the window, broad shoulders narrowing into slim hips. Hair, a little long, a little ragged, teased the collar of his white shirt.

She sensed he wanted another answer, yet was afraid to ask more of her. And she hesitated to ask more of him. Perhaps there was no more. She stood and put the baby to her shoulder.

"Mike, we have no one here, nothing to keep us. If I were to move away, maybe back to the United States, maybe to the east, no one would know what I was or what I'd done."

"You have me."

His words were soft, barely a whisper, so soft she wondered if she'd heard them at all.

He turned to face her. Jenny looked into his eyes. Did he mean those sudden words as she hoped he did? No. He looked as surprised as she to have found that he'd uttered them. Hope faded, replaced by disappointment.

"What do you mean, Mike?"

He swallowed. "I meant that I'm your friend. And Duncan and Sam. We'll be here to help you if you need it."

She wanted more from Mike Finnegan than friendship. Much more. But his intentions toward her were a mystery. She sensed an attraction, and yet he buried it beneath offerings of compassion. She was used to seeing the glimmer of lust in men's eyes, an element of attraction once they knew she was a forbidden commodity and sometimes, when he didn't know she was watching, she saw the same in Finnegan. But then there were times he looked at her in a way that made the tips of her toes tingle.

"Is that all you mean?" she pursued.

His eyes darkened and he took a step toward her. "No, I don't think so."

Her heart began a steady thud and the lower half of her body grew heavy as desire chased away common sense. His breath ruffled her hair. He leaned forward, over her, his arms at his sides, not touching her. She tipped her face back, her body straining with anticipation. Mere inches apart, he paused, his breath fanning over her cheeks.

She closed her eyes and waited, willing him to complete what he'd started, knowing she looked the fool. His mouth touched hers, warm and demanding. As he seduced her with uncommon practice, one arm slipped around her waist and urged her closer, the baby between them.

Somewhere around the edges of her passion, she heard a door open then close softly, but if Finnegan heard, he paid no mind.

The same hand that had urged her forward to press against him now smoothed up her back, depositing its warmth along the ridges of her spine, touching flesh yearning to be touched. He tangled his fingers in the hair at the base of her neck and moved her head to better accommodate his kiss, taking fuller access to her mouth. His tongue swept the inside, a tantalizing intimacy that sent quivers down her spine. She clamped a hand around his forearm, hard and sinewy beneath the soft fabric of his shirt.

Mike Finnegan was a man well-experienced at pleasuring a woman. Every part of her now knew this to be true. He was seducing her senseless without frantic clawing or heaving chests. There'd be no embarrassing fumbling in the dark, no half pleasures or disappointments with this man.

He drew away from her, pausing to bestow one last tiny peck on her lips. When she could think again, she opened her eyes to stare into his—cool and unrattled, as if the earth had not just moved.

"Are you all right?" he asked, his frown deepening as he studied her face, his brow furrowed in genuine concern.

"I'm fine," she countered, taking a step backwards before she couldn't. "I have to put the baby down."

She turned back to the makeshift bed and laid the baby in his drawer. All the while, she prayed her knees wouldn't buckle. Dear God, where had he learned to kiss like that?

Finnegan braced his hands on the frozen porch railing and looked up at the northern lights arching their ribbons of color across the night sky and eclipsing the beauty of the stars. He scooped a handful of snow and rubbed it across his face. A hard knot rode at the bottom of his stomach, ruining his appreciation for Sam's wonderful dinner.

Cold air threatened to freeze his damp skin. He dried his face with his shirtsleeve and tried again to bring to life the vague memory that had haunted him since he'd kissed Jenny. Like a wraith come to haunt him, the vision had appeared in his mind the moment his lips touched hers, intensified when his body tensed and hardened in response to her caress.

Huge green eyes, too large in a thin face. Thick chestnut hair tumbled around youthful shoulders propped against a lacy pillow case. The air thick with cigar smoke, casting a surreal feeling over the image. Somewhere in the background, a piano tune irritated its way into the memory.

He'd been drunk. Roaring, as a matter of fact. Rude and rutting, intent on his own pleasure, he'd paid her little attention except as a receptacle for his throbbing release.

Until afterwards.

THE HEALING

She'd lain there, her lips swollen, her cheeks reddened from the irritation of his three-day beard. Covers drawn up to her chin, she'd watched him with those bottomless green eyes, brimming with tears. Only then had he realized she was a child. Probably barely fifteen or sixteen. Not a virgin physically, but still, she'd had no idea how to pleasure a man except to lie beneath him and allow him free access to her body.

He'd treated her roughly, not cruelly, but with irritation that she'd done nothing to enhance his pleasure, used none of the skills other prostitutes had used to bring him to a shuddering and complete finality. Now, spent and more sober, he'd sat on the end of the bed and watched this fragile sprite watch him, her face lost in that cloud of hair, and wished he could simply disappear.

He turned away from the night sky, crossed his arms, and wondered what the chances were. . . .

No. He wouldn't even consider that possibility. It couldn't have been Jenny. Fate wouldn't be that cruel. Neither would God. Would he? He looked in the window to where Duncan had squeezed himself into the rocking chair and sat rocking his infant daughter. Would he ever deserve this? Would he ever know a peaceful day or night when memories and guilt from years of irresponsibility didn't wait for him to fall asleep so they could taunt and torture him like minions?

His thoughts returned to Jenny, how she'd looked up at him—the baby in her arms, her eyes large and green, her hair tumbled loose about her shoulders. . . .

The knot in the pit of his stomach tightened.

An insistent knocking woke Duncan from his peaceful sleep, Sam spooned against him in the curl of his body. He stared at the ceiling, wishing away the tendrils of sleep, hoping the banging was simply one of those remnants.

Bang. Bang. Bang.

He threw aside the covers, slipped on his pants, and eased down the stairs, hoping not to awaken the baby. He lit a lamp on a small table, threw loose the door bolt, and eased his revolver out of his holster hung on a peg on the wall. He opened the door. Tom, the errand boy from the Golden Nugget, stood on the porch, arms wrapped about his thin coat, stomping from foot to foot to keep warm.

"Mr. John says you gotta come right now and get Constable Finnegan afore Superintendent Steele gets wind of it."

"Wind of what?" Duncan peered into the dark behind young Tom and saw nothing.

"He's roaring drunk, Inspector." Tom leaned forward. "And he's in uniform."

"Dammit. I'll be right there. You want to come in and get warm?" Duncan stood to the side and held the door open wider.

"Nope, I gotta get back. Mr. John is there all by himself with the constable." Tom turned and

THE HEALING

trotted down the steps and back in the direction of town.

Duncan closed the door and set down the lamp, cursing under his breath.

"Duncan, what's wrong?" Sam asked from the first landing.

Duncan sat down in a chair and pulled on a boot. "Finnegan's in the Golden Nugget tying on a fine one."

"Finnegan's drunk? He never touches liquor."

"According to Tom, he's done more than touch it tonight."

"What would have set him off like that?" Sam asked, descending the steps.

Duncan shook his head, one boot dangling from his hand. "Only one thing'll make a man drink like that. And God help him if it's that."

The inside of the Golden Nugget was smoky and stale. At the end of the bar, John looked up from drying a glass and nodded at a pitiful figure hunched over the bar.

Duncan stepped to Finnegan's side and leaned one hip against the shiny brass railing. Finnegan stared into his empty glass, seemingly making an intense study of the bottom.

"You shouldn't drink alone, lad. Folks'll talk about you."

Finnegan raised bloodshot eyes and blinked several times to focus. "What?"

Duncan nodded at the glass. "How many of those have you had?"

Finnegan tipped the glass and looked inside again. "Too many, I know. Did John send for you?"

"Aye, he did."

Finnegan laughed a little too loudly. "I suppose that's the smart thing to do in his position. No barkeep worth his salt wants a drunk Mountie staggering around his bar."

"He's concerned for you. As am I. Want to tell me what brought this on?" Duncan leaned one elbow on the bar.

Finnegan glanced at John, wiping the other end of the counter and thankfully out of earshot, then back down at his glass. "I've slept with Jenny."

"Is that all this is about?" Duncan sighed deeply and quelled the imagined horrors spinning in his thoughts. "It's been obvious, lad, that you're in love with her. Does this happening surprise you?"

Finnegan twirled the glass, hesitating. "It didn't happen recently. It was years ago. When she was ... far too young to be thinking about such things, much less doing them with strangers."

Puzzled, Duncan frowned. "You knew her before she came to the Yukon?"

Finnegan snorted a laugh and shook his head. "Not knew, exactly. I was one of her customers," he said with a sneer. "I didn't realize it was Jenny until I kissed her. I still can't be sure, but ..."

Duncan pushed his hat back with one finger and wondered if he was talking to Mike Finnegan or a pint of John's finest. "I suppose that explains your

THE HEALING

thirst. Should I ask what brought on this realization?"

Finnegan shrugged and studied the wood grain of the bar. "I've had this feeling, ever since I saw her in Lucille's, that I'd known her from somewhere else. Then tonight, I looked in her eyes and knew it was the same girl."

"What are you going to do about it?"

Finnegan squinted up at Duncan. "Do about it? Well, I . . . don't know."

"Does she know?"

"No. And I don't want her to." His speech had begun to slur and his eyelids drooped.

Duncan took his arm. "Let's get you out of here before you make a fool of yourself—and me."

As discreetly as possible, Duncan lead Finnegan out of the saloon and down the deserted street toward Fort Herchner. To the Irishman's credit, he did a fine job of holding his liquor and staying on his feet. When they passed through the gates of the fort, Finnegan roused himself and walked on his own, nodding to the guard as they passed. Only a slight sway to his gait revealed that he'd consumed too much.

On the porch of the enlisted men's barracks Finnegan grabbed a porch post and hauled himself up the steps without aid.

"I can make it from here on me own," he stated, his brogue thick and slurring.

"You'll not remember a word I say, I know, but she'll hold nothing against you, I'd bet, lad," Duncan said as Finnegan stumbled toward the door.

He stopped, staring at the rough wood inches from his nose. "It won't matter. I'll know and I'll remember what a bastard I once was."

Without further comment, he opened the door and staggered forward, as consumed by his own guilt as he was by the darkness that eventually swallowed him.

Chapter Thirteen

"Constable, please. I do have other customers." Marge Grady stood with hands braced on her counter and glared at him over gold, wire-framed glasses.

Finnegan stared down at the three tiny dresses spread out on the scarred wooden countertop. A decision was impossible. "Tell me again what's different about them."

A collective groan went up behind him as waiting customers grumbled. He glanced over his shoulder at a pretty young woman with a baby in her arms. She smiled shyly at him. "Which would you choose?" he asked her.

"Well, how old is your baby, Constable?"

He could almost feel the group lean closer to hear his answer. "He's not mine, but he's about two weeks old."

Marge Grady pinned him with a gray-browed stare. "Is this for the McLeod baby?"

"Yes," he lied, shamelessly diving through the opening offered.

Marge turned, barely able to maneuver her wide hips behind the counter, and pulled down a stack of tiny garments. "Babies don't need fluff and nonsense at this age. All they need is something to keep them warm." She flopped a stack of tiny shirts on the counter.

Finnegan raised his eyes to hers. "I wanted this to be something special."

"That McLeod baby's got enough clothes for two." Marge leaned closer. "And didn't I sell you something back in November? A baby's layette and a woman's pink dress?"

Just who was the trained interrogator here? Finnegan wondered, resisting the urge to squirm under scrutiny. "Yes, Mrs. Grady, you did."

She watched him a moment longer—hoping for a confession, he supposed. "Let me know when you've made up your mind, Constable." She waddled off to wait on another customer, abandoning the inquisition.

Finnegan picked up one of the garments and poked his finger inside a tiny sleeve, marveling at the miracle that a baby was. He threw a glance toward Mrs. Grady and found her glaring at him over her glasses. Two other women stared as well, sweet smiles of understanding on their faces. Finnegan quickly dropped the garment and turned his attention back to making a decision.

THE HEALING

A tiny bell over the door at the far end of the store tinkled and the door closed with a click.

"May I help you?" Mrs. Grady called, the door hidden from view by aisles of merchandise.

"Yes, I'd like to see some clothes for a baby," came a familiar voice.

Dear God, it was Jenny. Finnegan stepped back from the counter, pivoted and sauntered down an aisle stacked tall with boxes and merchandise. He feigned an interest in boots and rounded the end of the aisle to position himself where he could see her and remain hidden.

"I'll be right with you, dear." Mrs. Grady's scissors snipped through a length of fabric which she folded and handed to one of the two women.

The woman placed two coins in Mrs. Grady's hand and the pair turned to leave, throwing Finnegan a curious glance and a smile as they did. He supposed he did look ridiculous perusing a display of patented medicines and peeping around a corner, all while in his uniform.

"Oh. These are exactly what I was looking for," Jenny said from behind the aisle. "Is someone else purchasing these?"

"There was a gentleman in here earlier, but I believe he left." The sarcasm in Mrs. Grady's voice would escape Jenny, but he knew the old gossip wouldn't fail to scent the trail of this tidbit, not with her fine nose for gossip.

"I'll take these and some of these. You can weigh gold dust, can't you?"

Finnegan's heart plunged and vague suspicions

grew into real doubts. She could have gotten gold dust anywhere, he told himself, maybe saved from her days in Lucille's. His stomach did an odd flip-flop at the thought and he quickly pushed away that line of thinking.

Scales clinked metallically as Mrs. Grady dragged them out from under the counter.

"Oh my, you have quite a bit there."

"We have a claim up near Eldorado. My husband was on the way to sell this, but I told him I had some shopping to do."

She'd lied so smoothly to the gray-haired shopkeeper that he wondered if she could have deceived him just as easily.

"I certainly wouldn't walk around with all that on me. Isn't safe in a place like Dawson City. That'll be ten dollars, dear."

The scales rattled softly. "Could I wrap that for you?"

Finnegan peeped an eye around the corner in time to see Jenny stuff the leather bag into the bodice of her dress. She cast a furtive glance over her shoulder and shifted little Michael to her other arm. Paper rustled.

"Thank you. I'm sorry, I didn't catch your name?" said Mrs. Grady.

"Thank you," Jenny replied and walked to the front of the store. Finnegan stayed hidden until the bell above the door announced her departure.

"You can come out now, Constable."

THE HEALING

Chagrined, Finnegan stepped around the end of the display.

"And I suppose you're going to tell me that this is all part of your job?" Mrs. Grady asked, watching his reaction over the rim of her glasses.

"That I am," he answered, a dozen explanations spinning around inside his head.

"Humph," she replied as she replaced the scale. "Do you want these?" She held out the remaining baby clothes.

"No, Mrs. Grady. I want you to make up a layette for me, all the things a baby might need. I'll be by later to pay for it."

She braced her beefy hands on the counter and leaned forward. "My husband and I came to Dawson City two years ago when there was nothing but miners and mud. Now we have a real town here and I don't want to see it sink back into the puddle of iniquity I found it in. I intend to see that morals are enforced here, Constable, and I would hate to think that one of the Mounted Police is engaged in something . . . shady."

"There's nothing shady going on here, Mrs. Grady. The clothes are for my brother's wife in Edmonton. Their baby's about the same age as the McLeod baby. I intend to send them out with the next mail run. As for the lady just in here, I'm suspicious of anyone carrying a large quantity of gold dust."

She eyed him warily. "I'll have your package ready tomorrow, Constable Finnegan."

* * *

"Jenny, please don't go. There's plenty of room here."

Jenny glanced down at the satchel at her feet, anything to keep from looking at Sam's stricken face. "This is *your* home, Sam. Not mine. It's time Michael and I found our own place."

"You don't want to raise a baby in a hotel. If you stay here, we can help each other."

Jenny smiled and put her arms around Sam. "I know your offer's sincere, but I need to find my own place, start over. Can you understand that?"

Sam pulled back. "Yes, I can. But I'll worry about you and little Michael in that dingy place. What businessman with half a brain would name their establishment the End of the Road Hotel. Sounds more like a funeral parlor."

Jenny laughed. "Aside from the name, it's decently clean and affordable. When I can, I'll move to something better or maybe rebuild my cabin when summer comes. It'll do until then."

The two women stepped apart, tears flowing down their cheeks. Duncan glanced at Finnegan, who shrugged his shoulders and picked up Jenny's satchel.

"You'll come for Sundays." Sam trailed behind them to the door. "Promise?"

"I promise." Jenny paused for a moment, then closed the door on Sam's tearful face. Her own pasted-on smile quickly faded.

THE HEALING

"Are you sure this is what you want to do?" Finnegan asked as he helped her down the steps and across the icy walkway. Clutching the baby, she stepped over dirty snowdrifts until they reached the long, plank sidewalk of Main Street.

"A rooming house would have been cheaper," he offered as they reached the dilapidated front of the End of the Road.

"There are no rooms available anywhere in Dawson City. Apparently, everyone else had the same idea." She grasped the brass door handle. "We'll be all right here. It's dry and warm and I've already made arrangements to work in the kitchen for part of my board."

"What about the baby while you're working?"

She shrugged. "He can go with me."

They entered the musty lobby, scented with old tobacco and wood smoke. The clerk looked up over tiny, gold-rimmed glasses, his face long and slim and disapproving "Mrs. Hanson. We were beginning to wonder if you were going to make the dinner hour tonight."

He slid a narrow key across the counter and Jenny picked it up.

Something in his voice rankled Finnegan, even though the words were benign enough. She must have led him to believe she was a widow. A smart ploy in a place like this.

"Yes, Mr. Clark. I'll be right down as soon as dinner is finished."

"May I help you, Constable?"

"I'm going to take Mrs. Hanson's bags upstairs."

The clerk hesitated as if considering stopping him.

"I trust there's no problem with that?" Finnegan asked, unreasonably irritated at the man behind the counter.

"No, Constable. None indeed."

They climbed the stairs, the threadbare carpet beneath their feet long since faded to oblivion from a red-and-gold pattern.

"I know it's not the best place in town, but the price was right," she said, as if to reassure herself rather than him. She unlocked the door and cold air swept out. The hearth was dark, ashes strewn across the stones. The bed was shoved against a wall, a faded, dingy bedspread covering it. In some ways, it was worse than her cabin.

"It'll do fine, Mike," she said, answering his unasked question, her back to him as she stacked wood on the hearth.

"I didn't say anything."

"No, but you were thinking it." She straightened and turned to face him. "I've been in worse places than this. Compared to some, this would seem like a palace."

He stepped forward and her expression grew wary. "Why do you settle for less than you should have, Jenny?"

She studied his face for a moment, her expression soft and open. "Because I learned early that the smart mouse is better off than the bold rat."

THE HEALING

"You're not a mouse. You're a smart, beautiful woman who could have all the world if she wanted it."

"And how would I go about getting those things? Marry money? Sell myself again to the highest bidder? Rob a bank? Strike gold?"

He didn't have an answer, at least not one he could voice.

She stepped toward him. "You owe me nothing, Mike. You've been a good friend and a gentleman. Your conscience, where I'm concerned, should be clear." She pushed a stray lock of hair off his forehead, just for the excuse to touch him. "I've never borne any false ideas about what I've done or what I am. And I know that the road to change will be hard and long. But this is the choice I've made, just as I made the choice to leave home all those years ago. No one forced me to go—I went willingly."

He caught her hand and pressed the tips of her fingers to his lips. "I don't want to be a gentleman with you, Jenny."

She looked up at him. "But you are."

"Not out of respect, although God knows I wish it was."

"Don't say any more."

"I've done terrible things in my life."

"So have I."

He stepped closer. "I've wanted you in ways . . . I'm no different from any other man who's ever looked at you."

Her heart pounding, Jenny struggled to keep control of the conversation as it careened toward disaster. "Did you expect to be?"

"I expected better of myself, yes."

Jenny laughed. "Dear, sweet Finnegan." She caressed his brow and he took off the broad Stetson.

"I'm neither dear nor sweet tonight, Jenny." He lowered his face toward hers.

She should back away, she knew, stop this before they both regretted the next few minutes. But his eyes riveted her where she stood. Deep blue in intensity, bright with desire, his eyes said things he could not. And yet she sensed something deeper, something she dared not even dream he felt.

Tossing his hat on the bed, he hooked an arm around her waist and pulled her against him. Casting aside any claims of gentlemanly behavior, he slipped his hand lower and snugged her hips against his, reassuring her that all he'd just said was absolutely true. His mouth closed over hers, pretending no semblance of decency.

One hand tangled in her hair sent hairpins flying to the far corners of the room. Her hair tumbled loose, the strands catching and remaining on the stubble of his beard.

So this was intimacy, she realized with a jolt. The planes of his body fit perfectly against hers. The faint scent and taste of the coffee he'd had at Duncan's house. The slight trembling of his hands as he held her, evidence of the intensity of his desire.

The scrape of his beard against her skin. The roughness of his lips, chapped from winter's wind. All the tiny, defining things he had shared with her alone.

Terrified, she sprang away from him just as an insistent hammering came at her door.

"Mrs. Hanson, I must insist that you attend to your duties in the kitchen. That was our arrangement. Am I correct?"

"Yes, Mr. Clark, it was and I'll come right down."

"See that you do."

Twisting her hair up on her head and hunting down her errant hairpins, Jenny finally straightened and raised her eyes to Finnegan's.

"I wanted to make love to you."

The honesty in his voice and on his face sent shivers up her spine.

"And I would have except that the baby's only..." He let the words drift off and blinked, apparently having only just realized the fact of her physical state. "Jesus," he breathed.

"It's all right, Mike." She slid in the last pin and stepped toward him.

He leaned over and retrieved his hat from the bed. "I guess that settles the issue of whether or not I've behaved like a gentleman."

"Mike—"

"God help women if we gentlemen treat them all this way." He seated the Stetson on his head and paused at the door. "I'll see you Sunday at Duncan's. Right?"

"I did promise."

He opened the door, stepped through, and shut it behind him. Jenny stared at the chipped wooden panels for several seconds, still tasting him on her lips. "I never said I wanted a gentleman."

Potted palms seemed oddly out of place in the glistening lobby of the Merrimack Hotel. Gleaming marble floors welcomed the well-to-do and polished brass rails edged the clerk's counter. Finnegan stepped up to the registration desk and stared at his reflection in the wide mirror behind.

"May I help you, sir?" the desk clerk asked, looking as if he'd choke in his stiff, white collar and sleeve garters.

"Mrs. Harriet Bentz's room number, please."

The clerk glared at him a moment before turning around to the assortment of pigeonholes stacked one atop the other. "Mrs. Bentz is in room 204, Constable."

"Thank you," Finnegan replied and mounted the steps.

How different from the hovel Jenny was in, he thought as he strode soundlessly down the carpeted hallway. Stopping in front of room 204, he rapped sharply on the polished door.

"Come in," a feminine voice sang.

Finnegan twisted the glass doorknob and the heavy door swung open. He swept off his Stetson and stepped inside.

THE HEALING

"Constable Finnegan. You received my note."

"Yes, ma'am. It was delivered this morning."

She uncurled herself from a round-back upholstered chair, making full use of an exposed ankle while delicately slipping her feet into her abandoned shoes. She stood, brushed down the wrinkles in her dress, and glided toward him, oozing seduction.

"I thought we might have a little chat," she said, stopping much too close. "And a little dinner, perhaps." She moved to the bellpull in the corner and gave it a yank. "I found life in my cabin, while refreshing, soon became boring."

"I can't stay for long," Finnegan said as she glided back toward him. "I have sentry duty tonight."

"Ah, what a pity. What I have to tell you might have taken all night long," she cooed, her meaning clear.

"Why don't you tell me what you called me here for." Finnegan sat down in one of the fireplace chairs, placing his hat on his knee.

"I have reason to believe that a whore of your acquaintance, Jenny Hanson, is the trollop who was living with my husband."

The implication in her words rankled, but he let the anger slide off him. "How did you come by this information?"

Harriet skimmed to the dresser and lifted a gold locket from the small china plate there. She walked across the room and held it out to Finnegan.

My dearest Jenny. Frank, the back read.

Heart hammering, Finnegan swallowed and struggled to keep his voice even. "Where did you find this?"

"Underneath a loose rock in the hearth. And . . . it was covered with gold dust."

He thought of Jenny, paying for the baby's clothes with gold dust, of her tale to Mrs. Grady that she and her husband had mined it. Cold, unavoidable truth crawled through him.

"Is this all you found?"

"All? What more proof do you want, Constable?" She sashayed around in front of him. "I have heard you've been seen in her company. Perhaps I should take this information to Superintendent Steele himself."

Finnegan looked up into her leering face. "Miss Hanson is a casual acquaintance of mine and I know how to do my job."

"I'll bet that's not all you know how to do."

Before he could protest, she perched on his lap, crushing his Stetson, and ran a finger underneath his chin. She looped an arm around his neck and nuzzled his ear. "A gentleman like yourself would never be seen in a house of ill repute, Constable, but surely you have appetites that need satisfaction. Perhaps we could work out a discreet arrangement? Once here in my room. Another time in a room of your choice. I assure you, I'm quite skilled in the arts of love." That said, she reached down and cupped him through his uniform pants.

THE HEALING 227

Finnegan stood, dumping her unceremoniously to the floor. "I'll see that Superintendent Steele is made aware of your concerns, Mrs. Bentz."

Harriet scrambled up from the floor. He expected her to come up swinging. Instead, she adjusted her dress, smoothed her hair, and stepped in his direction as if that sort of rejection was an everyday thing.

"You're a smart man, Constable, and in need of a woman. A man's words might say one thing, but his body says another."

Finnegan bent to sweep his crushed hat up off the floor. She flung her arms around his neck and kissed him, deeply and open-mouthed, thrusting and tangling her tongue with his. He set her away, ashamed that his breaths came quicker.

She smiled slyly. "Women have the advantage over men. They can keep their passions to themselves. Everyone can read a poor man's most private intentions."

"I'll keep you informed," he said, slipping the locket into his pocket and heading for the door. She followed him. Lightning quick, her hand shot out and snatched the locket from his coat. "Now I can't let you go off with my evidence, Constable."

A knock came at the door and Finnegan gratefully swung it open.

"You rang, ma'am?" a young man asked, attired in a faultless black suit and white shirt.

"I'd like to order supper," she said.

"For how many?" he asked, looking between the two of them.

"Only one," Finnegan answered and stepped out the door.

She slammed the door behind him and the young waiter jumped backwards to avoid being smashed in the nose. Her peals of laughter echoed down the hall. The waiter shrugged and headed back toward the kitchen.

A couple strolled down the broad hall, arm in arm. Finnegan quickly turned his back and pretended to straighten his hat, suddenly embarrassed to be caught in the company of Harriet Bentz, the irony of the situation not lost on him. The woman threw him a curious glance and whispered something to her companion. They continued on their way and disappeared down the steps before Finnegan followed.

Finnegan stepped out into the cold night air, grateful for the chill that ran through him. He headed for Fort Herchmer, disturbed still that Harriet Bentz's madness had appealed to a part of him over which he had little control. As he walked, he pushed aside the embarrassing exchange and tried to concentrate on what she'd said.

The locket could be a ruse, something to put him onto Jenny's trail, to raise his suspicions about her involvement in Frank's disappearance. Or, it could be true. But if the locket was indeed found along with evidence of gold dust, what did that

THE HEALING

prove? That she'd once lived with the man? Certainly not that she'd killed him. According to the mounting evidence, scores of people wanted Frank Bentz dead. Jenny would be only one of many.

Finnegan kicked at a lump of snow and watched it careen into the recently scraped street, then scatter. The thought of any other man touching Jenny raised his temper, despite lectures to himself that past was past and he had as many sins as she. And yet, the anger remained. She was his, the devil on his shoulder whispered, as surely as if he'd taken her to wife with vows and flowers. And yet he hadn't. Nor had he declared his love to Jenny.

He shoved his hands into his pockets and stopped at the sentry station just inside the gates of the fort.

"Things quiet?" he asked young Constable Harper.

Bleary-eyed from lack of sleep, the man nodded. "Nothing but snow and an occasional wandering dog. Are you on at midnight?"

Finnegan nodded. "I'll go and get my heavy clothes and be right back."

Leaving Harper, he trudged across the muddy, churned interior of the fort and eased into the sleeping barracks. Rows of bunks lined both walls and soft snores disturbed the quiet. Finnegan sat down on his lower bunk, cringing as the bed protested beneath his weight. He pulled off his boots and added a layer of socks. Then, with one boot in his hand, he paused.

He'd lived this way for better than ten years. Everything he owned could be picked up and loaded onto the back of a horse in minutes. His home was wherever Ottawa sent him. Before now, simplicity had been a welcome respite and responsibility didn't extend beyond tomorrow's orders. But now he wanted more.

He laced up his boots and hauled his heavy fur coat out of the foot locker at the end of his bunk. Then, picking up his rifle, he headed back across the parade ground to the tiny shack at the entrance of the fort.

"I'll be glad for a warm fire," Harper said as Finnegan checked the cylinder of his revolver. "How long have you been in the Force, Constable?"

"Ten years and some," Finnegan answered, locking the cylinder in place.

"Don't you get tired of sentry duty?"

Finnegan knew the real question on young Harper's mind was why he was still a constable after all these years. "Especially in the winter," Finnegan replied.

"Well, I'll see you at breakfast, then."

Finnegan nodded and the young man hurried away, eager for his bed and a fire. Pulling on beaverskin gloves, the thick pelt soft against his skin, Finnegan picked up his rifle and began a slow stroll around the circumference of the fort.

"Ben," he said with a nod to Constable Ben Matthews, standing a lonely, cold vigilance over

THE HEALING

thousands of dollars in gold stored in one small room awaiting shipment out of the Yukon.

"Finnegan," he replied, blowing hot air on his cold hands.

"Have you been here long?"

Ben grinned. "Relief's coming any time now. I got a pillow and a warm blanket waiting for me."

"Sleep well, then."

Finnegan moved to the back of the command buildings, checking with a glance the windows of Steele's quarters where the Superintendent of the Yukon slept peacefully. His boots crunching in the snow, Finnegan completed his round and emerged from behind the cluster of buildings back onto the wide parade ground.

Standing guard was almost a ceremonial responsibility now at Fort Herchner, except for watching the gold storehouse. In the early years of Fort McLeod and Fort Walsh, vigilance was a necessity as the Mounted Police fought off whiskey traders in the Cypress Hills and on the wide, high prairies. Then, a man's mind was occupied with staying alive and determining what waited beyond the next coulee, leaving little time to mull over one's shortcomings.

Somewhere along the trail to the Yukon, that had changed. In the early days, men of the Force were forbidden to marry, although as soon as that rule was set in ink, several men challenged it and won. Still, Ottawa frowned on its men taking on the responsibility of wife and family and taming western Canada, yet several had done so and done so successfully without impeding either their careers or the structure of the Force. Duncan was a perfect example, happily wed and commanding his own detachment.

Finnegan eased his tired body into a chair inside the guardhouse and tipped it back on two legs. Placing his rifle across his knees, he crossed his arms and set his mind to wait out the night. But peaceful preoccupation didn't last long. Thoughts of Jenny came calling, stirring up self-doubts and banked dissatisfaction.

Who was he to administer justice or offer himself as a husband and father? He'd left behind a string of mistakes and even now, struggled to keep his beasts in control. Every day required concentrated effort to stay on the straight path, even though the task had grown easier as years passed. Still, the temptation to drown his sorrows lurked in the shadows, waiting to spring.

The fire had nearly gone out in the small woodstove in the corner. Finnegan propped his rifle against the wall and opened the door with a squeak. He tossed in a stick or two and shut the door. Shadows danced against the wall and the metal firebox groaned and ticked.

Hands shoved into his pockets, he moved to the window that looked across open ground just beyond the fort gates. Most of the men who'd enlisted with him were either out of the Force or else promoted to inspector. Advancement had never held the charm for him it did for some. An

THE HEALING

increase in rank meant an increase in responsibility and his life was fine the way it was. Until now.

A gnawing discontent crawled through him, routing out his well-established safeguards and upsetting the perfect balance he'd worked so hard to get and keep. He did his job and did it well. All his waking hours were devoted to just that. There was no time for anything else, no time for reflection or regret. To pause and study one's shortcomings, or lack of them, meant taking out and examining the very things that made one a man. And sometimes those things did not bear close examination.

Jenny made him want to examine what had shaped him into the man he was. She made him want the answer he'd never sought for his wasted years and his appetite for alcohol and self-destruction. Again, the green-eyed innocent returned to haunt him—the frightened face of the too-young woman peeping at him over tumbled bedclothes.

He hunched his shoulders to ease a nagging ache and wished for morning and his bed. Too many ghosts floated loose in his consciousness with only himself for company. Too many half-remembered embarrassments and bitter regrets came back, asking to be taken out and reexamined and explained.

Regrettably, his thoughts returned to Jenny and he knew at that moment that she had forever changed him. From now on, she would be his constant companion, whether he chose that union or not. Was this how Duncan had felt about Sam on those nights he'd paced through the barracks, a silent, barefooted ghost wreathed in pipe smoke?

Had she haunted his every thought as Jenny now haunted his? Duncan's only salvation had been to marry his tormentor. Was he doomed to the same fate?

Chapter Fourteen

The banks of the Yukon's wandering, gold-rich streams were deserted, frozen in winter's grasp. Here and there, smoke rose from a cabin chimney where a sourdough guarded his claim through the long, lonely winter. Finnegan included visits to these isolated souls in his patrols when he could, making sure they had food and that the dark days and the solitude hadn't stolen their sanity.

Elbert Hawkins's cabin sat at the head of a ravine, shielded from the wind and obscured from sight. Only the telltale curl of gray gave away the cozy cabin's location as Finnegan swung his dog team onto the well-worn path that paralleled the stream blown clear of snow by two days of howling wind.

An oddity among the community of constantly shifting faces, Hawkins seemed to enjoy his solitary lifestyle—relish it, in fact. In the summer he worked his claim to modest results and in the winter he holed up in his cabin, surrounded by creature comforts more typical of a fine English cottage than a miner's shack. Woolen blankets woven in tartan patterns covered crude, handmade furniture. A leather-covered ottoman with elephant's feet for legs crouched beside a chair made of cut-and-bent willow reeds. Rich, colorful rugs lay across a floor of rough, uneven boards. Mr. Hawkins, it seemed, was a well-traveled gentleman, a man whose word could be relied upon. And yet, despite his hermit-like existence, he seemed to keep a close eye on the comings and goings among the gold fields.

Finnegan brought the team to a stop, stepped off the runners, and pulled off his gloves. He climbed the steps up to the porch and rapped on the door. A stirring came from inside before the door opened and Elbert Hawkins, his pipe firmly clenched in his teeth, filled the doorway.

"Constable Finnegan. Come inside." He seemed unremarkably surprised despite the fact that more than likely he hadn't seen another human for months. He moved out of the way and Finnegan stepped into the warm room. An odd aroma swirled up to meet him, a comforting mixture of leather, old books, and wood smoke. Bookshelves filled with leather-bound volumes arranged according to size and color filled one wall and the other three were covered with elegantly framed pictures and souvenirs from faraway and mysterious places.

"Routine patrol, Constable, or has some trouble brought you to my door?" Elbert smiled, squinting dark eyes lost in bushy brows. He wore a faded but once elegant smoking jacket over worn buckskin pants, an odd but somehow fitting combination.

"Routine." Finnegan strode to the fireplace and chafed his hands together over the flames.

"Ah, and how goes business with the Mounted Police?" Elbert asked as he closed the door.

"Things are quiet. Winter, you know." Finnegan turned around, reveling in the warmth that spread across his back.

Elbert sat down in a chair and picked up and closed the book he'd obviously been reading.

"How long have you been here, Hawkins?"

"Three years, give or take a few months."

"Ever hear of a fellow named Frank Bentz?"

Hawkins smiled and laid his pipe in a handy bowl. "The nefarious Mr. Bentz. Mr. Bentz and I have talked on occasion. Most recently when I forced him off my property at the end of that Kentucky long rifle hanging there above the fireplace."

Finnegan glanced up at the ancient but well-kept weapon, its oiled stock gleaming in the firelight.

"I heard someone finally dispatched Mr. Bentz to the reward he's so richly earned."

"Supposedly so, but Old Frank didn't see fit to leave behind his body," Finnegan said.

Hawkins leaned back in his upholstered chair. "A swindler to the end, eh Constable?"

"Looks like. What did you know about him?"

Hawkins steepled his fingers and smiled. "Frank Bentz made a living preying on others. He never did a day's work in his life, as best I could tell, except for wading through streams to get to sluice boxes."

"Is that where he got his gold? From sluice boxes?"

"Filched it right out from underneath the owners' noses, most of the time. He was slick, that one, and hard to catch in the act. I was the only one that ever caught him red-handed."

"Why didn't you kill him?"

Hawkins looked astonished. "Kill him? And miss the pleasure of looking down the barrel of my rifle as he ran down the ravine, his finely tailored coattails flapping behind him? Come now, Constable, there are some things more precious than gold."

"Was he mixed up in anything else? Something more serious than stealing gold dust?"

Hawkins rose, went into his kitchen, and rustled around in the cabinets until he found a tin of tea and set it on the small, cloth-covered table. "You'll stay for a cup, of course?"

Finnegan nodded.

"I always thought Frank Bentz capable of more evil than he demonstrated. We crossed paths a time or two in more gentlemanly pursuits—before I threatened to shoot him, of course. We were competitors once in an all-night card game at the Golden Nugget. He was quite an accomplished gamester, very smooth in his deceit. A less practiced eye than mine would never have known he was dealing from the bottom of the deck that night."

"What did you do about it?"

Hawkins placed a kettle on his cookstove and shoved another piece of wood into the firebox. "I outcheated him, of course, and no one was the wiser. Except him and me." Hawkins turned, leaned against the table, and crossed his arms over his chest. "I've dealt with many a gaming man, some gentlemen, some not. Most are basically petty thieves, clever and shallow. Mr. Bentz has a black soul. Or rather had, if he is indeed dead. A black soul and a deep, eating anger at some bad hand life has dealt him. A dangerous combination."

"What about women?"

The kettle jangled for attention. Hawkins lifted it clear of the stove and poured water into two cups. "He likes to knock the whores around. Makes an issue of announcing he's going to do it, too."

"Did he ever do serious damage?"

Hawkins stirred the delicate china cups with a gleaming spoon. "By serious, I take it you mean lasting damage? Rumor was he killed a girl once, a prostitute in a house in Seattle. Nothing was ever proven, though. The body disappeared—as well as Bentz." He lifted a cup, took a sip, and announced it ready with a wink.

Finnegan took the cup Hawkins offered and stared into the swirling bits of leaves, empathy for the fear Jenny must have known at Bentz's hands creeping through him. How many times had she felt blood-chilling fear for her life and that of her baby?

"Are you investigating his murder? Or is it a disappearance?" Hawkins asked, sipping his tea.

Finnegan shook his head. "Not sure. He's disappeared is all we know." Finnegan glanced at Hawkins. "Do you know anything about the last woman he was keeping company with?"

Hawkins nodded and set down his cup. "She was a looker. I met her once. Seemed too smart for the likes of Bentz. But she stayed with him, is the way I heard it. Over there, across Chandler's Ridge. Are you thinking she's the one that did away with Frank?"

Finnegan paused, wondering how much he should divulge. "I can't say. I've been to the cabin. There's bloodstains on the floor and an empty grave in the yard."

"You sure it was Frank's place?"

"His wife says so. She's moved in and moved everything else out."

"Frank had a wife?" Hawkins threw his head back and laughed. "Now that's fitting punishment if I ever heard it. Did she come up to catch him in the act?"

"No, she came up to find him—or so she says. At first she seemed convinced he was still alive. Since then, she's changed her story and now insists he must be dead."

"And what do you suppose changed Widow Bentz's mind?"

"I think Frank has experienced a resurrection the likes of which we haven't seen in nineteen hundred years."

Hawkins looked shocked. "You think Bentz is still alive?"

THE HEALING

"I've seen things to make me think that."

"So why would he stage his own death?"

"I don't think he set out to. I think the shot went awry and he saw an opportunity."

"Gives new meaning to the words *operating behind the scenes,* doesn't it?"

"I suspect he'll return to his old ways, as soon as there's gold dust to steal. But until the thaw, I'd bet he'll resort to robbery, breaking into cabins and claims looking for hidden gold dust. Keep your eyes and ears open, will you?"

Hawkins took another sip of his tea. "Sure."

"I'll be back this way now and again. Thought I'd stop at some of the claims along the way and ask the same question."

"Do you have a particular interest in the woman who killed, or tried to kill, Frank?"

"What makes you ask?" Finnegan frowned, wondering what rumors had preceded Jenny's arrival.

Hawkins shrugged. "Just heard some things is all."

"What sort of things?"

Hawkins took another sip of his tea, savoring both the flavor and his answer. "Rumor is she killed him for his gold, and a considerable amount of it, too."

The steam-filled air reeked of sour food and unwashed dishes. Jenny plunged her chapped hands into the pan of dishwater and wrinkled her nose when the smell worsened. She swiped a cloth around a dirty dish and squished her toes in her soaked shoes.

Placing the dish in a rack to dry, she cast a glance at the long preparation table where Michael peacefully slept in his dresser-drawer bed. Bless him, he'd been little trouble during her nights of kitchen duty, almost as if he knew this was something they had to do together.

"Here's another load." Dishes splashed into the pan, sending a slosh of water over the edge and onto Jenny's already soaked feet.

"Dammit, Isabelle. You should have warned me." Jenny picked up a towel and dabbed at the now-drenched front of her dress.

"You're the dishwasher, ain't you? You're supposed to be looking out for more dishes. It ain't far from closing and when that clock says eight o'clock, I'm going home."

Buxom and obnoxious, Isabelle took delight in tormenting and bullying the entire kitchen staff, placing her station as waitress above those who cleaned up the messes.

"You seeing anybody tonight?" Isabelle grinned at her, a gold front tooth shining. "Maybe that Mountie man that hangs around here?"

Jenny looked up from her suds. "What Mountie?"

"I seen him nearly every night, waiting out there in back. He ain't looking for no robbers, I'll bet. Bound to be you he's a-waiting for. Sure ain't me or Ralph."

THE HEALING

The cook glanced up from the smoking pan on the stovetop and mouthed what passed as a smile around a tortured cigar butt.

"I don't know what you're talking about." Jenny kept her attention on the soapy water, but her thoughts raced. Had Finnegan been lurking around the hotel keeping an eye on her? And if so, did she like it or did she want to box his ears?

"He's mighty fine, too. Redheaded. I like redheaded men." The gold tooth flashed again.

"Your order's ready," Ralph growled from one corner of his mouth.

Isabelle loaded her hefty right arm with plates and sashayed away through the swinging doors.

Jenny placed the last dish in the rack and dried her hands on a towel just as the baby began to stir and fuss. She spread the towel to dry, picked up the drawer, and climbed the back stairs to her room. Footsteps behind her made her blood surge. She whirled around. Finnegan stood just behind her, his hat in his hands.

"What are you doing here? And so late?" Isabelle's observation rang in her memory.

"Could I speak with you a moment?"

Jenny frowned as she unlocked her room door. There was something odd in his behavior, something different.

The room was cold, the fire long dead when she swung the door open. Jenny put Michael's drawer on the bed and hurried to the hearth. Now in full squall, Michael wailed at the top of his lungs, demanding to be fed.

"I'll get him," Finnegan said as he placed his hat on the bed and picked up the baby.

"What's the matter, little one? Dinner isn't coming fast enough?"

Jenny glanced over her shoulder. Finnegan held Michael up, hands under his armpits. One fist lodged in his mouth, Michael studied the face before him with comic seriousness, his hunger temporarily forgotten.

As she turned back to the fledgling fire, she heard Finnegan chuckle softly and mumble some nonsense in a thick Irish brogue.

"You should get married and have children," she said over her shoulder. "You'd be a good father."

"You think so, do you?"

When she turned, he watched her pointedly. "Yes, I do," she replied, meeting his gaze.

Michael, having lost his fascination with Finnegan's face, began to squirm in his grasp.

Jenny took the baby. Finnegan sauntered to the window, his back turned, while she sat down, opened her dress front, and spread a blanket across her shoulder. "What did you want to talk to me about?"

He walked back and sat on the bed opposite her. "Did you know Frank Bentz?"

So, her secret was finally found out. She should have known Finnegan would ferret out the facts, given enough time. Inwardly, she heaved a cleansing breath of relief. Outwardly, she prepared to defend herself. "Yes."

Finnegan's expression didn't change, although she thought she saw him flinch.

"Do you know where he is?"

She took a deep breath, part of her grateful that the lying was about to be over. "He's buried in a shallow grave in the yard of a cabin behind Chandler's Ridge."

"Did you kill him?"

"Yes."

Finnegan rose and returned to the window to gaze out into the darkness. "Why?"

She looked down at Michael, asleep at her breast, a smear of milk on his cheek. If she hadn't killed Frank, what would her alternate fate have been? Would baby Michael be here now? Would Frank have used his fists and caused her to miscarry? Or would he have taken the newborn and disappeared, abandoning her to frantic desperation?

She rose, buttoned her dress, and placed the sleeping baby in his makeshift bed, tucking the blanket in securely around him, noting each action, wondering if it would be the last time and if she's spend the rest of her life in jail. She moved the drawer to its place nearer the fire, then straightened and turned to face her future. Finnegan waited, watching her with a veiled expression that gave no hint to his internal thoughts.

"When I first met Frank, he was a two-bit gambler in whorehouses and saloons," she began, her fingers threaded together in front of her to quell their trembling. "There was a kindness in him then, someplace, buried beneath the greed. When we came here, following the gold, gambling wasn't enough. He started disappearing at night and coming back before daylight. And he always had gold dust, lots of it. I found out eventually he was stealing the gold from sluice boxes. The local miners suspected him but couldn't catch him in the act." She unclasped her hands. "When I found out I was pregnant, I wanted out."

"Frank's Michael's father?"

"Yes."

Finnegan leaned back against the wall and crossed his arms and ankles. "That's not much of a reason to kill a man."

This was Finnegan the interrogator, not Finnegan her friend. The shift was frightening.

"I killed Frank because he would have eventually killed me or the baby or both. I'd do the same again under identical circumstances."

"Did you love him?" Finnegan looked up, drilling her with his icy gaze.

She met his gaze, knowing she owed him honesty. "Once, a long time ago."

He looked down at the toes of his boots. "Tell me what happened in the end."

She related the events of that terrible night. Of the threats and her fear. The roar of the gun, the splatter of blood on Frank's shirt, and the ensuing puddle at her feet. Of dragging Frank's body through the snow and finally burying him beneath a pile of rocks. Finnegan listened without a change

THE HEALING

of expression, but Jenny was trembling when she finished.

"What about the bag of gold you risked your life to save from the cabin when it burned?"

"It's Frank's, gold he'd stolen over the last few months," she admitted. "It's all I had to give me a new start, so I took it."

He didn't comment, just sighed and looked down at his boots.

"What's going to happen now?" she asked.

He looked up, his expression softened. "I imagine he'll sleep there until morning." He nodded toward Michael's tiny bed.

Jenny frowned at the slow smile that crept across Finnegan's face, hesitant to believe he wasn't hauling her off to jail.

"What would you say if I told you I don't think Frank's dead?"

Fear slammed into her with the force of a December gale. Cold sweat popped out on her forehead, whether born of relief or panic she couldn't untangle.

"Not dead?"

He shook his head. "I've been to that cabin, Jenny, and there was no body there."

"Wolves—" she began, but he interrupted her with a shake of his head.

"No, there was nothing there when I examined the grave. No body, no bones. Nothing." He pushed away from the wall and stepped in her direction. "Did you know he had a wife?"

Jenny swallowed. "I suspected he might, but he never said."

"And you stayed with him anyway?"

"Lust makes one do foolish things."

"Aye, it does," he said softly and took a step closer. "His wife is here in Dawson, demanding that I find out what happened to her husband." His voice returned to a normal pitch. "She's living out in the cabin, supposedly alone, but I have my doubts. She showed me a shirt with a bullet hole through the shoulder. Of course, she didn't realize what she was showing me."

"But . . . there was so much blood . . . on his chest, everywhere."

"Did you see that you'd shot him fatally?"

"No, I didn't examine the body, if that's what you mean. I just wanted him out of the cabin and buried."

He took a step closer until he was within arm's reach. "I think old Frank's alive and well and living with his wife on Chandler's Ridge. But knowing it's one thing. Proving it's another."

"What do you suggest?" she asked, looking up into his face.

He shrugged. "Wait for him to show his hand. And he will. Greed'll get the best of him and sooner or later he'll go back to his sluice box filching."

He seemed to want to say more, but he looked down at her instead, conflicting emotions in his eyes.

"Is that all, Constable?"

THE HEALING

Her question hung between them, floating on the tension that awaited his answer.

"I don't think so." Finnegan the Interrogator slipped away into obscurity. He cupped her elbows in his palms and drew her toward him until his breath stirred her hair.

"You're a curse on my soul, Jenny Hanson. You make me want to do all the things I swore I wouldn't."

She tipped back her head to look into his face, her pulse hammering at the base of her throat. He kissed her, his arms slipping around her waist, settling at the small of her back, pulling her against him. And she went. Without hesitation. Without doubt. This is where she belonged. In his embrace and within the circle of his protection. And he within hers.

She circled his waist with her arms, the muscles of his back tensing at her touch. Only a man too long unloved, too long untouched, would flinch at a caress. How many walls of resistance had he thrown up? And how long had he hidden behind those walls?

She kneaded the stiff serge of his tunic, soothing the tightening of his back. He relaxed in her embrace, molded against her, his kiss softening into a smooth, heated seduction.

"I love you," he whispered as he released her mouth and pulled the pins from her hair. "I won't tell you it was love at first sight, though."

"No?" she said as he untwisted the knot of hair

on the back of her head, her mind refusing to believe the words he'd just said.

"No. I thought you were foolish and stupid and mercenary to put yourself in such a position."

"Really?" She tipped her head back and watched his gaze flit down to her lips, then return to her eyes.

His hands returned to her hair, combing, sliding, arranging it across her shoulders. "But then you started to grow on me."

"Did I now?" She raised an eyebrow and smiled at the brief twinkle in his eye. "Even with all my sins?"

He abruptly released her and stepped away, further confounding her. "There's confession due on both sides." He crossed to the mantel, propped one hand on the rough-hewn surface, and unbuttoned his jacket with the other. "I'm not the man you think."

"None of us are the people others think us, good or bad."

"I left Ireland because I had to. I can't go back because there's a murder warrant waiting for me." He draped his coat across the back of a chair and looked up.

"Murder? You? I'll never believe that."

His grip on the chair tightened, his knuckles whitening. "Whiskey was my curse back then. A drunken lad staggering about the pub was cheap entertainment on a Saturday night. So they bought me drinks. All I could hold."

"How old were you?"

THE HEALING

"Fifteen."

The same age as she'd been when reality came calling.

"A fight broke out one night—two drunk blokes that made fighting into a game. I don't remember just what happened, exactly. I hit one with a chair and he went down. An accident, to be sure, but I was charged nonetheless, mostly on my reputation for trouble rather than the facts."

"And so you ran?"

He smiled. "Aye, run I did. Straight to the docks and the first ship leaving for Canada. But changing countries didn't do much to change my ways. I worked in saloons, sweeping up, running errands. Worked my way up from saloons to whorehouses. There, I discovered women."

"Mike, you don't have to—"

"Yes, I do," he countered sternly, turning to face her. "I want you to know before you give me an answer."

She waited, a sense of unease sweeping over her.

"Ten years ago I was in Seattle for a short time before I came to Canada. And I spent a great deal of time in a place called The Velvet Rose."

Seattle. A stir of recollection, long ignored, awoke and returned like a wisp of smoke. The madam of The Velvet Rose in Seattle's red-light district had taken her in off the street when Dave Marcus abandoned her. There she'd learned to market pleasures of the flesh and there she'd left her childhood behind. Jenny swallowed, her uneasiness turning to outright dread.

"There was a girl there with big, green eyes and beautiful chestnut hair. And she was young, Jenny, far too young."

His eyes asked the question his words did not, seeking an answer he desperately needed.

Chapter Fifteen

Jenny looked into Finnegan's eyes and saw his certainty that their paths had crossed before. She studied his face, but no memory floated back. There'd been so many back then and their faces were now a haunting collage. But search as she might through those half-forgotten images, she couldn't remember anyone who might have been Finnegan in his youth.

He waited for her answer, for confirmation to his theory. She'd been that green-eyed innocent at one time in her life and to too many men. She couldn't change the past, but she could accept it and hope Finnegan did, too. "I had to eat."

"So it was you?" She saw no condemnation in his eyes, only mild surprise and satisfaction that his suspicions had been proven true.

"It could have been. I worked there for several years."

"I remember the room was wallpapered in roses, little pink roses. Almost like a child's room."

The blood left Jenny's face. She hadn't thought of that room in years. Nor had she thought of the conflicting emotions staring up at that paper always stirred. A child's life lived inside a woman's body.

He took her in his arms and pressed her cheek to his chest.

"I'm so sorry," he whispered, a catch in his voice.

"You've no reason to be sorry," she replied. "I made that decision."

"You don't make decisions like that when you're fifteen. Life makes those for you."

The loss of her innocence was her last concern in those days. The source of the next meal was a more pressing worry.

"You were so thin, thin and delicate," he continued. "And I . . . I don't remember much about me. Except that I was drunk."

There was an expectancy in his eyes, as if he wanted either confirmation or exoneration.

She placed a palm on either side of his face. "I don't remember you at all, Mike, if that's a comfort."

Not much of an answer, she had to admit. But it must have been what he was looking for. Some of the tension eased from his shoulders.

She didn't want to remember how it felt to be held in his arms, didn't want to imagine intimacy

THE HEALING

between them—two awkward, groping adolescents.

Seeking to break the spell and sensing he wanted to say more, she changed the subject.

"So how did you come to be in the Mounties?"

He gave her a puzzled look, stepped out of her arms, and returned to the fireplace. "The paper in Seattle ran an article about the Mounties, how they were a tough bunch, disciplined, sent out into the wilderness, far away from temptation." He shrugged one shoulder. "It seemed like the thing to do. The next day I scraped together what money I had, boarded a train north, and eventually ended up in Regina. I enlisted and in their ignorance, they took me. It was my salvation."

Finnegan turned away from the fire, hands by his sides, a vulnerability in his eyes she'd never seen before. "There hasn't been a woman since I joined, Jenny." There was a sad honesty in his voice that touched a responding sorrow in her own collection of regrets. Wiry Mike Finnegan had just laid at her feet everything she wanted. A home, family, love. Did she have the good sense to bend down and pick it up? Or would she, like him, allow old ghosts to chase her away.

"I've spent my adulthood trying to separate love from lust. I never knew the difference before." He raised his eyes. "Now I do," he said. "Will you marry me, Jenny?"

She hadn't expected a proposal of marriage and hadn't wanted one. The word *marriage* carried a connotation of servitude and submissiveness, something she'd already had enough of. Over the years she'd hardened her heart against commitment and developed herself a fine arsenal of excuses. But now, faced with the honesty in his eyes, she couldn't clearly remember even one of them.

"I don't have much to offer a wife." He held out his hands, palms up. "The housing's poor and the life's hard. But you'll have my heart, Jenny, and there's never been a truer one."

No doubt rose to challenge the truth of his words. He'd be a loyal husband and a devoted father to little Michael. As much as old habit urged her to say no, she wanted to say yes.

"Have you ever slept with someone you were in love with?"

"No."

She stopped in front of him, his white shirt glowing softly in the firelight, marred only by the dark slashes of his suspenders. Fingers trembling with anticipation, she slid one of the wide elastic straps off his shoulder. "I'd like to know what it's like. Wouldn't you?"

"What about our wedding night?"

Jenny laughed at his perplexed expression. "Now, that's a little like shutting the barn door behind the horse for both of us, wouldn't you say, Constable?"

"I thought you might want to wait," he said as he pulled his arm around and let it dangle in a loop at his side.

"Life's too short."

He clasped her wrist with a firm grip, the skin

THE HEALING

of his palm rough against her skin. "Is that a yes to my proposal?"

Their gazes locked, each reading the other's thoughts. An unnerving thing, having someone anticipate one's thoughts.

"Yes, it is."

He hauled her against him and bit at the base of her neck, rolling the sensitive skin between his teeth, sending waves of gooseflesh dancing down her arms. "I love you."

She slipped her arms around his waist, urging him closer. "I love you, too." The words were easier to say than she'd imagined.

He pulled back and smiled. "Should we count our collective sins?"

Another ripple of desire spread through her, jarring in its intensity, oddly enhanced by the humor in his voice. "I don't think we have enough fingers between us."

"We could resort to toes."

She stopped and looked up into his face. "We'd have to take off our shoes."

"I'd planned to take mine off anyway." He lowered his head and claimed her mouth again. Tender at first, the kiss deepened and his breaths grew ragged as his control ebbed away. Jenny fumbled with the buttons on his shirt until the fabric opened, revealing his soft knit suit of winter underwear. She snapped off his other suspender, then raked his shirt over his shoulders and down his arms.

He released her mouth, shook off his shirt, and

dropped it to the floor. Eyes bright, his breaths were shallow and quick and where he touched her, his grip trembled. Abruptly, he turned and walked away from her.

"We're going too fast," he said, his back turned. "Too fast."

She pursued him and walked around in front of him. Hands on his hips, he stared at the floor, obviously fighting for control.

She touched his shoulder and he flinched. "You won't disappoint me."

He raised his head, seemingly surprised she'd read his thoughts. "I've just realized that I know plenty about sex and nothing about love."

"It's not something you study, Mike." She traced a finger down the rounded pearl buttons of his undershirt and smiled when he quivered under her touch. "It's something you learn from practice."

He studied her a moment, then lifted her hair and pushed it behind her shoulders, sliding his warm fingers against her skin. He undid the buttons on her dress until it hung open to her waist, revealing her thin chemise underneath. Frowning, he ran a fingertip across the scar that skirted the top of one breast. "What's this?"

"A gift from a customer who didn't feel he'd gotten what he was looking for."

Finnegan leaned forward and kissed the puckered skin. "He was obviously looking for the wrong thing."

Jenny threaded her fingers through his hair as he pushed the lace-edged fabric off her shoulders.

"I want to see you," he said as the material slid beneath her breasts and lay at her waist. She stood before his gaze, her breasts tingling as her body responded to the baby's sleepy whimper.

Her body less than perfect, producing milk for a child of another man's seed, she suddenly wondered how on earth Mike could find this reality sexy. Her passion faded and she moved to step away in anticipation of his rejection. Before she could, he bent his head forward and captured one breast in his mouth. She put a hand on his shoulder to push him away, but he caught her forearm and raised his head.

"It's all part of you, Jenny. I'm not thinking any further than that and neither should you."

He backed her toward the bed until the hard rail of the side pressed against the back of her legs. Aroused nearly to the point of speechlessness, she looked up into his face, soft in the firelight. Only with Frank had she allowed her body to respond to passion. And then only in their early days before his abuse robbed her of even that. But Frank had never elicited from her the sweet desire now racing through her blood. But then Frank had only aroused her body. Finnegan had aroused her mind and her heart as well.

He crouched in front of her and undid the button that held her dress tightly to her waist. Her remaining clothes slid to the floor and she stood before him, naked and chilled.

His gaze roamed over her boldly, then he dropped to his knees. "What's this scar?" He pointed to the ugly red scar that bisected her lower abdomen.

"Another gift from a customer, a priest, set on destroying harlots, as he called us. Only he had no qualms about sampling the forbidden fruits first."

"Dear God," she heard him whisper and he pressed his lips to that sensitive skin. She flinched. He was far too close to forbidden areas.

She reached for the buttons on his trousers, but his hand closed around hers. He stood and removed his remaining garments himself, his gaze locked with hers as if measuring her response to his body by degrees.

A scattering of red hair lay across his chest and muscular forearms. Here and there scars marred the softly freckled surface of his skin—evidence of a physical and difficult life. He moved the hair off her neck and put an arm around her waist to urge her closer. Teeth nibbled at the top edge of her ear as he stroked her back, drifting lower and lower with each caress until he pulled her hard against him.

"Jenny," he whispered brokenly, moving closer, reminding her of his need and revealing his desperation.

Jenny ran the palms of her hands across his hips and up his back to knead the tight muscles there as he'd once done for her. "Slow down," she whispered against his cheek, then stepped back away from him.

His cheeks blazed with color—from embarrassment or desire, she couldn't decide—but she

THE HEALING

lifted his hand and kissed the open, scarred palm. "We have the rest of our lives."

He released her and stepped back, the raging color drained from his face until he was nearly pale. He bent, picked up his trousers, and rummaged in the pocket. He took her hand and pressed into her palm a French shield, protection from another pregnancy.

She looked up into his expression, a mixture of expectation and study awaiting her reaction. "You thought of this?"

He shrugged one shoulder, obviously ill at ease. "I wasn't taking any bets on my behavior once you were in my arms." He caught her arm as she turned toward the bedside table. "Are you sure about this?"

There was a vulnerability in his eyes she hadn't seen before and obvious doubts circling his thoughts. Rising on tiptoe, she ran her fingers through his hair. "Never surer about anything in my life."

He backed her toward the bed until the bed rail pressed against the calves of her legs. Together, they tumbled into the tangled quilts, nested together against the cold. He pressed her close, his warm arms encircling her, protecting her. She sighed and rubbed her cheek against the soft skin of his shoulder, surprised at the contentment she felt just lying beside him.

But Mike wasn't content to simply lie close. He moved over her, pinning her beneath him. Thus trapped, she looked up into his eyes and slid a hand between them to touch him intimately. He jumped and caught her wrist in a firm grip, frowning. Surely he'd been touched this way before, caressed by a woman's hand? Was his concern a matter of urgency or trust?

"It's all right," she soothed, and caressed him past the strangeness of her touch. His tender parts balanced in her palm, she felt powerful and yet humbled to be the recipient of his trust and love. And undeserving.

She shoved at his shoulders and he obediently rolled to his side. While he watched her, she applied the French shield, noting that his gaze never left her face.

"I've never used one of these before," he said into the silence between them.

"Never?"

He shook his head.

"You should have."

He smiled slowly. "That wasn't the first thing on my mind in those days."

Such protection was common enough in the more reputable houses, insisted on in some, since shields had become widely used and accepted. She smiled down at him, enjoying the role of teacher.

But soon, the teacher became the student as he rolled her beneath him and took her slowly, cautiously, easing past the soreness. Once impaled, Jenny waited as he stilled and cupped her face in his hands. He seemed about to say something, but then his lips brushed hers lightly, then more firmly, as if he would consume her there and then. His

THE HEALING

body moved within hers with torturing deliberation. It was as she'd thought. Mike Finnegan did indeed know how to pleasure a woman.

Despite the barrier between them, he struggled to wait, slowing and stopping their pace when necessary, but never sacrificing her pleasure with his pauses. She applied her arts, hard won and dearly sacrificed for, wondering if all the past, all the pain had been for this moment, this joining. For he loved her with a tenderness she'd never imagined, much less hoped for. As his own pleasure increased, so did he make sure hers followed. By his own admission, Mike Finnegan hadn't been with a woman in a long time, but he surely hadn't forgotten the nuances of the act.

Years of sorrow had passed since she'd been a virgin, but tonight, being held so tenderly, so adoringly by the man she loved was as foreign to her as if she'd never loved before. He swept her past the simple act of sex, past the physical satisfaction and into a realm of contentment and well-being she'd never imagined was possible in any man's arms.

"Are you all right?" he whispered, his breath hot on her ear.

She nodded, speech long ago an impossibility.

His hands moved over her head to grip the posts of the headboard, shifting the angle of his body. She covered his rough knuckles with her fingers and stared up into his face as he quickened the pace of their lovemaking, clearly aware of and measuring her response. Hands still clutching the headboard, he closed his eyes as he brought them both to pleasure.

Trembling with the effort of holding his weight off her, he rolled them to the side and snuggled her against him without withdrawing.

"We almost broke the bed," she whispered into his hair.

"That we did, lass." His voice was husky and rough, tinted with humor and arousing in its honesty.

She pulled back a little to examine his face. "Regrets?"

He kissed the end of her nose. "Are you joking? You?"

She shook her head.

He started to withdraw and she stopped him with a hand on his hip. "Not yet. Please?"

He pulled her closer, tucking her head beneath his chin. "We can't stay like this, you know."

"We can for a little longer."

"I'm afraid that'll take care of itself eventually, lass."

Safe in his arms, she memorized the last few moments. The rumble of a chuckle deep in his chest. The scrape of his stiff chest hair against her cheek. The scent of their lovemaking, clinging to them both. She committed every detail to memory in case some circumstance of life sprang up between them and the future as she willed it never came to pass.

They lay cradled in each other's arms, naked, sated, and marked with each other's scent, until the fire burned low and the room grew chilly. Finally, he sat up on the side of the bed and looked back over his shoulder with such tenderness that she wanted to cry and cling to him, to forbid him ever to leave her arms again.

He flipped the tumbled quilt over her, pausing to tuck it firmly to her side. A tiny motion, but one that said much about the man. Suddenly the world was far more dangerous and uncertain than it had been thirty minutes ago.

He dressed in silence while she watched, admiring the way shadow and light played across the rise and fall of his back. Such commonplace motions—picking up a shirt, sliding on a pair of pants, buckling a belt—everyday tasks performed in the privacy of bedrooms and witnessed only by those intimately trusted. So simple and yet so endearing. She committed the images to her growing mental album. Then he came to sit by her again on the ruined bed frame and the tousled sheets. He cupped her cheek with his palm. "I'm holding you to your promise."

She covered his hand with hers. "And I'm holding you to yours."

He sobered and she felt the specter of reality creep into their world. "I want to put Frank behind us before we're married, draw him out somehow, make him show his hand."

Her hopes sank. Frank was far too crafty to fall for a ruse. "How do you intend to do that?"

He stood and the bed shifted with the loss of his

weight. "I'll think of something." He bent and brushed a kiss across her lips. "Don't worry."

The door swooshed shut behind him, leaving her alone in the gentle glow of firelight. A sense of loss filled her, however temporary, and she yearned to have him back at her side. She glanced over at the baby, sleeping peacefully in his bed, and then slid further beneath the quilts. The faraway dream of hearth and home became a growing hope.

If Frank was truly still alive, why was he playing dead? What could he want from her? What would draw him out? Money would draw Frank out, money and success. Hers. His need to control and manipulate would override his sense of caution. She'd bet her stash of gold dust on it.

Chapter Sixteen

"She's beautiful, Sam." Lizzy McLeod leaned over the cradle and tickled her baby sister's chin. "Was it a hard labor? What was the delivery like? Did it hurt much?" She fired questions at her stepmother, dropping her parcels to the floor, forgotten.

Jenny watched the family reunion from Sam's bedroom doorway, feeling more than a little out of place. Although dark like her father, Lizzy McLeod's face had an exotic quality, a fineness of line and stature that made her a rare beauty. Sally, younger by several years, was the picture of her father, but light-haired and blue-eyed.

"Does she cry much at night?" Sally asked with a skeptical frown.

Duncan and Sam exchanged knowing glances.

Apparently, Sally McLeod always shot straight from the hip.

"And how was your trip up with the mail carrier?"

Sally's sober expression melted into a broad grin and sparkling eyes. "Just wonderful, Pa. We raced through the snow and the trees whizzed by."

"I should shoot young Harper for allowing you to make the trip over the pass with him this time of year."

"Don't scold him, Pa. We made him bring us. We really did. He was in Skagway and we just couldn't wait for you to come for us."

"Despite his youth, he's a constable in the Mounted Police. The pleading of two young women shouldn't make him do anything."

As if on some silent cue, all three McLeod women turned to stare at Duncan as if he'd just uttered the most insane piece of nonsense they'd ever heard.

"Duncan. Think of what you're saying," Sam scolded with a smile.

Duncan looked uncomfortable for a moment, then smiled sheepishly. "I suppose you want me to say I'd have given in to the likes of you two if I'd been Harper."

"Of course you would have, Pa," Sally said with a frown that asked how he could have done otherwise.

Sam guided Lizzy by the elbow over to Jenny. "Lizzy, this is Miss Jenny Hanson. She's a friend of Finnegan's."

THE HEALING

Lizzy seemed nonplussed by the fact that Jenny was a "Miss" with a baby and no "Mr."

"I'm very pleased to meet you," she said with a smile and a raised eyebrow. "So, you're a friend of Uncle Mike's?"

"Yes." Jenny grasped Lizzy's extended hand, surprised at the strength in the young woman's slim fingers.

Speculation sparkled in Lizzy's dark eyes. "A very good friend?"

"Finnegan was kind enough to bring me up from Skagway on his mail run."

Disappointment replaced curiosity. She'd obviously expected more. "Oh."

Sam caught Lizzy's arm and led the three of them away from Duncan and Sally, who were leaning over the cradle. "Miss Hanson has a business proposition she'd like to discuss with you."

"Sam, can we do this later?" Jenny said, feeling oddly out of place.

"Nonsense, now's as good a time as any."

Jenny looked up into Lizzy's expectant expression. "I've recently moved here and I'd like to open a seamstress shop. Sam tells me you'd like to do the same. I thought we might go into the venture together."

Lizzy's eyes snapped with pleasure. "I've dreamed for so long of having a shop of my own, sewing my own designs. And I'd love to have a partner. Pa frowns every time I talk about doing it on my own."

Snowflakes swept into the room as the door burst open and a bundled figure stepped inside. "Uncle

Finnegan!" Lizzy and Sally chorused and flung themselves at him. He caught them in both arms, clasping them to his heavy fur coat while they covered his cheeks with kisses.

"Has the big city spoiled the two of you?" he asked, setting their dangling feet onto the floor.

"You know I love the Yukon," Lizzy said. "And now I'm going to have my own dress shop." She turned a dazzling smile on Jenny.

Finnegan followed her gaze to Jenny's face. "You are?"

"I want something of my own, something good," Jenny said.

He watched her for a moment, taking in this new information. They'd told no one of their plans, hoping Frank Bentz, if he was indeed alive, would show himself. At the same time, Finnegan pursued every wisp of evidence, every whisper of rumor hoping to find someone who'd seen the gambler since his miraculous rebirth.

"I think that's a good idea," he finally said.

Lizzy grasped Jenny's elbow excitedly. "We'll begin our plans tomorrow."

Duncan stood in ankle-deep snow, his sleeves rolled up to his elbows, pipe clamped in one side of his mouth, a pencil in the other. Freshly milled boards lay at his side and a gaping square hole yawned from the front of the barn's hayloft.

"I'm building Sam a trellis for roses," he mum-

THE HEALING

bled around his mouthful when Finnegan walked up to his side.

"In February?"

"Can't wait till the last minute."

"What about the hole in the barn?"

Duncan glanced up at the barn, then back to Finnegan. "Don't buy the story, huh?"

"Not for a minute."

Duncan removed the pencil from his mouth and dropped it into his workshirt pocket. Then he took his pipe out of his mouth and grinned. "Sam talked me into making the top half of the barn into a place for Jenny. Think she'll take us up on it?"

Finnegan looked up at the tall structure. Here, she'd be watched over. Sam was only a few steps away in case there was a problem with the baby. She'd be out of the hotel and out of the dishwashing business. It was a nearly perfect solution; the only drawback was that he couldn't live there with her yet as her husband.

"Come look at this." Duncan grinned and led Finnegan around to the back. A half-finished stone chimney stood against the side. "She'll have a woodstove upstairs and I'll have one downstairs when Sam runs me out of the house."

"You'll have to think of an awfully good excuse to get her here."

"The lying I leave up to my missus," he said, clamping the pipe stem between his teeth. "That's her territory."

* * *

"Duncan wants to rent it out and I don't want just anybody back there. It's taking quite a bit to house everybody, what with the baby and the girls coming back soon. I thought of you right away. We could be such a help to each other."

Jenny stared at Sam over her steaming cup of tea and wondered how much of the spiel she'd just heard was true. They felt sorry for her, thought she couldn't look after herself and little Michael. They didn't know how close to the truth they were. Working in the kitchen at night and tending Michael at the same time was proving impossible. Clattering dishes kept him awake and she lived with the constant fear someone would spill hot water on him. This was a way out. Would her pride let her take it?

"Let me think about it."

"Please, Jenny. We could take turns keeping the babies. And Sarah and Lizzy would help. It would be so much easier on you. And me," she quickly added.

Jenny assessed her options. She could dip into her savings and move to another hotel, but that would dwindle her nest egg. She could sell the land and add that to what she already had, but even that wouldn't last for long. Her only hope was to help Lizzy get the dress shop established. And she'd need extra hands to help with that. The very help Sam was offering.

"All right, it's a deal."

THE HEALING

Sam leaped from her chair and embraced Jenny, spilling her tea across the already dingy rug. "Duncan says you can move in on Saturday. He'll have everything ready by then."

Jenny jarred awake to the baby's wails. Scrambling to get to the dresser drawer that served as his bed, she stumped a toe against the leg of the bed and swore under her breath. Michael was red-faced and squalling breathlessly by the time she picked him up. Opening her gown, she placed him at her breast, but he refused, crying louder.

She checked his diaper and found him dry and clean. Even walking the floor did no good. A rough knock came at her door. When she opened it, the desk clerk glared at her over his glasses. "Mrs. Hanson, you are going to have to do something about that brat of yours. I've had three complaints already."

"I know. I don't know what else to do." She bounced the baby as she spoke, making his cries bob up and down in pitch.

"Well, think of something or you'll have to leave this establishment." He raised his glasses and peered at the baby, illuminated in the faint glow of the hall lamp.

"That child has smallpox!" He backed away into the center of the hall. "You'll have to get out of here."

Jenny stepped into the light and pushed back

the baby's blanket. Round, red spots covered his face and chest.

"If you don't get out, I'll have the constables throw you out," he threatened in a quivering voice.

"You can't throw a baby out into the cold night."

"I'm not having you stay and start an epidemic in my hotel, either."

"You couldn't talk the Mounted Police into something like this."

"If the constables won't come, I know men who will," he said, edging toward the top of the stairs.

Jenny quickly gathered her things and the baby's rather than risk his threats. The clerk pressed his back against the wall and waited for her to pass before slamming shut her room door.

"Don't stop. Go right on outside," he ordered, clumping down the stairs behind her.

She stepped out into the cold and Michael stopped crying for a moment as the cold air struck him. She had nowhere to go and snow was beginning to fall. There was a surgeon at Fort Herchner. And Finnegan was there. She turned and trudged toward the fort at the end of the street, using moonlight as her guide. It must be well past midnight, she thought sleepily, noting that all the street lamps had been extinguished.

Two sentries guarded the fort entrance.

"Is your surgeon here?" she asked, shielding the baby against the increasing snowfall.

"No, ma'am. He's down at Skagway."

"Could you get Constable Finnegan for me?"

Eyeing her warily, the constable led her to the

THE HEALING

main barracks, now quiet and dark. "Wait here," he said and disappeared inside.

"Finnegan." Someone shook his shoulder, stirring him from a deep sleep and a dream about Jenny.

"What?" He sat up and wiped a hand across his face.

"There's a woman and a baby outside to see you," Constable Harper whispered furiously.

"A woman and a baby?" he parroted, realization beginning to dawn.

"Does the young'un have red hair?" a voice in the dark said and a round of chuckles echoed in the room.

Pulling on his pants, Finnegan half hopped, half walked to the door as he followed the sentry outside, barefooted.

"Jenny! What are you doing here?" he asked, running a hand through his hair. "Why are you out in this weather?" He gazed off at the thickening snow.

"The baby's sick," she whispered. "The desk clerk threw us out of the hotel because he thinks it's smallpox."

Finnegan shut the door behind him. "Are you sure that's what it is?"

"No. That's why I'm here. I don't know how to tell. Do you?"

"I don't know. Wait here against the wall, out of the snow. I'll be right back."

He moved quickly and soundlessly, gathering his clothes, boots, and coat. Then he left the barracks and finished dressing on the porch. "We'll go to Duncan's."

"No. What about Skye?"

"Not in their house. In the new room over the barn."

They made their way down the street, heads bent against the driving snow. Duncan had built a set of stairs to the top floor of the barn. Finnegan helped Jenny up, holding her arm to keep her from slipping on the slick steps. The odor of fresh, new wood poured out when he pushed open the door. A single lamp sat on a small table. Finnegan quickly lit it and replaced the chimney. Soft light poured forth.

"Give him to me," he said, taking Michael from her arms and laying him on the table alongside the lamp. He pulled away the layers of blankets. Tiny gooseflesh popped up on the baby's skin, sprinkling the fiery red blotches.

"I don't think it's the pox," he said, rubbing a finger across the sore. "It looks different. But I don't know what it is."

"We need willow bark for tea to keep his fever down," Jenny said, "and I don't have any."

"We can buy it in the store now. It's called aspirin. But I wouldn't know how much to give a baby. I think the best thing to do would be to put him in a bath to keep the fever down. The surgeon's in Skagway, but we're expecting a new lad in a day or two, right out of medical school."

"A day or two might be too late." Her eyes were

THE HEALING

huge and dark in the poor light, fear rolling off her in waves.

He rewrapped the baby carefully and cradled him in his arm. The chill of being undressed had momentarily stopped his crying, but now he frowned and pitched in anew.

"Poor little lad. You shouldn't worry your mama this way," he said as he tucked the blanket securely around him.

"I don't think I could bear losing him."

Finnegan looked up to meet her eyes and was reminded again of the frightened innocent who'd stolen his heart so many years ago. "Don't think about that. Not even for a second. Understand?"

She nodded and Finnegan put the baby into her arms. "Hold him until I get back. I won't be long." He disappeared out the door, only his muted footsteps remaining behind, and then silence. He was back in a few minutes, his arms loaded with wood. He strode to the far end of the room and knelt before a small, black woodstove she hadn't noticed before. The firebox clanked as the wood struck the sides. Finnegan struck a match and soon had a fire going.

"I'm going up to Duncan's for a pan and the other things we'll need."

She caught his forearm. "You can't go in there. You might give it to them."

"I'm not." He started away, then turned back and kissed her. "Don't worry," he whispered and disappeared for the second time, leaving her alone with the silence and her fear.

* * *

Thwack.

Something struck the bedroom window.

Thwack.

Duncan stirred beneath the quilts, hooked his arm around Sam's waist, and held her against him, spooned in the curl of his body.

"What was that?" she whispered in the dark.

"What was what?"

"That."

Thwack.

Duncan threw back the warm covers and padded to the window. Something sailed toward him and hit the window with a splat, leaving lumps of snow clinging to the glass.

"What the hell—" Duncan yanked open the window and dodged another snowball that splatted against the side of the house.

"Duncan, what's going on?" Sam asked, sitting up in bed.

"Finnegan's downstairs throwing snowballs at the house." Duncan poked his head outside. "What's wrong?"

"Come downstairs," Finnegan said, looking up.

Duncan shut the casement and scrambled around for his pants and boots.

"Duncan. What is it?"

"I don't know. Something's wrong," he said as he hurried out of the room and down the stairs.

Cold swept in as he pulled open the door. Fin-

THE HEALING

negan stood on the walkway, several feet from the porch.

"Jenny's baby's sick," he said before Duncan could ask. "It could be the pox. They're upstairs in your barn. The hotel threw her out when he started to cry."

Duncan stared at Finnegan, remembering, and knowing he did, too, the epidemic they'd endured in the Blackfoot village in the winter of '96 and the ensuing terrible, lingering deaths.

"Damn." Duncan looked down at his boots.

"This was the only place I could think to bring her."

"No, of course you did the right thing. What can we do?"

"I need a pan and a bucket for water so we can keep his fever down."

"Finnegan, what's the matter with the baby?" Sam came out onto the porch, pulling her wrapper closed.

"He could have smallpox. I don't think so, but I'm being cautious."

"She can't stay out in the cold with a baby. You bring her in here right now." Sam squirmed past Duncan and started for the steps.

"Sam. No." Duncan grabbed her arm.

She turned around. "Why?"

"Because Finnegan and I both know what an epidemic of the pox does. He's right. They should stay isolated until we know."

"You can't possibly think to leave her up there with no heat, no bed, nothing."

"Finnegan's taking care of them. This is the way it has to be. Think of the girls."

Sam looked between them, panic and hopelessness on her face.

"Jenny decided this before I did, Sam," Finnegan said. "She knows this is what is best."

"What do you need?"

"I've told Duncan what I need."

"Then I'll just add a few things you don't," she said as she brushed past Duncan and went back inside.

In a short time, Finnegan's arms were loaded down with blankets, a pan, a bucket, two cups and a package of tea. For his second trip, Sam had laid on the porch a pillow, clothes for the baby, and soft cloths to bathe him with.

"That young surgeon we were expecting is in Skagway. Steele got a wire yesterday afternoon. It'll take him a day or two to come up with the mail carrier. I'll send him over as soon as he arrives."

Finnegan nodded, his arms loaded.

Duncan propped a hand against the porch post, hating the helplessness he felt at his feeble efforts. At his side, Sam shivered, her trembling quivering against him. "Come get us if you need us," he said.

Finnegan waded through the snowfall, soft, new snow filling up his partially untied boots. He shoved open the door with his foot and stepped into the room, his arms laden with supplies. Jenny stood by the stove, swaying with the whimpering baby.

She turned as he entered, her eyes shadowed and large.

"Any change?"

She shook her head.

"I'll get some snow to melt." He dropped his load and took the kettle and the bucket back downstairs.

The kettle steamed on the stove while Finnegan went back to the McLeods' front porch to retrieve the rest of the things Sam had set out for him. When he returned, a rocking chair sat amid various other things including more blankets and a dresser drawer for the baby to sleep in. By the time he'd transported it all upstairs, Jenny had filled a pan with snow and was pouring hot water from the kettle over it. She knelt by the pan, laid the baby on a blanket, and unwrapped him. Finnegan saw her pause and fear cross her face as the last of his wrappings fell away, revealing the extent of his illness.

Red and angry, the blotches covered the tiny body, barely a finger's width of skin not affected.

"He's burning up with fever," she said, lifting him free of his diaper and easing him into the tepid water. The move brought a fresh round of squalls.

Finnegan took off his coat and hat and hung them both on a nail by the door. Then he rolled up his sleeves and stepped to her side. "Here, let me."

She surrendered easily, as if relinquishing responsibility, if even for a short time, was a much-needed relief. Finnegan's hands replaced hers holding the slippery infant. Jenny moved a short distance away, leaned against the warm wall, and crossed her arms over her chest.

Finnegan scooped water into his hand and let it trickle over the baby's tiny chest. Michael gasped, eyes wide, and stopped crying. Finnegan chuckled, his heart doing an odd flutter in his chest.

"When I found out I was pregnant, I considered not having him," she said softly. "Now I can't imagine life without him."

"No, I don't suppose you could."

"Did you ever want children?" she asked, as he dribbled more water over the baby's angry, splotched skin.

"Not until I met you."

She met his eyes briefly before he turned his attention back to the baby.

"My sister and her family lived with us for so long that I felt like I'd already raised a family by the time I left home. And then you came along and made me want all kinds of things I hadn't wanted before."

"Do you think he'll die?" She hadn't meant to ask the question out loud, only allow it in her heart, and she was surprised to hear her words echo in the empty room.

"I don't know," Finnegan answered honestly after a pause.

He lifted the now calm baby out of the water, quickly wrapped him in a clean diaper and blankets, and handed him to Jenny. She shed her coat,

THE HEALING

fed the baby, and tucked him into the dresser drawer to sleep.

Finnegan sat down and leaned against the wall, warm from the glowing stove. "Come here." He raised an arm to indicate a place for Jenny. She wriggled into the space by his side and he draped an arm across her shoulders, snugging her against his side. Held so, safe and warm and exhausted, she soon fell asleep, leaving him to stare at the shadows alone.

His fingertips began to tingle from lack of blood flow. He raised his arm, eased away from her, and laid her on a quilt he'd drawn close for later. Restless with worry, he stood and checked the stove. Then he checked on the sleeping baby, curled into an angelic pose, one fist tucked beneath a pink cheek. He reached out a finger to touch him, then thought better and withdrew his hand.

He walked to the wide front window that looked out over Duncan's house and the ridges of mountains beyond. A clear night and a full moon did great justice to the distant rugged peaks, touching each summit with a frosting of luminescent snow.

Movement in the shadows below caught Finnegan's eye. He squinted into the darkness that lay between the barn and Duncan's house. A solitary figure stood halfway between them, bundled in a heavy coat, the glowing end of a cigarette delineating him from the surrounding shadows. Hands shoved deep in pockets, the figure seemed to be studying the barn, making no move to enter or to leave. Suspicious, Finnegan walked to the door, eased it open, and stepped out onto the stair landing. But the figure was gone, swallowed by the night, leaving behind only a wobbly path of footprints in the snow.

Chapter Seventeen

Baby Michael stared at the adult face hovering above him with the focused concentration only an infant could summon, a fist shoved into his mouth, his wailing forgotten.

Surgeon Witchell smiled, one hand disentangling Michael's chubby fingers from his stethoscope tubing while the other held the diaphragm to Michael's splotched chest. "It's not the pox," he said, leaning back in his chair. "I suspect it's a mild form of measles. His fever's down and he should be fine in a few days, granted the fever doesn't worsen." He ran a finger down Michael's bare chest and the baby squirmed and squealed with delight. "Gave your mama a scare did you, fellow?"

Finnegan met Jenny's eyes across the table where Michael lay and saw the relief he felt mirrored there. "Do you suppose there'll be any lasting effects?" Finnegan asked, again seeing the same question in Jenny's eyes.

"I doubt it," the surgeon said, leaning forward to tickle the baby again, his trained eyes carefully assessing the baby's reactions to his touch. "He looks fine to me."

A swift knock on the door drew Finnegan's attention. Duncan opened the door a crack, shielding the opening with his body. "What's the verdict, Doc?"

"It's not smallpox."

Duncan stepped into the room, the expected grin absent. "If all's well, then, could I see you a minute, Finnegan?"

Finnegan snared his coat off a nail by the door and stepped outside into the snow-brightened morning sun. Hands shoved into his pockets, Duncan's expression was unusually glum. "Steele wants to see the both of us in his office right away."

Finnegan cast a glance toward Jenny, barely visible through the crack in the door. She held Michael to her shoulder, his tiny, dark head pressed against her cheek. Everything in Finnegan strained toward that scene, longed to be part of the love and gratitude there. But duty had to come first.

"Do you know what he wants?" Finnegan asked, swinging his gaze back to Duncan's face.

Duncan shook his head slowly. "He didn't say, but from the look on his face, I'd say it wasn't good news."

THE HEALING 287

They walked the short distance to Fort Herchner in silence, crunching through the new snowfall side by side. A dozen possibilities spun through Finnegan's thoughts, but nothing seemed more prominent than another. Perhaps Frank Bentz had surfaced. Perhaps Harriet had been up to more mischief. Or perhaps Hawkins had brought information to the fort.

"Have a seat, gentlemen," Steele said as soon as he opened his office door. Uncharacteristically out of uniform without his scarlet jacket, Steele stepped to the side to allow them to enter. His wide, blue suspenders glared dark against the pristine white of his shirt.

Duncan and Finnegan sat in two unyielding, straight-backed chairs aligned to face Steele's desk. Their commander walked around the mahogany piece and sank into his own chair with a sigh. "Of all the duties I have carried out as an officer in the Mounted Police, this is my least favorite." He leaned forward, rested his elbows on the desk, and laced his fingers together. "I've received some disturbing information, Constable Finnegan, about your activities prior to your joining the North West Mounted Police."

Finnegan's heart sank, leaving a huge, hollow spot in his chest and a warped sense of relief. "I would imagine that to be a warrant for my arrest, sir."

"It is indeed." Steele picked up a folded document and then flopped it back onto the desk without looking at it. "And I understand that its appearance now has something to do with a letter you wrote almost a year ago."

Finnegan closed his eyes and swore softly. Last winter, victim of cabin fever and an overly sensitive conscience, he'd been consumed with regrets for his actions and overwhelmed with the desire to, once and for all, have a clean slate. So, he'd written a letter to the sheriff of his county in Ireland, explaining the situation of his accusal so many years ago and asking for a solution. When spring released him from his prison of self-doubt, he'd forgotten he'd ever written the letter. Until now.

"I wish that you had discussed this with me before writing that letter, Constable."

"So do I, sir. Am I to be arrested?"

"No. In light of your position as a North West Mounted Policeman, I was able to convince Sheriff Darby that you were a poor risk for escape and he has agreed to turn the matter over to a circuit judge and abide by his decision. I received the papers from Ireland in today's mail. The judge will be here in three weeks to conduct your trial. Until that time I am placing you under the supervision of Inspector McLeod. He will see to it that you are at that trial. Am I right, Inspector?" Steele glared across the desk at Duncan.

"Aye, sir. He'll be there, all right."

"Constable, would you like to tell me your side of the story?"

Finnegan related the events from the now dim past, describing the actions of a young man filled with frustration and anger, a young man so

THE HEALING 289

unknown to him now that he could have been describing a stranger.

Steele leaned back in his chair and listened, crossing his arms over his chest, his face noncommittal. Finnegan kept his explanation factual and short and when he'd finished, Steele continued to stare up at the open, beamed ceiling in contemplation.

"Given your exemplary record, Constable, I wouldn't expect the judge to be harsh, but I'd be prepared for anything."

Not much comfort in those words, Finnegan thought as the possibilities rolled past in his imagination.

"We'll speak again before the trial. You're dismissed for now."

"And me thinking you were a virginal youth when you enlisted all those years ago."

Finnegan threw Duncan a slanted glance as they retraced their steps down the snowy street and smiled. "You didn't know I was a fiery-tempered Irishman with a past, now did you?"

"No, I'd have kept a closer watch on my daughters had I known you were a scalawag."

"There's not much scalawag left in me these days."

"You've put ten good years in the Mounted Police. I can't imagine the judge'll hold you responsible for something that happened fifteen years ago and with dubious evidence to boot."

"Murder is murder and must be atoned for. So says the queen and God."

"I can't speak for the queen, but I'm not sure even God can sort out the guilt in a bar fight." Duncan draped an arm across his shoulders. "How about some coffee?"

Rosita's Cafe was an oasis of good food and freshly starched tablecloths amid the mud and confusion that was Dawson City. Sitting there at one of her finely set tables, life seemed oddly a-tilt and deeply uncertain, perhaps more so than at any other time in his life. Finnegan turned his coffee cup, absently aligning the bottom with the red-and-white plaid pattern of the tablecloth.

"I asked Jenny to marry me," he said, his eyes on the coffee cup and how the bottom rim matched a stripe of red.

"I suspected as much wasn't far off," Duncan replied. He swallowed his coffee and set his cup down. "And did the lass say yes?"

Finnegan smiled. "She did. We didn't tell anyone. We both wanted the issue of Frank Bentz resolved first. Now, I guess this is one more thing to overcome."

"Does she know about any of this?"

Finnegan nodded. "She knows it all. I told her everything before I'd let her give me an answer."

Duncan nodded to the hovering waitress, who refilled his cup. "And the lass said yes anyway? You must have done something right, lad."

Finnegan laughed. "Yes, I suppose I must have."

"What are you going to do about the question of Mr. Bentz's immortality?"

Finnegan rotated his cup. "I'm convinced he's alive. From the shirt Harriet showed us and what Jenny's told me, I don't believe her shot was fatal. Bentz is waiting out there somewhere for the right opportunity to return and claim what he believes to be his."

"Jenny and the baby?"

Finnegan shook his head. "The gold."

"Gold? What gold?" Duncan frowned and leaned forward.

"Jenny took a bag of gold Frank had stolen. He knows she's got it and so does Harriet. I know for a fact that Harriet's turned the cabin upside down looking for it."

"How much gold are we talking about?"

"I didn't ask. But it can't be too much. I've seen the bag and there's only a couple hundred dollars left."

"Why would he risk exposure for so small an amount?"

Finnegan raised his eyes to meet Duncan's gaze. "Because he sees it as his, just as he sees Jenny and Michael as his. Amount doesn't come into consideration. Only possession."

Bright bolts of cloth were unloaded from the wagon parked in front of the newly painted storefront. The door to the store opened and she stepped out. Her clothes were stylish and modest, tailored to her slim figure. She was excited, beaming a smile at the men unloading the supplies while nervous hand motions accentuated her words. If he listened carefully, he could even catch a word or two, Frank Bentz realized, and he strained to pick her voice out of the din on the street.

Throaty and mellow, deeper than most women's voices, Jenny's low tone and soft speech never failed to deeply stir him. But with that pleasure had always come a wisp of dissatisfaction, an uneasiness he'd never experienced with any other woman. She was confident in a way that was unnerving, sure of herself and what she wanted. Even in his worst rages, even when she cowered from his temper, there was in him a mutinous, lingering doubt that he'd completely conquered her. And the possibility that he hadn't drove him crazy.

He returned his thoughts and senses to her, to the picture she presented standing there in the morning sun, obviously having very nicely picked up the pieces of her life after his "death." With the aid of his gold, he thought with a tightening in his gut.

He pushed away from the post against which he'd leaned and angled his way across the muddy, rutted street to a spot down the sidewalk from her shop where he took up his surveillance again. From here he could hear her voice plainly, the highs and lows of her speech sliding across his thoughts, teasing to life passionate memories of her, of them.

Did she still believe him dead? Surely, she did. He had no reason to think she was suspicious of

THE HEALING

his disappearance, no reason at all not to assume she believed herself a murderess. And yet she had the nerve to open a shop on Main Street, to pass herself off as a businesswoman, an upstanding member of the community, when he knew what she really was. The knowledge that she'd pulled off her charade further galled him.

A slight, dark-haired woman stepped from the shop to Jenny's side. Together they were light and dark, one complementing the other in form and color. This new woman also spoke with authority, bobbing her head in answer to questions from the deliverymen. Whatever their venture, they were apparently in it together, he gleaned from snatches of their conversation. Women tended to band together that way, he'd learned from hard experience, and could present a formidable front when challenged. If he wanted to catch Jenny alone, he'd have to somehow draw off her partner. The two women disappeared inside the shop, leaving only the plodding trips of the deliverymen to entertain Frank.

And then Fate favored him. The dark-haired woman appeared again, her reticule in her hand, a short cloak about her shoulders. She was leaving and presenting him with the chance he needed.

Frank pushed away from the post he leaned against, his interest caught and held. Should he wait, bide his time, and savor the knowledge that he could step back into Jenny's life and put an end to her well-laid plans with a word? Or should he appear to her now, deliver his intentions, and watch her squirm at the end of his string? Both possibilities were intriguing.

But the prospect of finding Jenny alone, of seeing her surprise turn to horror, was too tempting to pass up. He strode down the sidewalk, relishing his deceit, and stopped at the glass-paneled door. Inside, Jenny leaned over a crate of supplies. She straightened and held up a length of ribbon to admire, taking advantage of a patch of morning sun, and he remembered, with a painful twinge of conscience, how much he had once loved her.

She was delightfully unaware that he watched her, her movements and the slow smile that spread across her face unguarded and natural, without suspicion or wariness. Standing there, hidden from her view by the dirty glass and the scrolling gold letters, a small corner of his conscience regretted that he was about to strip her of her blissful ignorance. And yet a larger part wanted to snatch away that mantle of confidence she wore. Was there another man? Was that small smile merely the result of momentary pleasure from the articles she held in her hand or did it go deeper? Was she loved and safe in that love? The thought angered him, giving him the courage that had faltered for a moment.

The bell above the door jingled, marking his entrance sooner than he'd have liked. She turned and froze.

"Hello, Jenny."

"Frank." She whispered the word as if he were

a ghost and saying his name might truly conjure him from the dead.

"Aren't you going to say 'Frank, you're not dead'?"

She quickly roped in her surprise and traded it for wariness. "That's obvious, isn't it? How did you pull this off?"

He moved toward her, expecting her to cringe backwards, but she stood her ground. No sign of surrender crossed her expression. "You're a bad shot. Got me clean through the shoulder, that's a fact. Painful but not fatal."

"You *let* me bury you?"

He shrugged. "All a part of the charade."

"And you had the presence of mind to think all this up after I shot you?"

"Nothing like being dragged across a hard, snowy yard to quicken one's mind."

She let the ribbons slide from her hands, but still, there was no sign of fear on her face. "I wouldn't have thought even *your* mind, Frank, could invent such a ruse on such short notice."

"One must never miss an opportunity, my dear."

"What do you want from me?" She met his eyes with an unwavering, green-eyed stare, going straight to the heart of the matter, a habit he'd often found unsettling.

"I want what's mine. My gold. Our baby. You."

"You don't want me, Frank. And you never wanted Michael. And as for the gold," she held out her hands, palms up, "I just sank the last speck in the lease on this place."

The gold had never been the issue, Frank acknowledged to himself, but making her give it back was. And suddenly punishing her seemed overwhelmingly important.

"I could have you arrested for attempted murder, say you tried to kill me for the money."

"And how would you explain that it took you four months to decide I *had* attempted to kill you, Frank? And that the gold was stolen in the first place?"

Her response caught him off guard and at a momentary loss for words and strategy. A change of tactics was called for.

"I see you're not making your living on your back and have taken up shopkeeping instead. Do you think this is good use of your best skills, Jenny? Can you feed my child on what you'll make here?" He moved away from her, strolling through the piled boxes and crates.

When he turned, she stared at him with her arms crossed over her chest. "What do you want, Frank? Or did you come here just to insult me?"

What did he want now that she wasn't cowering in fear before him? Did he want her back? Want the responsibility of a woman and a baby? Oh, he wanted her all right, wanted her in his bed, always submissive to his wishes, sexual or otherwise. And when that was over, he wanted the freedom to move on to another woman, another conquest, and leave no tracks.

No tracks.

He'd left behind a child and he had no idea if

THE HEALING

it was a son or a daughter. Until this moment, he hadn't cared. Even now, the fact was merely fodder for conversation. He felt nothing for the seed he'd planted except a remembered satisfaction in the act that had created it.

"I want you to pay me back for the gold you stole."

"I don't have it, I told you."

"Then get it."

"Or what?"

"Or else one night your lover won't come home. I burned the cabin, you know."

She blanched and the earth dropped out from under his feet. So there *was* someone, someone who'd put that soft color in her cheeks and the life back in her eyes. He'd casually thrown the comment at her, expecting her to deny it. Upon her denial, he'd been prepared to back that up with a threat to the baby, a sure way to secure her cooperation. But as he watched the roses disappear from her cheeks and the defiance from her eyes, a strange sense of loss and jealousy welled up inside him, threatening to rob him of his satisfaction.

"So, there is someone." He hadn't meant to say the words out loud, only allow them one brief trip through his thoughts. But now that he'd said them, he met her eyes with a steady gaze and awaited her answer.

She tipped her chin up slightly, an unconscious act of defiance that moved him more than she could know. "Yes, there is."

He forced a sneer, surprised at the slash of jealousy that cut through him. "Does he leave money on the bedside table?" The gibe sounded childish and desperate, even to his ears. One look at her face said she thought so, too. Unruffled, she continued to study him.

"I'm sorry that you've made yourself such a hard bed, Frank, but you knew what you were doing. You have a wife, I understand. She came all the way to the Yukon to look for you. Why don't you take what's left of that marriage and try to make something for yourself?"

The words, more mature than any he could have conjured, fell like blows from a stout stick across his back. Used to having the upper hand, he felt out of control. Foolish. Belittled. And all by the woman he'd once thought he controlled.

There was a serenity about her now that was unnerving. He sensed no greed or shrewdness, no cruel ambition. She seemed simply at peace.

"Remember what I said," he repeated as he moved toward the door, "every cent. And soon."

"I'm not afraid of you any longer, Frank," she said as he opened the door, ignoring the irritatingly joyous tinkle of the bell.

He was halfway out the door, and glad of it, when her voice stopped him in his tracks. "I knew it was you who burned my house. But you did me a favor, you know."

He stopped, one hand on the door.

"Don't you want to know if you have a son or a daughter?"

No, he didn't want to know. Without knowing

the sex, he could put no face to the bit of life he'd helped create and therefore no images would haunt his conscience. "Sure," he said and cursed himself for a coward. "What?"

She remained silent, watching him for a moment, pity in her eyes. "You have a son, Frank, a healthy baby son."

"I've come to see to his prosecution meself."

Sam Steele looked up from the folded papers and wished he'd gone on that hunting trip after all.

"Sheriff Darby, I thought that you and I had reached an agreement about this months ago."

"Aye, that we did, Superintendent, but then I got to thinkin' that 'twould be a pity if the bastard got off after all these years."

Steele leaned back in his chair with a grunt. The little man before him reminded him of a rat terrier his mother had once owned—all mouth and little sense. And the similarity didn't stop there. Each one seemed to take special pride in torturing whatever was judged to be the enemy of the moment. "I've released Constable Finnegan into the custody of Inspector McLeod. He's led an exemplary life these last ten years and has a spotless record since joining the Mounted Police. I predict that the resolution of this case is hardly worth your traveling halfway around the globe to oversee."

"He's a murderer, Superintendent—allegedly, of course. And hardly trustworthy."

"Sheriff, Constable Finnegan has been dispensing law and order without benefit of judge or court for ten years on the Canadian frontier. His trustworthiness is not in question."

"Were his trustworthiness not in question, there'd be no need for those papers, now would there?" Sheriff Darby pushed back a ragged bowler hat and smiled, his eyes glittering with triumph. "The circuit court judge is due here in two weeks. He's agreed to hear the case then."

"That'll give me ample time to prepare me case, then."

Steele slowly shook his head. "The evidence is ten years old, Sheriff. What more information could you gather here?"

Darby paused dramatically, drew himself up slightly, and stepped to the window, where he planted his fists on his hips. "Much can be seen about a man by the company he keeps."

Warning bells clanged in Steele's head and a pain began as an annoying prick between his eyes. "What do you mean?"

"Mike Finnegan always had a way with women, even as a young man, and I've information that says he hasn't changed that habit."

Steele rubbed the ache between his eyes. "Get to the point."

"I left Ireland the day I got your letter. Finnegan left quite a trail across Canada and into the United States. Did you know he frequented a brothel in Seattle called The Velvet Rose?"

"I'm not responsible for the morality of my men

before they enlisted, Darby, only for what they do afterwards."

"Would you have signed up Constable Finnegan had you known of his background?"

"No."

Darby smiled. "And so he's duped the both of us because he's keepin' the company of a whore right under your nose, Superintendent."

Darby seemed so pleased with his tidbit of information, Steele longed to wipe the smirk off his face with a right hook. "Miss Hanson's former occupation is none of my concern. She nor Constable Finnegan have given me reason to believe that their friendship is anything other than honorable."

"Honorable. Is that the term they're usin' for it now?"

"Until the behavior of one of my men infringes on the reputation of the Force as a whole, I stay out of their business. I suggest you do the same, Sheriff Darby."

"You don't spend as many years routing out the rubbish as I have, Superintendent, and not come to know that there's some that never change their spots."

"And I suppose you consider Constable Finnegan one of those?"

Darby shrugged. "Seems to me he's sniffing after skirts as bad now as then. Sure an' he brought some of his other sins with him."

A full-fledged headache now claiming his thoughts, Steele hauled himself to his feet and leaned both hands on his desk top. "Do what you must, Sheriff, to prepare your case. But remember this—Constable Finnegan is a member of the North West Mounted Police. We take care of our own."

Chapter Eighteen

Candlelight softened the raw yellow of the newly stripped logs and the soft warble of a scratchy graphophone recording filled the small room.

"Duncan, it's wonderful!" Sam flung her arms around Duncan's neck. "Where did you get it?"

"I ordered it from Sears Roebuck before Christmas. I'm afraid it didn't arrive until now."

"You and Finnegan brought this all the way back from Skagway?" She pecked Duncan on his cheek and danced back over to the wide, black horn projecting a Brahms symphony. Jenny turned to Finnegan, standing on a rug by the door, snow melting off his shaggy coat. "Was the weather very bad?" The question was inane, she knew. Obviously the weather had been bad, but her real question to him was asked in the tone of her voice and his answering wink. He was all right, his patrol safely completed one more time.

"Finnegan, get that dripping coat out of here," Sam admonished as she adjusted the angle of the horn.

He opened the door and stepped outside. Jenny followed him into the January cold. Duncan's cabin had once been on the edge of burgeoning Dawson City. Since then, a street had been cut in nearby and oil-lit street lamps installed. Now, that light served to illuminate the gentle snowfall, casting a ghostly blue over the landscape. Ribbons of color arced across the night sky, bowing in submission to some unseen hand and rivaling the stars.

"No, the weather wasn't so bad," he answered, draping his coat over a rocking chair. "Some snow and wind. We brought back quite a bit of mail." He turned toward her, his face barely visible in the dim light, and yet she felt his concern for her reaching her in some unspoken manner. "How have you been?"

How simple the question and how complex the true meaning of the words. Even as he asked it, she knew he'd already satisfied himself that she was fine physically and had moved on to making her intimately aware of her every action by the silent communication passing between them.

Jenny walked to the porch railing and brushed away the small rounding of snow accumulated there just to have something to do with her hands. "I'm fine and the baby's fine, too." She didn't want him to read in her eyes the fact that Frank

THE HEALING

had threatened her. And she knew that Finnegan's finely tuned instincts would pick up on her distress the moment their gazes met.

"How are you getting on, living over the barn?"

She smiled and looked up at him despite her own cautions not to meet his eyes. "It's wonderful having my own place again."

He reached into the pocket of his serge jacket and withdrew a small, velvet bag. Into the palm of her hand he poured a ring of twisted gold, two tiny threads intertwining into a large, sturdier strand. "I bought this in Skagway. Don't you think it's time we let everyone else in on the secret and set a date?"

The warmth and acceptance she'd anticipated at the public announcement of their union was lessened by the shadow of Frank's words, but she pushed away the disappointment lest Finnegan see evidence of it in her eyes.

She looked up into Finnegan's face and saw that he loved her as she'd always wished to be loved. He held no reservations about her, no illusions about her past, no doubts about their future. The importance of Frank and his threats lessened.

He kissed her and as she turned to go inside, he caught her elbow. "Jenny, wait."

A cold chill of premonition ran up her spine.

"There's something you should know." He moved away from her and leaned back against the porch railing, distancing himself, she sensed, for something unpleasant.

"What is it?"

He crossed his ankles and looked down at his boots. "I've been arrested for murder."

"The old charges from Ireland?"

He nodded, arms crossed over his chest. The air left her lungs and her world seemed to fall away in great, cold chunks.

"How did they find you?"

He set his jaw and shook his head. "I led them right to me with a well-intentioned letter." He related the contents of his letter of confession. "I had hoped that my time in the Mounted Police would count for something, that they would understand I'm no longer that man. I wanted the matter cleared up and forgotten. Apparently this is how they want it done."

"What happens now?"

"I've been released into Duncan's custody. The rest is up to the circuit judge when he comes to hear the case."

"You mean there's going to be a trial? They're going to try you for a murder you're not even sure you committed fifteen years ago?"

"There's no time limit on murder trials, Jenny. And Sheriff Darby himself has come to see justice done."

In the space of seconds, her dreams had been give life, then dashed into pieces.

"What do you think will happen?"

Finnegan shrugged, his expression set and resigned, wearing that noncommittal mask that served him so well in his career. "I don't know.

Darby seems set on making a point that no transgression goes unpunished in his county."

She'd gone from thinking herself a murderer to facing the possibility of Finnegan being accused. How bizarre were the twists and turns life took!

He pushed away from the railing and reached for the door. She stopped him from opening it with a hand on his. "Maybe we shouldn't. Not until we know how this will turn out."

"I don't intend to wait for you a minute longer than I have to. Let Sheriff Darby and the circuit judge dispense justice as they see fit." He hooked an arm around her waist and drew her close. "I intend to announce my intentions to make an honest woman of you."

As they stepped through the door together, Sam turned from bending over the fireplace, a poker in her hand. A slow smile spread across her face as she anticipated their news—probably from the silly grins on their faces, Jenny mused.

"Jenny has consented to become my wife," Finnegan managed before Sam launched herself at them, arms flung wide.

"When's the wedding?" Lizzy chimed, rising from her chair and dumping her sewing unceremoniously onto the floor.

"We haven't decided." Jenny threw Finnegan a questioning look.

"We'll have a double wedding," Lizzy exclaimed, her eyes shining. "We're getting married next month, just before the miners begin to pour into town. That's not too soon, is it? It'll just give us time to make your dress. And we'll just double everything else."

Jenny glanced over Lizzy's head at Finnegan. Next month she could be his wife—for her a dream once so distant it had seemed an impossibility. Or he could be on a ship bound for an Irish prison. He watched her, waiting.

"What do men know about weddings, anyway?" Lizzy asked with a playful glance at Finnegan.

"Next month sounds fine." As Jenny spoke the words of agreement, a chill of uncertainty stole her joy.

Sam stood back and fluffed out the skirt of light blue silk. "It turned out well, don't you think? Even if we did have to hurry." The layers of fabric settled in a soft pool around the foot of the dress form.

Jenny looked up at the clock from where she sat cross-legged on the rug, putting in the last stitches of her rolled hem. "Court convenes in an hour."

"And the weddings convene tomorrow morning at nine. Finnegan's told you to keep your mind on that."

"Finnegan's mind is on the wedding night and, besides, he doesn't understand what it's like to feel so helpless."

"Oh, he understands, all right. He's just like Duncan. They think if they ignore the problem it'll just work itself out. And besides, who cares if he's thinking of the wedding or the wedding night? He's thinking about you. That's what's important."

THE HEALING

Sam raised her eyebrows and smiled but Jenny couldn't join in on the humor.

"He should be thinking about the trial."

Sam picked up a needle, threaded it, and flopped onto the floor beside Jenny. "He's put all that into Sam Steele's hands. Capable hands, I might add."

Jenny watched the mantel clock tick off the minutes of her life, the delicate, dark hands moving with jaunty deliberation. Twenty-four hours from now, when the clock face read ten o'clock in the morning, what would her life be like? Would she be promising to love and cherish the man beside her or would she be saying good-bye?

The bell on the door of their shop jangled and the door closed with a solid click. Jenny unfolded her legs, untangled her dress, and rose. "I'll see who it is."

She stepped out of the back room and froze. Frank stood in the center of the shop, twisting a bowler hat in his hands as he looked around, amazement on his face. Her heart plunged. She'd completely forgotten about Frank and his threats.

Glancing over her shoulder to the back room where Sam was hidden from view, she quickly crossed the rug-strewn floor, took Frank's arm, and guided him to a sunny corner by the front glass before she spoke.

"I don't have your money, Frank, but I'm trying to put it together. We've only just opened three weeks ago. I need more time."

There was no mocking arrogance in his expression when she finally met his eyes and the surprised registered slowly.

"I didn't come for the money."

Years rolled back and for the breadth of a moment she saw again the man she'd once fallen in love with. "What do you want, then?"

He glanced down at the hat in his hands, worried it another turn, then looked up. "I came to say good-bye."

Thunderstruck, Jenny could only stare in disbelief. "Good-bye?"

He smiled then, a slow, soft smile completely foreign to any of the facial expressions in Frank Bentz's carefully cultured collection. "Harriet's pregnant."

Harriet, the practiced seductress of Finnegan's description, was carrying a child? Frank's child? And Frank was pleased? What miracle could have wrought such changes?

"I can't imagine that," she replied before she thought.

"Neither could I." He widened his smile. "And neither could she until we found out. We're going back to Seattle and try and make a life there. Once upon a time, I was a decent clothier, before the gambling bug bit." He nodded to the interior of the shop. "I once owned a shop much like this, catering to men's clothes, of course. Thought I might give it another try."

"Well, Frank, I'm amazed."

His expression sobered. "About the baby."

"Our son?" She couldn't resist the jibe.

THE HEALING

He reached into his waistcoat pocket, extracted a sealed envelope, and handed it to her. "This is legally drawn up by a solicitor. It gives my permission for Finnegan to adopt him once the two of you are married."

She took the smooth envelope from his hands and noticed that his fingers quivered ever so slightly. "Do you want to see him?"

"No." His answer was sharp and immediate, accompanied by a frown. Then his face relaxed. "No, I think it's better I don't." He studied her face for a moment longer. Was he remembering their few but memorable good times together?

"I'm sorry, Jenny, for anything I might have done to hurt you." He held up a hand when she started to answer. "I know that doesn't even begin to make up for what I've done, but I wanted to say it anyway. Nothing can make up for what I've put you through and I won't make any excuses for my behavior, recent or past. I'm a new man, Jenny. I hope that you will always serve as my example as to how one should live their life."

With those words, he plopped the hat on his head, turned on his heel, and was gone into the morning sun, leaving only the tinkling of the bell as the door closed behind him.

"This court will come to order," Constable Harper announced. "This is the district court of the Yukon Territory, circuit court judge Albert Metz, presiding."

The jammed courtroom clambered to its feet with much scraping and sliding of chairs. White hair frizzed out at all angles, Judge Metz stepped behind the desk and waved the crowd to sit with a thin, bony hand. "Sit down, sit down, all of you."

Jenny's stomach tightened another notch at the irritation in the judge's voice. Apparently, he'd been on the circuit for some time and was tired, irritable, and due to retire when he returned to Ottawa. This, in essence, was his last case.

At the table in front, Finnegan sat ramrod straight, his scarlet jacket impeccable, staring ahead. Sam Steele sat at his side, seemingly relaxed. Beside them at the other table, Sheriff Darby slouched in his chair, an arrogant smile riding his lips.

"Now, what have we here?" Judge Metz said out loud, dragging the stack of papers toward him and pinching a set of gold-rimmed glasses onto his narrow nose. "Ah, alleged murder. Good God, this case is fifteen years old. Sheriff Darby, did it take you this long to catch your man? And I see you netted a Mountie for your trouble." The judge peered over his glasses and between two strands of white hair.

"Aye, that I did, Your Honor. Constable Mike Finnegan here did commit a murder in the Cock and Bull Pub fifteen years ago, stabbing one Red O'Leery." Darby delivered the information like a carnival barker, his voice rising and plunging for emphasis. Judge Metz was unimpressed.

"I'm too damned tired and cold to listen to theat-

THE HEALING

rics, Sheriff. Limit your comments to the facts or I'll decide the case myself while you sit outside."

"Of course, Your Honor." Darby's face blanched.

"Constable Harper, swear in Constable Finnegan."

"Your Honor, I believe it is my place to call the witness," Darby said.

"Whose damn courtroom is this, Sheriff?"

"Yours, Your Honor."

"Remember that, Sheriff."

Finnegan walked to the front of the room, placed his hand on the Bible, and swore to tell the truth.

"Now, I see this happened fifteen years ago. Long before you were a member of the North West Mounted Police. Is that right, Constable?" the judge asked.

"Yes, Your Honor," Finnegan answered.

"How old were you, son?" the judge asked, peering over his glasses.

"I was fifteen that year."

The judge studied the papers before him and Jenny recognized Steele's looping hand.

"You want to tell me your side of this?"

Finnegan quickly related the sketchy details of the alley attack.

"It says here you were living on the streets at the time. Where were your parents?"

"Both were dead by that time, Your Honor."

"Please drop the 'Your Honor.' By the end of my circuit, even the words make my head hurt."

"Yes, sir."

"Now, at this point both parents are dead and you're a street urchin, by all measures."

"Yes."

"So, I'm intrigued as to how you wound up in the North West Mounted Police."

Finnegan related the events from his flight from Ireland on the first available ship to his sordid and winding path to the Force. One cheek propped on his hand, the judge listened without comment until Finnegan had finished.

"If I didn't have Sam Steele's signature here, I'd swear that was a lie," the judge said, leaning back in his chair. "Sheriff, what's your story?"

"Your Honor, you've not conducted this trial as it should be done," Darby blustered. "I should have presented my accusations first."

"I beg your pardon, Sheriff, for my ignorance. Please, present your side."

Yanking his pants a little higher on his ample hips and with quite a flair for the melodramatic, Darby etched a sordid and manipulative scheme to dispatch the long-dead Red O'Leery. When he was finished, the judge regarded him with a cold, expressionless stare . . . then burst into laughter. "That's the biggest load of blarney I've ever heard, Sheriff. Has it taken you all these fifteen years to work that many conspiracies into your theory? Dear God, man, you've implicated everyone but the queen."

The judge leaned forward and affixed his glasses more firmly on his nose. "Here's my decision."

Jenny's heart slammed against her ribs and she

THE HEALING

twisted her hands into the skirt of her dress. Through the folds of fabric she felt Duncan's warm hand give hers a squeeze.

"While Mr. O'Leery's death is a tragedy, I see from your description, Sheriff, that Mr. O'Leery was a frequent visitor to this pub and participated on more than one occasion in getting the young Mike Finnegan roaring drunk for the mere purpose of amusement for the rowdy crowd. Mr. O'Leery was no stranger to this lifestyle and should have known the chances he was taking frequenting this sort of establishment. Therefore, as far as I'm concerned, Mr. O'Leery bears a good deal of the guilt in his own death and Constable Finnegan merely defended himself. I find Constable Mike Finnegan not guilty."

The tiny courtroom erupted in cheers and scrambling chairs. Somehow through the ensuing melee, Finnegan pulled Jenny into the safety of his arms. Her cheek pressed against the rough serge of his tunic, she watched the swirl of humanity around them and said a soft prayer of thanks.

The woodstove settled into the deep night with comforting pops and groans, its glass-fronted door emitting soft light to shadow the lines and planes of her husband's bare back. Satisfied and happy, Jenny feigned sleep in their tousled bed so she could watch him undetected.

Finnegan sat on the side of the bed, silently staring off into the encroaching night, his thoughts in some faraway male place she could only pretend to understand, she supposed. He'd claimed her as wife with compassion and sweetness, and a passion deep and enduring. Now, she wondered what he thought. Was he lingering in the glow of satisfaction as was she, or was he critiquing his performance? She smiled beneath the quilt she peeped over and marveled at the wonderful differences between man and woman.

He rose, his hips bare and narrow, and reached for his pants, abandoned on the floor. A shawl of freckles lay across his shoulders and here and there a scar marked the broad expanse of his back. She watched with unabashed admiration as he stepped into the blue uniform pants, their broad yellow strip glowing in the dim light, and half fastened them, slinging the garment low across his hips.

Floorboards creaking, he walked barefooted toward the tiny dresser drawer where baby Michael had been kind enough to sleep through their lovemaking. He sat down in the rocking chair and leaned forward to peer into the makeshift bed, his elbows propped on his knees. He remained so for so long, Jenny began to wonder if he was having second thoughts about taking on a family.

As if in response to her thoughts, he leaned forward and lifted a now stirring Michael into his arms, murmuring something softly as he cradled the baby. He leaned back, setting the chair to swaying, and continued his one-sided conversation, spoken in soft tones, heavy with the Irish accent he'd almost lost.

THE HEALING

She could catch bits and pieces of the story, some exaggerated bit of nonsense, not unlike others he'd whispered to Michael at odd times when he thought he was unobserved. But now they'd settled into a rhythm together. Michael's soft coo said he was awake and curious, his attention captured by Finnegan's tone, if not his words.

The coos turned to frets and she heard the soft sway of the chair stop and the boards creak under Finnegan's steps. The quilt and its accompanying blanket of warmth slid down her body and let in the night chill.

"Let's see if Mama has anything for you," he said, laying the baby next to her bare breast.

As the baby began to nurse, she opened her eyes and stared into Finnegan's. He slid into the bed beside her, careful not to disturb the baby. "There's a line forming for your attentions, Mrs. Finnegan," he said, propping his jaw in his palm and undisguisedly watching the baby at her breast.

"Mrs. Finnegan. Now that's an odd-sounding name."

He smiled but his brows dipped into a slight frown. "What do you mean?"

"Well, I've always heard you called by your last name instead of your first. I'm not so sure about being *Mrs.* Finnegan."

"Well, what would you like to be called?"

She smiled. "The what doesn't matter so much. I'd like you to call me often, though."

He leaned forward and answered her remark with a kiss. "My wife makes wisecracks."

She glanced down at the baby. "Do you think we can build the cabin back some day?"

He pulled back to look her full in the face. "I thought that would be the last place you ever wanted to go again."

"Not at all. Michael was born there. And if Frank hadn't burned it down, I might have lived a lonely spinster's life right there in the bend of the river—without you. So, it's sort of a monument to man's foolishness, don't you think?"

Finnegan smiled slowly. "You just want it built back because it's yours, right?"

"A girl has to plan for a rainy day, doesn't she?"

He leaned forward, his mustache tickling her cheeks. "There'll be no more rainy days in the Finnegan household. Right, *Mrs.* Finnegan?"

COMING IN OCTOBER 2002 FROM ZEBRA BALLAD ROMANCES

__A BICYCLE BUILT FOR TWO: Meet Me At The Fair
by Alice Duncan   0-8217-7278-3 $5.99US/$7.99CAN
A handsome city swell like Alex English isn't looking to marry a girl who spends her nights telling fortunes at the Fair—and Kate Finney isn't any man's toy. Yet, he refuses to be ignored, insulted, or rebuffed by her. Kate realizes that she had better put him in his place, before he melts her icy armor and steals her lonely heart!

__AN UNFORGETTABLE ROGUE: The Rogue's Club
by Annette Blair   0-8217-7384-4 $5.99US/$7.99CAN
Alexandra Huntington said goodbye to her war-bound groom on the steps of the church. Bryceson Wakefield, Duke of Hawksworth, was too aristocratic to survive. Alex is penniless because he neglected to provide for her in his will. Now she is on her way to the altar once more, with Bryceson's enemy, the Viscount Chesterfield.

__A LADY BETRAYED: . . . And One For All
by Kate Silver   0-8217-7387-9 $5.99US/$7.99CAN
Courtney Ruthgard gave her heart—and much more—to a dashing Musketeer. Breaking her heart was one thing, but Pierre de Tournay stole papers incriminating her father in an illegal scheme. Courtney's only desire was to take revenge on the man who had betrayed her . . . and infiltrating the King's Guard was the perfect method.

__THE RUNAWAY DUKE: Reluctant Heroes
by Susan Grace   0-8217-7373-9 $5.99US/$7.99CAN
Jonathan Carlisle has retreated a rural hunting lodge—only to be kidnapped. Wounded in his escape, he awakens in the home of a country physician and his daughter, Melanie. Trusting no one and feigning amnesia, he cannot deny the passion he shares with Melanie. And yet, he is unaware that Melanie is burdened by a secret . . .

Call toll free **1-888-345-BOOK** to order by phone or use this coupon to order by mail. *ALL BOOKS AVAILABLE OCTOBER 01, 2002.*

Name _____
Address _____
City _____ State _____ Zip _____
Please send me the books that I checked above.
I am enclosing $_____
Plus postage and handling* $_____
Sales tax (in NY and TN) $_____
Total amount enclosed $_____
*Add $2.50 for the first book and $.50 for each additional book.
Send check or money order (no cash or CODs) to: **Kensington Publishing Corp., Dept. C.O., 850 Third Avenue, New York, NY 10022.**
Prices and numbers subject to change without notice. Valid only in the U.S. All orders subject to availability. **NO ADVANCE ORDERS.**
Visit our website at **www.kensingtonbooks.com.**

Experience the Romances of
Rosanne Bittner

__Shameless $6.99US/$7.99CAN
0-8217-4056-3

__Unforgettable $5.99US/$7.50CAN
0-8217-5830-6

__Texas Passions $5.99US/$7.50CAN
0-8217-6166-8

__Until Tomorrow $5.99US/$6.99CAN
0-8217-5064-X

__Love Me Tomorrow $5.99US/$7.50CAN
0-8217-5818-7

Call toll free **1-888-345-BOOK** to order by phone or use this coupon to order by mail.
Name_____
Address_____
City_____ State _____ Zip _____
Please send me the books that I have checked above.
I am enclosing $_____
Plus postage and handling* $_____
Sales tax (in New York and Tennessee) $_____
Total amount enclosed $_____
*Add $2.50 for the first book and $.50 for each additional book. Send check or money order (no cash or CODs) to:
Kensington Publishing Corp., 850 Third Avenue, New York, NY 10022
Prices and numbers subject to change without notice.
All orders subject to availability.
Check out our website at www.kensingtonbooks.com.